D1049744

# KINGDOM of SECRETS

# Kingdom of Secrets

CHRISTYNE MORRELL

DELACORTE PRESS

This is a work of fiction. Names, characters, places, and incidents either are the product of the author's imagination or are used fictitiously. Any resemblance to actual persons, living or dead, events, or locales is entirely coincidental.



rhcbooks.com

Educators and librarians, for a variety of teaching tools, visit us at RHTeachersLibrarians.com

*Library of Congress Cataloging-in-Publication Data*
Names: Morrell, Christyne, author.
Title: Kingdom of secrets / Christyne Morrell.
Description: First edition. | New York : Delacorte Press, [2021] | Audience: Ages 8–12 years. | Summary: "When her father is arrested for a crime she unwillingly committed, Prismena will do anything to save him, taking her on a high-flying and shadowy adventure"— Provided by publisher.
Identifiers: LCCN 2020020587 (print) | LCCN 2020020588 (ebook) | ISBN 978-0-593-30478-5 (hardcover) | ISBN 978-0-593-30479-2 (library binding) | ISBN 978-0-593-30480-8 (ebook)
Subjects: CYAC: Hot air balloons—Fiction. | Adventure and adventurers—Fiction. | Secrets—Fiction.
Classification: LCC PZ7.1.M67265 Ki 2021 (print) | LCC PZ7.1.M67265 (ebook) | DDC [Fic]—dc23

The text of this book is set in 11.75-point Adobe Garamond Pro.
Interior design by Carol Ly

Printed in the United States of America
10 9 8 7 6 5 4 3 2 1
First Edition

FOR HARPER

# THE STRANGER AND THE SCARF

Abigail Smeade arrived like a black eye: sudden, fierce, and blossoming under my skin. When I met her, I was sitting in the shade of an old oak tree, minding my own business. I'd just removed a burlap sack from a hollow in the tree's trunk and poured its contents out in the grass—scraps of metal, twisted brackets, and a few strips of a stretchy material called rubber. Most people would've described those things as junk fit for the bin, but I knew better. Pieced together just right, that "junk" would become more than the sum of its parts. And figuring out which way was *just right* happened to be one of my favorite pastimes.

But Father didn't like me tinkering with the odds and ends I gathered (and sometimes even pinched from his workshop). It wasn't proper, he said, and making something nobody had ever seen before might get a person looked at twice, which was the last thing we wanted. That's why I kept my collection stashed inside an oak tree in the middle of Fletcher's field. Nobody but Mr. Fletcher and me ever wandered into that field anymore, if you didn't count the sheep.

At the bottom of the bundle, rolled up tight, was a scarf, a single piece of fabric more precious than all the rest of it put together.

I unfurled it across my knees, and the silk shone and rippled like running water. It was cool to the touch, but the pattern—in shades of blue and yellow and purple—made me think of places drenched in sun. The kind of faraway places Mother liked to visit when she was flying hot-air balloons. In fact, the scarf had been a souvenir from one of her trips. She'd had a weakness for beautiful, unnecessary things. She'd filled the house with them once.

"Peanut brittle?"

Startled, I crumpled the scarf and crammed it back into the sack. Then I whipped my head left and right, hunting for the owner of that voice. It wasn't until I looked up that I spotted her, sitting on a branch of the tree and kicking her legs like she was lounging on a swing. She peered down at me with shrewd, glittering brown eyes. Without prompting, she extended a half-eaten shard of candy through the leaves. It glistened with a semicircle of saliva where she'd taken the last bite.

"No, thanks," I said.

"Your loss." She wedged the peanut brittle into the far reaches of her mouth and cracked off a piece. It rattled against her teeth as she spoke. "What's that?" She pointed down at one of my projects, something I was still trying to get just right. A small flying machine I'd made using those strips of rubber Mr. Dudley had given me.

"Excuse me . . . who *are* you?" I asked. She looked about my age—long-limbed and gangly, with light brown skin. Her hair had been pulled into a ponytail that erupted at the back of her head in a burst of copper corkscrews. She wore several layers of clothes—an apple-green vest, a striped jacket two sizes too small, and two gauzy skirts that looked like petticoats that had been dyed pink and cut short. Her scuffed boots kicked at the air over my head.

"Abigail Smeade, at your service," she said. "You can call me Abi." She smiled with a mouth full of crowded, crooked teeth, each one shoving its way to the front. She stretched her arm down to me again, this time offering her long, tapered fingers for a handshake. As though it were completely normal to meet someone while perched in a tree. I unpretzeled my legs and stood on tiptoes to give her hand a single uninspired shake.

"I'm Prismena," I said. "What are you doing here?"

"Same as you," she said. "Trespassing."

That response almost knocked me backward. She was correct, legally speaking, but I'd spent so much time in that field it felt like part of our own property. Mother and I used to stretch out in the long grass here to get the best view of the balloons taking off, when she wasn't flying one herself. I could still picture her that way—in profile, with bits of twig clinging to her strawberry-blond hair. She'd always gasp at the first sliver of color cresting over Fletcher's Mill, as giddy as a child on Savior's Day, and we'd watch that sliver grow and grow until it filled the sky and overtook the Wall, which didn't look so impressive then. Our hot-air balloons made one hundred feet of stacked stone look no more imposing than Mr. Fletcher's puny fence.

"You didn't answer my question," said Abi, jerking me out of my memories. "What *is* that thing?"

I fumbled for the words to explain my amateur flying machine to this strange girl, but it didn't matter. Abi was already moving, zipping down the branches of the oak tree. In an instant, she stood beside me, holding it in her hands, which—I happened to notice—were caked in dirt. "How does it work?" she asked. Once again, she didn't give me a chance to answer. She started twisting it roughly in ways it wasn't meant to twist.

"Stop," I shouted, yanking it away from her. "You're going to break it! Just watch me."

It was simple, really—a tight roll of parchment with a thin strip of rubber threaded through it, end to end. On one side, the rubber was attached to a lightweight propeller, and when I spun it, the rubber twisted around on itself. When I let go, it uncoiled, spinning in the opposite direction and thrusting the machine forward. Like I said—simple. It rose in a wobbly arc, glided for an instant, and crashed into the dirt.

"Wow," said Abi. "You built that?"

"Yes," I said, the heat rising in my cheeks. "But it's not quite right yet."

"Looks all right to me," she said. "Why do you keep it hidden out here?"

"It's not *hidden,*" I said. "It's just . . . it's where I store my things."

"Oh. Like your Tuleran silk scarf?"

I inched closer to my sack, as if that would protect the scarf inside it. "I don't know what you're talking about."

"Sure you do," said Abi. "How'd a Lollyhill girl like you wind up with a piece of the finest fabric in the kingdom? Something like that must be pretty expensive."

"That's none of your business," I snapped.

In truth, that scarf *was* expensive. Mother had brought it back from a flight to Tulera. An import like that would fetch a king's ransom now that the borders were practically closed. But that wasn't why it was so valuable. At least, not to me.

"You're not supposed to have it, are you?" asked Abi, eyeing me like she could see every thought in my head, written out like a diary. "Your daddy doesn't know you took it, does he?"

I froze where I stood. How could she possibly know that?

I didn't blame Father for selling Mother's things. With the war in the South plodding on and the travel bans grounding most of his flights, he had to sell anything we didn't need, just to keep food on the table. So, gradually, Mother's knickknacks disappeared—the cobalt-blue bottle from Rivelle; the pink lace from Chinchester; the peach pit from Palma, carved into the shape of a tiny bird. That's why, when I found Mother's silk scarf tucked away at the bottom of a drawer, I swiped it. I couldn't bear to see it traded for a handful of coins or a crate of onions, no matter how much my stomach may have disagreed.

Abi's eyes flicked to something in the distance. She squinted at it. "Is that him?" she asked, shielding her eyes from the sun. "A bearded man in a leather apron, kinda scrawny and mean-lookin'? Is that your dad?"

I gasped and spun around. If Father caught me out here, he'd give me a going-over I wouldn't soon forget. Worse, he'd destroy my collection—all except the scarf, which he'd sell quick as a heartbeat. Then he'd lock me in my room until I was old enough for him to kick me out.

Luckily for me, it wasn't Father who had ambled into the field and was staring at us trespassers. It was a lone sheep, braying softly, in search of a fresh patch of grass.

"Are you daft?" I said to Abi, relaxing. "That's not my—" I stopped short when I realized that *I* was the daft one. I looked down, and, sure enough, my sack hung open in a wide O of surprise, just like my slack-jawed mouth. Abi stroked the pristine silk of Mother's scarf against her soiled cheek.

"It even feels expensive," she said.

I lunged at her, but the edges of her skirts slipped through my fingers. "Give that back," I growled. "That's mine!"

"Is it?" Abi smirked. "When someone sneaks around like a common thief, it's usually because they are one."

"I am not!"

"If you say so," she said with a shrug. She wound the scarf around her thick curls and tied it there. As if she needed *more* clothing. "As it turns out, I *am* a common thief, but that's not why I'm here. I don't want your mother's scarf. I need your help. If you do what I ask, I'll give it back."

My stomach clenched so tight I thought I'd be sick right there in the field. "How'd you know it was my mother's scarf?"

"I know everything," she said. "I know your dad's the balloonist—the only one left who doesn't work for King Michael. I know you sit out here every day, tinkering with piles of junk, then you go home and sew balloons and look after an old man who hardly says two words to you. And I know following you is one of the most boring jobs I've ever had."

"*Following* me?" I yelped. She'd been *following* me? How had I not noticed her? Abigail Smeade didn't exactly blend in. "What do you want from me? How can I possibly help you? I'm not rich or anything."

"That's for sure," said Abi, sizing up my plain brown frock and drab wheat-colored hair as she strutted around me. I definitely wasn't the kind of girl you'd target for blackmail. "But I need your help anyhow. I have to send a package to Tulera on tomorrow's flight. A teeny-tiny box. Nobody will ever even notice it."

"Wh-what? You want me to smuggle something for you?"

"Exactly. Do as I say, and I'll give you your fancy scarf back as soon as the balloon takes off. Do we have a deal?"

My head went woozy as I tried to make sense of it. "I—I'll call the Royal Guard," I stammered. "I'll tell them you stole my dead mother's scarf!"

"Go ahead," said Abi, not the slightest bit ruffled. "I've been following you for three days without you noticing. Do you really think I can't escape from some bumbling soldiers? And if you do call the Royal Guard, you'll never see the scarf again. Maybe I'll even tell your dad about the stuff you're hiding in that little nook of yours. What's that stretchy stuff called? Does he know you have it?"

"You're a horrid girl," I cried.

Abi smiled sweetly. "Don't worry, Prissy. All you have to do is get my box onto that flight, and nobody will ever know about your little treasures. Not even your dad."

My stomach twisted into an even tighter knot. "Balloon shipments have to comply with strict regulations, and any deviations from the flight manifest could get Father in big trouble. Besides, he checks his inventory carefully. What you're asking for is impossible."

"Don't sell yourself short," said Abi. "I've seen what you can do." She motioned to the flying machine, which looked flimsy and childish to me now. "So are you in?"

I bit my bottom lip as she smiled at me, calm as a windless sky. If I put a box of who-knows-what on Father's balloon, I'd be betraying him. But if I let that smug little sneak walk off with Mother's scarf, I'd be betraying *her.* I balled my fists so tightly my fingernails bit into my palms.

"Fine," I said through clenched teeth. "I'll do it."

"Good," chirped Abi. "I'll see you tomorrow." She popped the last bite of peanut brittle into her mouth and gave me another toothy grin. As she skipped off and hopped the fence from Fletcher's field into a neighboring farm, the silk in her hair shimmered blue and yellow and purple, and I longed more than ever to be someplace else. Somewhere far, far away.

# WHAT A REAL BALLOONIST KNOWS

I plodded back home, wishing the fields would stretch like rubber so I'd never arrive. Our land was smack in the middle of Lollyhill, a neighborhood of Oren set high on a hill and marked by sprawling farms and fresh air. It was a stark contrast to the crowded interior of the kingdom. Father settled here because the open spaces were perfect for launching and landing hot-air balloons. Plus, he liked the peace and quiet.

Father's workshop was a stone building set apart from our house, so big that a hot-air balloon could fit inside, spread out from end to end. The huge room practically invited a person to run around with abandon—if the person weren't too old for such things, of course. At the entrance, Father stored the soft materials—hay and other kindling for the burners, reams of fabric, and balloon tarps in every conceivable color (except purple, which was reserved for the royal balloons). It looked like a rainbow had been pulled down to earth and neatly folded. Deeper into the workshop, the bright colors gave way to the formidable gray and black of machinery, where the clang of metal was the building's beating heart. This was where Father constructed the frames that attached the wicker baskets to the giant silk envelopes. Most people think balloons are just drifting baubles in the sky, but a real balloonist knows they're sturdy and strong. Even dangerous.

Father was stationed at the forge when I entered. His body was bent over a cast-iron anvil, on which he had balanced a thick strip of metal. It was black at one end, but glowing red at the other, where he pounded away at it. His gloved hand kept it steady, while his other hand wielded the hammer that shaped it to his whim. I'd seen him do it hundreds of times, but it always left me awestruck that my mild-mannered father could turn the most solid material known to man into something pliable.

"Get back," he shouted over the whoosh of the fire. I'd crept too close to the shower of crimson sparks that erupted when he struck the metal. I stepped away as he quenched the finished piece in a tub of cold water, releasing a gush of steam into the air. He removed his leather glove and used it to mop his brow, which was coated in sweat and ash. Then he strode over to another bucket of water—this one for drinking—and downed a ladleful in one long swig.

"*Saint Ursula* needs mending," he said after he drank his fill. *Saint Ursula* was our apple-green balloon. Like all the others, she'd been named by Mother, who never explained why she'd named a balloon after a saint. I'd noticed *Saint Ursula* spread out on the ground when I entered—how could I miss a bright-green tarp bigger than my house?—but had hoped she wasn't for me. My eyes darted back and forth between the deflated balloon and the hunks of metal crowding the forge.

"Can't the hired girls do the sewing?" I asked. "I'll be more help to you here, with the pipes and fittings." I didn't have anything against needlework per se—it was downright necessary for my inventions—but I'd already done my share of mending envelopes. I wanted to try something new. I wanted to get my hands on all the different parts of the balloons so that someday I could build one, top to bottom, like Father did. And then I'd fly it.

"No," said Father, with a firm shake of his head. "Too dangerous."

"But what about—"

I almost brought up Guernsey, Father's second-in-command and his unofficial choice to take over the workshop someday. Just last week, Guernsey had failed to wipe down an anvil, his pipe had slipped, and he'd smashed his thumb with a nine-pound hammer. And though Guernsey had memorized the components of the Dudley Valves used to steer the balloons, he couldn't describe how or why they worked—I knew because I'd asked him. I wanted to point out to Father that such ignorance was far more dangerous than a little fire. But I caught the look in his eye and knew I'd be wasting my breath.

"Those hired girls aren't as good as you," said Father, ignoring my brush with insubordination. "They didn't have your mother for a teacher." Mother used to toil beside Father in the workshop, too, sewing and weaving baskets. But such work didn't suit her, either. She was happiest when she was flying, and she was a better pilot than any of Father's men. She volunteered for every voyage, even though Father always grumbled about it. She had a knack for soothing his grumbles away, and it served her well. She flew all over the world in hot-air balloons.

Unfortunately, I didn't have the same knack. If Mother were here, maybe she could talk him into letting me help at the forge. If she were here, maybe he'd be grooming *me* to take over as the balloonist, instead of clumsy Guernsey. But Mother wasn't here, and suddenly everything was "too dangerous."

"Get to work," said Father.

"Yes, sir," I said, turning toward *Saint Ursula.* But before I could set to my sewing, I recalled with a sinking stomach the other thing I had to do. "By the way, who's flying to Tulera tomorrow?" I asked, trying to sound casual.

"Guernsey," said Father.

"Which balloon is he taking?"

*"Percival." Percy* was our navy-blue balloon, as valiant and reliable as a fairy-tale knight, according to Mother.

"And, uh, what time will he leave?"

Father's eyes narrowed in on me. "Why the sudden interest in the Tulera flight?" he asked. The furnace fire cast an eerie glow on his features, which made him look hollow and haunted. He was much too thin these days. With Mother gone, it fell to me to look after him, and I'd done a wretched job of it. And now, by getting myself into this fix with Abigail Smeade, I'd failed him more than he knew.

"Um, it's just that . . . Ms. Stoneman said rain is coming. She said she can feel it in her joints." I wasn't accustomed to lying to Father. It tasted bitter in my mouth.

"Bah," he bellowed, shaking his head. "Ms. Stoneman doesn't know weather. Tomorrow afternoon, the wind will be high. It'll be perfect for flying. It should be a steady clip all the way there. Though Guernsey has been known to get blown off course in still skies."

"Have you heard about this substance called rubber?" I blurted out. I immediately wished I could reel the words back into my mouth, but it was too late.

Father, who'd been poised to take another gulp of water, paused with the ladle halfway to his mouth. He arched an eyebrow at me.

"It's just . . . something I heard about at the market," I went on. "I thought maybe we could use it to push the balloons through the air, even without wind. It's stretchy, and if we could build propellers—"

"Have you been talking to Mr. Dudley again?" he asked, shaking his head. "Don't get carried away by that man's ideas, my girl. It'll only get you into trouble. Do you hear me?"

"Yes, Father."

"Once you've finished the sewing, I need you to get started on the paperwork for the Ministry."

A groan slipped past my lips. Filling out paperwork for the Ministry of Balloons—in triplicate, no less—was far worse than sewing. Almost anything you wanted to do in Oren required a permit, and ballooning over the Wall required about seventy-five of them.

"Is there a problem?" asked Father.

"No," I said quickly, the lie coming more easily this time. I coughed. "Something caught in my throat."

"Hmph," said Father. He picked up the metal rod he'd recently bent. It was dripping with the water he'd used to quench it. "Look at this."

I looked. It was a completely ordinary piece of metal, as far as I could tell.

"This bar is heavy," he said. "And solid. Nothing about it suggests that it should be able to fly. Yet it does. And do you know why?"

I shook my head, not sure where he was going with this.

"It can fly because it connects the brazier to the basket. And the brazier holds the fire. And the fire creates the heat that lifts the balloon. This"—he thumped the rod against his palm, showing off its heft—"can fly because it's part of something larger than itself. But if any of the individual parts break down, the whole balloon crashes."

This time, I nodded. He was describing precisely what I loved about hot-air balloons, the beauty that had nothing to do with silks and bright colors. The inner workings that only a real balloonist would understand.

"A kingdom is the same way," said Father. "Everything must work together for a common purpose. Laws steer us to that purpose. It's not our place to question them. If everyone did as they pleased, and obeyed only the laws they liked, the whole thing would fall apart."

"Yes, Father."

"In triplicate."

"Yes, Father."

Without another complaint, I trudged off to do my part.

# APPLE SEASON

*Wren's story, as far as she was concerned, began on Market Day. Once a week, every vendor in Oren descended on the square in front of the palace to sell their goods, and the whole kingdom convened to amble, gawk, and barter. The clamor flooded Wren's senses—the colors of piled-high produce, the scent of fresh-baked bread, the whinny of tethered horses. Roaring voices filled the air, the loudest peeling off from the rest: "Fresh eggs 'ere!" "Best in Oren!" "Daisies for the missus!"*

*Wren never tired of it. Everywhere else, she was someone's daughter or someone's potential wife. But at the market, she was just Wren. She moved along streets packed with people, the limbs of her countrymen jabbing her, the weight of their flesh sometimes squeezing the breath from her body. To be part of it was nothing short of intoxicating. And that was* before *she met Jaxson.*

*The first time she saw him, he was standing at a stall brimming with apples, their shiny skins glinting in the midmorning sun. Red, pink, gold, green—the array of colors and sizes astounded her. And the boy selling them? He outshone the ripest among them, with his shaggy, sandy hair; bronzed skin; and clever blue eyes. She cleared a path to his booth—indelicately, with her elbows prodding anyone who stood in her way. She stumbled into the apple stand and nearly sent a mountain of fruit toppling to the ground. Not quite the first impression she'd hoped for.*

*The boy didn't seem to notice, or mind, her awkward approach. "Apples, miss?"*

*"Yes. I'll take . . . your finest apple." She hoped it sounded natural. In truth, she couldn't name a single variety.*

*"Hmm." The boy tapped his chin and studied his produce with a slightly pained expression, as if he'd been asked to select a favorite child. "The Candlers are sweet and crisp, but the Dolbys have a unique tartness to them. It all depends on your mood. Do you prefer sweet? Or tart?"*

*"How about one of each?"*

*A smile curled his lips. "It's always wise to hedge your bets. If you can afford it, that is." After some deliberation, he plucked two apples from the cart and held them out to her, one in each hand. She fumbled for the leather purse lashed to her belt and pushed out two coins. Her last two coins, which she'd borrowed from Greta. The sugar-dusted doughnut she'd been craving would have to wait until next week. She tucked the fruit into the sash slung across her body.*

*A commotion stirred behind her. She turned as the crowd split down the center, as if sliced by a blade. Two ladies in fine clothes, with parasols balanced over their heads by careful servants, stepped daintily through the path that had been cleared for them. The nearer one noticed Wren and frowned at her simple smock, stained at the hem. The lady swung her nose into the air, as if to breathe the purer scents there.*

*"Hmph," snorted the apple seller. "They've come to look down at us for sport. I guess it must be rather boring, getting what you want all the time."*

*Wren grinned, liking him even more. "Perhaps they've run out of people to scorn inside the palace walls."*

*He chuckled, and she swelled with pride at having caused such a sound.*

*"I'm Jaxson," he said.*

*"I'm Wren," she replied, praying the heat building in her cheeks wasn't turning her redder than his Candlers. She quickly turned to go. For some reason, she wanted to remain in his presence and hide beneath a rock, at the exact same time.*

*"Wait," he called. "Here." He held out a small brown object—a peach pit, intricately whittled into the shape of a rose. "It's a hobby of mine," he said. "Mr. Hillman brings peaches from Palma for us to sell. I carve the pits for my little brother."*

*"It's lovely," she said, tracing its smooth curves. She handed it back, thrilled and terrified that her fingers might brush against his.*

*"Keep it," he insisted. Her blush deepened as she placed it in her sash.*

*Needless to say, she ate more than her share of apples that season.*

# A BRIEF HISTORY OF THE KINGDOM OF OREN

I stared out the classroom window, tracing the path of the sun higher and higher in the cloudless sky. All morning, I'd been watching it, barely aware of Ms. Stoneman's lessons on geography, reading, and what passed for math. How could I concentrate on school when every inch of the sun's rise brought me closer to *Percival*'s flight? Closer to my betrayal of Father. Closer to . . .

*Abi?*

She appeared as suddenly and inconveniently as she had the day before, standing right outside the schoolyard, less than fifteen feet away from where I sat. She was doodling on a poster nailed to a tree, her tongue poking out of the side of her mouth as she worked. She wore boys' riding clothes—breeches with holes at the knees and a loose lace-up shirt, which she'd tucked and tied so it looked like something else entirely. Something rather fashionable. And, of course, she'd topped it off with a familiar silk scarf woven into her hair. When she finished whatever she was doing, she angled back to admire the result. Then, as if she sensed the weight of my panicked stare, she looked up and gave me a big vivacious wave.

My gaze swung to the schoolmistress, who was lecturing from

the podium about the history of Oren. I looked back at Abi and shook my head, hoping she'd get the message: *Go away.*

She didn't. She gestured for me to come outside. I shook my head again, more forcefully this time. Still, Abi waved me out, getting more animated and more annoyed in lockstep. Clearly, that girl had never been to school.

"Prismena Reece!" snapped Ms. Stoneman. Somehow she'd moved from the podium to my desk without my noticing, which I could only assume was some schoolmistress magic trick. She peered down at me with intense disapproval. Which, to be fair, was how she always looked. Her lips were drawn into a perpetual pucker, all bunched up in the center of her face like someone had tried to sew them shut. She wore a high-necked dress cinched with a leather belt that occasionally left its mark on a student's backside. "What are you looking at?" she demanded.

"Nothing, ma'am," I muttered, keeping my eyes lowered. I resisted the urge to check if Abi was still there. I wasn't sure what would happen if Ms. Stoneman discovered my blackmailer waiting for me outside, but I knew it wouldn't end well for me.

"Good," said Ms. Stoneman, whose voice was as brittle as Abi's hard candy, but with none of the sweetness. "Now answer the question." She turned sharply and clicked to the front of the classroom in her heels, which gave me one last chance to look outside. Thankfully, Abi was gone. Then I cast desperate glances around the classroom, hoping someone would feed me the answer Ms. Stoneman wanted. Or even just the question. All I got was a stuck-out tongue from Alfie Stewart, the nastiest boy in class.

"Ms. Reece?" barked Ms. Stoneman, whipping around again to face the class. "Answer, please." The chalkboard displayed the lesson in Ms. Stoneman's blocky handwriting: *The Great Peace.* So I grasped at the most obvious answer.

"The Palmerian War?"

"Is that a question, or is it the answer, Ms. Reece?"

"The answer?"

Ms. Stoneman squinted at me skeptically. "Correct. And what caused the Palmerian War?"

"The abduction of Princess Catherine," I replied.

Ms. Stoneman nodded and smoothed the slick hair of her tight bun. "Benjamin Warren!" she called. I exhaled in relief, but poor Benji winced like he'd been hit. Splotches of red crept from the collar of his shirt and traveled up his neck, like mercury rising in a thermometer. "Why did the Palmerians kidnap Princess Catherine?"

"Um . . . t-to try and steal the Oren throne after K-King Reginald fell ill," he said. By then, the color had reached his hairline, making his head look like a plump, sputtering tomato.

"Precisely," said Ms. Stoneman. "Oren was vulnerable because King Reginald had only one child, a teenaged daughter. The Palmerians snatched her from the castle in the night and took her south to their kingdom, where they held her prisoner in a foul dungeon. Lydia Kincaid!" The schoolmistress spat the name out of her mouth so quickly Lydia yelped like a kicked puppy. "How did Oren respond to Palmerian aggression?"

Lydia recovered quickly, plastering a smile on her face and folding her hands demurely on her desk. "Princess Catherine's new husband, Lord Michael, sent troops into Palma to rescue his beloved. And in her absence, he built the Wall to keep Oren safe from further attack. He eventually became king, and he never stopped fighting for the woman he loved. Two years after she was taken, Queen Catherine was rescued by King Michael, and they have ruled together ever since." When she said that last bit, Lydia got a dewy-eyed, dreamy look on her face. It was widely agreed that King Michael's rescue of his queen was the most romantic thing that had ever happened in Oren. Or perhaps anywhere.

My gaze drifted back out the window, and I almost toppled out of my chair. I was greeted by Abi's scowling face only inches from my own, right on the other side of the glass. She held up the palm of her hand, where she'd written a single word in smudged charcoal: *NOW!* I lifted my shoulders in a gesture of helplessness, trying to convey to her that I couldn't simply walk out of school in the middle of a lesson. Abi's expression conveyed back to me that she didn't care.

"Ms. Stoneman!" called Alfie, thrusting his hand into the air. "My brother said the Palmerians have a weapon so powerful it can blast through the Wall. He said they captured lightning from the sky and will use it to attack us. Is it true?" The other children gasped, but Ms. Stoneman glared them into silence.

"Don't be a dunce," she said, skewering Alfie with a sharp look. "The Palmerian army, like any other, is no match for the Wall. What's more, they are losing the war, and soon we will celebrate an Oren victory. But people with nothing to brag about will often invent something to make themselves sound impressive. They are fools, but so are we if fall for it. Right, children?"

"Yes, ma'am," everyone said. Everyone but Alfie, who stared glumly at his desk.

Outside, Abi raised her other palm and held it up to the glass. *I'll scream!* was written on it in thick black lines. I had no doubt Abi would do exactly that if I didn't join her soon.

"We are lucky we live in Oren," Ms. Stoneman went on. "And we must express our gratitude with obedience." She scanned the sea of heads compliantly bobbing. When her gaze landed on me—thief, liar, future smuggler—it lingered there, as if she knew. My mouth went dry, and sweat slicked my palms.

From the corner of my eye, I saw Abi suck in a deep breath, preparing to carry out her threat. My hand shot into the air. "Ms. Stoneman," I blurted out. "I have to go!"

The schoolmistress's eyebrows rose sharply.

"Uh . . . there's a flight to Tulera this afternoon, and Father needs my help," I said. It wasn't unheard of for Father to keep me home on flight days, but Ms. Stoneman didn't approve of such practices. She studied me for a moment, and I was certain my lies had finally caught up with me. But then, with a disgruntled sigh and a flick of her wrist, Ms. Stoneman dismissed me from the room, promising to take it up later with my father.

# THE ART OF ABIGAIL SMEADE

"What were you thinking?" I roared, tearing out of Lollyhill Day School and storming over to Abi, who was leaning casually against the tree. "Now I have to deal with Ms. Stoneman, who is definitely going to tell Father I left school early. How am I supposed to explain that?"

"Aren't you happy to see me?" Abi asked, pouting slightly. I couldn't tell if she was really wounded or just putting me on. Either way, I didn't have time for her nonsense.

"We've got plenty of time before *Percival*'s flight," I said. "You've got no business with me until then. What are you doing here?"

"I wanted to make sure you didn't get any big ideas about standing me up. Besides, I had other important matters to attend to in Lollyhill."

"Like what?" I huffed. "Defiling posters?" The parchment over her shoulder was an announcement for the annual Savior's Day celebration, taking place in ten days' time. Savior's Day was Oren's most important holiday, marking the day King Michael placed the final stone on the wall surrounding the city. Every year, the entire kingdom turned up at Savior's Gate for dazzling entertainment, spectacular food, and general merriment, all while the royal family waved down at us from the top of the Wall. The poster provided the details of the event alongside stately portraits of King Michael and Queen Catherine. But someone had embellished their familiar royal faces. Someone had given both of them thick black mustaches. Abi stood beside her handiwork and grinned.

"What have you done?" I cried. "Defacing a picture of the royal family could get you in big trouble."

"I can't get in trouble unless someone snitches on me," she said, her smirk fading. She stepped toward me with a menacing gleam in her eye. "Are you gonna snitch on me?"

"No," I mumbled.

"Like I thought," she said, backing off. "Besides, I think I've improved them. Anything to cover up the king's face. Don't you think he looks like a sticky bun with eyes? And an undercooked sticky bun at that."

"Of course not," I said. I couldn't deny that King Michael's face had a doughy quality, but I wouldn't dream of comparing the savior of Oren to a baked good. Not out loud. "And what about the queen? Surely you don't think her looks are improved by facial hair?" Even Abi—who seemed to be disagreeable for the mere sake of it—had to admit that Queen Catherine was beautiful, with her flowing black hair, alabaster skin, and delicate features.

"The Mad Queen?" said Abi. "Yeah, she's pretty. But her soul is empty. Just look at her eyes. Cold and lifeless. Now her outside matches her inside—ugly!"

Once again, I couldn't disagree with Abi's description. The queen's eyes *were* unsettling. According to rumors, the once-beloved Princess Catherine had been utterly changed during her years in the Palmerian dungeon. People said she'd been hardened, her innocence turned to callousness. Now they shrank from her and spoke of her in whispers as the Mad Queen of Oren.

"Did you know she wears her hair down to hide a deformed ear?" said Abi. "She tried to cut it off with sewing shears when she didn't like one of her musician's songs."

"That's ridiculous," I said.

"The truth often is."

"Well . . . maybe you'd be mad, too, if you were stolen from your home and held captive in a foreign dungeon!"

"Ha!" Abi crowed. "I'd have broken out before anybody knew I was gone."

"Yeah, right."

"Never you mind about that. Just worry about getting my box on that balloon today."

"Fine," I groaned.

Abi stood upright, and I noticed something unusual about the patch of bark she'd been leaning on. I stepped in closer and saw that a short poem had been carved into it:

PINK TO HEAL YOU.
RED TO FIGHT.
GREEN TO KEEP YOU
WARM AT NIGHT.
BLUE TO FEED YOU.
WHITE TO RUN.
YELLOW FOR THE
RISING SUN.

"I've seen this before," I said, running my fingers over the words. "On another tree, just last week. Did you do this?"

"Of course not," she said. But once again, I couldn't figure out if she was duping me.

"I wonder what it means."

"What do *you* think it means?" she asked. She was staring at me strangely, like she really expected me to answer.

"I don't know," I finally said with a shrug. "Sounds like a bunch of drivel to me."

"Then that's exactly what it is," she replied. And she bounded off ahead of me, in the direction of the launch site.

# WHAT HOPE FEELS LIKE

"I remember when balloons were invented," Mother said to me once. We were in Fletcher's field, watching our red balloon, *The Flame,* soar over us. "I thought they were something out of a dream," she said. "How else could such things float around in the sky without strings or magic? I used to run after them, chasing them for miles to see what treasures they carried from distant lands. Those deliveries were never meant for me, but I always hoped that someday, just maybe, a balloon might bring me something special."

"And did it?" I asked. "Did a balloon ever bring you anything?"

"Of course it did," she said. "It brought me your father."

"Oh," I muttered. "Is that all?"

At that, Mother laughed, and the sky split open with the sound. She had a bold, from-the-belly laugh—nothing like my timid one. I had to shrink back just to give it room.

"Father would've been enough," she went on. "But the balloons brought me more than a husband. All my life, I'd been staring at the same blue sky—so predictable, so boring—and suddenly it was full of color. If that could happen, I figured, what *couldn't* happen?" She put her hand on top of mine. "That's what hope feels like."

If I closed my eyes, I could still picture us there—lying in the grass as *The Flame* swallowed up the sky for a breathtaking moment, then shrank again and eventually disappeared.

But when I saw *Percival* after school, hope was the very opposite of what I felt. He was strung up between the masts, the two giant poles Father had constructed to keep the deflated balloons upright. He waited there with an empty belly, ready to be pumped full of fire.

"Whoa," breathed Abi. She gaped at him for an instant, then changed course and marched to a clump of bushes near the launch site, where she presented me with a box. It was stamped with the name Winston Vickers and a fancy Tuleran address. It was neither teeny nor tiny.

"*That's* the box?" I gasped. "That thing will throw off the balloon's equilibrium for sure!"

"It will?" she said, doubt passing over her face for a split second.

"Yes," I cried. "As I've been trying to tell you, this is a bad idea!"

"Then I guess it's a good thing I've got my very own balloon expert," she said. "Please make sure my box doesn't throw off the . . . whatever you just said."

"I'm not a balloon expert!"

"You'd better become one in the next few hours," she said, "or me and my new scarf are out of here."

"Argh! Fine. I'll go check on Father and figure out how to get that thing on board. You stay here!"

On my way into the house, I nearly collided with Father, who was moving briskly in the other direction. "Hi!" I said in an unnaturally high-pitched voice.

"What are you doing here?" he asked. "Shouldn't you be in school?"

"Yes . . . technically. But I couldn't remember if I filled out the Ministry forms in triplicate or only in duplicate. So I came home to double-check."

"Hmph," he grunted, giving me that suspicious look again.

"Where are you going?" I asked.

"Guernsey's late. He tends to get carried away at the tavern before a flight, so I'm going to round him up." Father shook his head. "Sometimes I wonder about that boy."

"You and me both," I muttered, but if Father heard me, he didn't react. He trudged to the stable.

As soon as Father rode off toward the tavern, Abi and I wasted no time lugging the box onto the platform. In addition to being big, it was heavier than it looked. "What's in here?" I asked. "And who's Winston Vickers?"

"Never you mind," replied Abi.

I stopped suddenly, dropping my end of the box and causing her to stumble. "You know that balloons run on *hot air,* right? Fire? I need to know what's in that box, or someone could get hurt."

"It's perfectly safe," she insisted.

"What's in the box, Abi?"

"It's . . . candy." Even she didn't sound convinced.

"Abi!"

"It's candy! Winston Stickers is my grandfather. I'm sending him a birthday gift."

"Winston *Vickers*! And are you trying to tell me you blackmailed me to send a box of candy to your grandfather? That's insane."

"Grandpa Winston loves candy."

"Wait a minute . . ." I gasped. "Do you even know what's in this box?"

"All you need to know," said Abi, "is that it's completely harmless. Besides, you don't have much choice in the matter, do you?" She ran her fingers along the shimmering scarf in her hair.

I huffed at her. Then I lifted my end of the box and heaved it into the basket.

Father had carefully arranged the packages bound for Tulera by height and weight, but we dismantled his hard work in minutes, unstacking them and hiding Abi's box on the bottom. Then we put it all back, trying to make it look exactly as we'd found it, like putting together a puzzle with one extra piece. We even pocketed some of the inventory to rebalance the weight. When we finished, sweaty and panting, the illegal package was buried beneath crates of beets, kumquats, and squash. The next time someone uncovered it, it would be on the ground in Tulera, on its way to Winston Vickers. At least, I hoped it would.

"Nice job," said Abi. "You might have a future in the smuggling business."

I didn't dignify that comment with a response. Instead, I held out my palm. I'd done what she asked, and now I wanted Mother's scarf. I planned to put it back where I'd found it, at the bottom of a drawer, and let Father discover it himself. No more lies.

Abi was reaching to the nape of her neck to untie that slip of silk at last, when her eyes suddenly widened. The faint sound of a galloping horse was growing louder. Over Abi's shoulder, I saw Father riding toward us.

"Relax," I said. "It's only Father coming back from the tavern. Just hurry up!"

"It's not your dad!" she cried, staring past me in the opposite direction. "Hide!" She grabbed my arm and dragged me off the platform, into the same cluster of bushes she'd used to stash the box. We disappeared into the foliage just as a group of royal guardsmen thundered up the road to my house.

# THERE MUST BE SOME MISTAKE

The soldiers arrived at the same time as Father. Through a veil of leaves, I watched them dismount and approach him, making him appear small and frail next to their black boots and bulk. He listened to them and nodded. Then he rushed into the house and returned with a bundle of paperwork—the same bundle I'd filled out in triplicate the night before. He handed it to the officer with the most medals pinned to his chest, and they all walked toward the balloon. Toward us.

I'd heard about the Ministry of Balloons doing unannounced inventory checks, but I'd never witnessed one before. I told myself it was a mere formality. Not a big deal.

As long as the balloonist wasn't smuggling contraband, of course.

"You said it would be fine," I hissed at Abi.

"It will be," she said. "They're not going to check every single box."

"Are you sure?"

"I'm . . . pretty sure."

If my eyes had been weapons, Abi would've keeled over dead at that moment. Instead, she lived to watch those stone-faced soldiers unload every item in the basket, one at a time, checking each against the paperwork in their hands. As they neared the bottom, I thought I might keel over myself, from the stress of it. Finally, one of the soldiers uncovered Abi's box and consulted his list. He frowned and checked again. Then he alerted the officer in charge.

I stopped breathing altogether then.

Father's face registered confusion, then shock, then a brief flare of anger that he quickly tamped down. "There must be some mistake," he said. "I confirmed this inventory myself." He took the papers and shook his head. He looked even smaller.

I rose halfway, to go to him, but Abi pulled me back by the hem of my dress. "There's nothing you can do!" she said.

The lead officer called for a crowbar, and the men pried open the box. One of the soldiers dug his hands inside and removed two handfuls of small wrapped squares. "It's . . . chocolate!" he said.

"It really is candy," Abi gasped, and I wanted to wallop her more than ever.

"What's going on here?" growled the officer. "Is this a bribe? To . . . Winston Vickers? The Tuleran ambassador to Palma?"

"Wh-what?" sputtered Father. "I am a balloonist. A workman. I have no interest in foreign affairs. I—I can't imagine how this box wound up in my balloon."

"Has anyone else had access to this vessel?"

"No, no one else," stammered Father. "My pilot hasn't arrived yet. He's late."

"So your pilot—Jamison Guernsey—hasn't had access to this cargo?"

"No," said Father.

"Very interesting," said the officer. He paused for a beat and came very near to smiling. "This flight is grounded. And you, sir, are under arrest."

"What?" Father croaked. He swayed, then steadied himself against one of the masts. Once again, I resisted the urge to run to him. "I've done nothing wrong."

"You're being charged with smuggling," said the soldier, "and on suspicion of treason."

"Treason?" whispered Father. One of the soldiers roughly gripped Father's shoulders and secured his hands behind his back with a length of rope.

I couldn't stay put any longer. Abi tried to stop me, but I shook her off and bolted to Father, startling him and the other men.

"Let him go," I cried.

"Who is this?" the officer snapped.

"I'm his daughter, and he didn't—"

"This is no matter for a child."

"But I—"

"Stand back."

With a warning look from Father, I did as instructed. But I continued to protest. "You can't do this! He's innocent." My heart raced. My blood whooshed in my ears.

"We certainly *can* do this, and we *are* doing this," said the officer. "If your father's story clears, he'll be promptly released. Now get this prisoner and the evidence into the wagon."

"Yessir," mumbled one of the soldiers through a mouthful of chocolate. He crumpled an empty candy wrapper and tossed it to the ground before carrying the box to the waiting wagon. The other soldier nudged Father in the same direction.

"May I have a word with my daughter before I go?" asked Father, his watery eyes pleading his case. "Please?"

"Fine," said the officer. As soon as the word left the man's lips, I ran to Father at full tilt and threw my arms around him, almost knocking us both over.

"They can't do this!" Hot tears flooded my face and soaked Father's shirt. "I'll go to the palace and tell them there's been a mistake, and—"

"You'll do nothing of the sort," Father snapped, leaning back to look me in the eye. "I'll not have you getting mixed up in this. Do you understand?"

"But, Father, I'm the one—"

"Do you understand?" he barked.

"Yes, Father."

"Go inside, lock the doors, and pull the curtains."

"Yes, sir."

"Don't leave the house. Don't go into town. Don't put yourself in any danger."

"Yes, sir."

"Do nothing until I return."

"Enough!" growled the officer. One of the soldiers wrenched me away from Father by the arm. His fellow soldier ushered Father to the wagon. A moment later, in a blur of dust and tears, they were gone, galloping down the winding road that led to the heart of Oren.

I collapsed where I stood, shaking and sobbing. Father would be tossed into a foul prison cell, where he'd be starved and humiliated, kicked and beaten. He was too old and broken to endure such abuses. And it was all my fault.

As my teardrops hit the ground, something shining in the dirt caught my eye. It was the soldier's discarded candy wrapper. And there was writing on the inside. I picked it up with trembling fingers and smoothed it out. It said: *Celebrate Savior's Day with a BANG! When the sun rises . . .*

The rest of the message was illegible, smeared with dirt and chocolate, but I'd seen enough. The candy wasn't just candy after all. It *was* treason. I recalled the Palmerian weapon that Alfie had mentioned in class, the one that could break down the Wall. Did the Palmerians intend to attack Oren on Savior's Day? Was Abi plotting with them? Was she a traitor?

Worse yet, was *I* a traitor now, too?

The very thought made my blood run cold at first. Then it began to boil.

I stormed to the bushes, ready to confront the one person more deserving of blame than me.

But true to form, Abigail Smeade was already gone.

# ANOTHER MESS TO CLEAN

I gathered the kumquats that had rolled away, rudely kicked by soldiers' boots. Overturned boxes and stray produce littered the ground around *Percival,* and because I couldn't help Father or scream at Abi, I did the only thing left to do. I tidied up.

A rustling in *Percival*'s basket stopped me in my tracks. At first, I thought it might be Guernsey, but he wasn't the type to turn up while the Royal Guard was nearby. It had to be a critter, then, come to sample the spilled food. I wasn't eager to fight off a raccoon, but the least I could do was protect the shipment so Father could make his delivery when he returned. Besides, no animal was as scary as the men who'd just left. I moved cautiously toward the basket's swinging door and pulled it open.

There, ravenously hunched over a chocolate bar, was Abi.

"You!" I roared. I dropped the kumquats in my arms, sending them scattering into the grass again. I jumped at her, but she scooted out of my reach.

"Whoa!" she shrieked. "Is this the thanks I get?"

"*Thanks?* What is wrong with you?" I would've gone after her again, only I wasn't sure what I'd do if I actually caught her. She was skinny but strong, and I suspected she could lick me.

"While you and your dad were getting all teary-eyed, I snuck over to the soldiers' wagon and got our box back. I hid it somewhere they'll never find it. Now they've got no evidence to prove your dad did anything wrong. You're welcome."

"You really are a piece of work, you know that?"

"Thanks."

"It's not a compliment! You have to go to the prison—right now—and tell the Royal Guard the truth. Tell them you were the one who put that box in the basket. Tell them that Father didn't know anything about it."

"Not on your life," she said, taking another bite of chocolate. "That would ruin the whole plan."

"What plan?"

"That's for me to know and for you to never, ever know."

"You're only saying that because *you* don't know, either!" I said. "You walk around acting like a big shot, when really you're just someone's lackey, aren't you?"

"I am not!" Her face was turning red, her lips pressed tight together.

"Then tell me what you're planning. Let me see what's written on that candy wrapper!"

"No!"

I lunged for the slip of paper, but she held it over her head, out of my reach. "You won't get away with this!" I yelled, standing on tiptoe. Even that only put me at eye level with her chin. "I'll tell! I'll turn you in!"

"Your father told you not to get involved, remember? So why don't you listen to him? Go inside and lock the door like a good little girl."

"Argh!" I sank down onto my heels.

I didn't want to admit it, but she was right. I'd promised Father I'd stay out of it. I couldn't disobey him now, not after everything else I'd done. I backed away from Abi, who ripped the candy wrapper into tiny pieces and let them scatter to the ground. Another mess to clean up, courtesy of Abigail Smeade.

"You're not going to get away with this," I said softly. "Whatever you're planning, King Michael will stop you."

"You don't know what you're talking about," she said. She shoved past me on her way out of the basket. "Stick to what you're good at, Prismena. Mending holes in balloons and hiding behind locked doors. That suits you."

She walked off the platform, but her words echoed in my head. And they stung—more than they should have, coming from her. I picked myself up and watched her bound toward the road as if she didn't have a care in the world.

*Don't leave the house,* Father had said. *Don't put yourself in any danger.* What he'd meant but didn't say out loud was *Don't end up like Mother.*

Abi had almost reached the corner. If she turned and I lost sight of her, she'd disappear, as she seemed to be so good at doing. Then I'd lose my chance to clear Father's name and get him out of jail. Despite the voice in my head—Father's voice—telling me not to do it, I bolted out of the basket and ran after her as fast as I could.

# THE WEDDING GIFT

*The rest of Oren was still in bed as Wren crept along its deserted streets. Sunlight was just seeping in at the seams of the sky, and a rare feeling of calm shrouded the kingdom. But it was far too quiet for Wren's liking, as if she were the last person left in all the world. She shuddered at the thought.*

*She arrived at the meeting spot breathless and nervous. Jaxson—the boy she'd met at the market just six months earlier—was already there, sitting in a wagon beside a kindly gray-haired farmer from Palma named Mr. Hillman. They could trust him, Jaxson assured her, as he helped her climb onto the seat beside him. Wren untied her sash and cradled it in her lap. She'd brought only what she could easily carry—some clothes and a few coins to start a new life.*

*"Are you sure you want to do this?" asked Jaxson. Even in the dark, he must have noticed the tracks of fresh tears that streaked her face.*

*"I'm sure," she said. She sat up tall and bit her lip.*

*Mr. Hillman cracked the whip, and they trotted off toward Trader's Lane. They skirted the center of the city, taking the long way through the fields of Lollyhill. In the twilight, the rolling farmland looked like a big blue quilt resting on the sleeping form of a giant. It made Wren think of her father, in his bed at that very moment. He'd wake in a few hours to find her room empty, the bedsheets smooth. He wouldn't know where she'd gone, but he'd know why.*

*She didn't blame him. Everyone in Oren—from the humblest peasant to the queen herself—obeyed tradition, which dictated that a father selected a husband for his daughter. Only widows and castoffs married for love. So Wren was officially a castoff now. She felt for the simple copper band around her finger, the one Jaxson had placed there the day before, and stared at a countryside that would soon become a memory. Then Jaxson took her hand and pressed something into her palm. Small and smooth and intricate.*

*"A wedding gift," he said. "It's a wren." And so it was—a delicate carved bird. She closed her fingers around it and held it close to her heart.*

*"Must I take up whittling when I get to Palma?" she asked. "Does everyone there carve peach pits?"*

*"Not a single one," chuckled Mr. Hillman, overhearing. "Jaxson's the only person I've ever met with the patience for such a task." Wren smiled at her new husband.*

*"I left one for my brother," said Jaxson. "A dragon. He likes to believe they might exist. He'll find it when he wakes." His words were laced with sadness. Wren wasn't alone in missing Oren already.*

*"Tell me again about Palma," she said, nestling into him. She needed to think about something other than Jaxson's brother, waking to find he had nothing but a small trinket to remember his brother by. Or Father in the doorway of her room, his chin trembling even as he refused to surrender to tears.*

*"Palma is the loveliest place in the world," said Jaxson. "The air is warm and soft, like an embrace, and the breeze is gentle, like*

*a whisper. The trees are tall, with wide green leaves for shade, and fruit that falls down at your feet when it gets ripe, like an offering from the gods."*

*"Tell me about the ocean," said Wren, letting her heavy eyelids slide shut.*

*"The water is every kind of blue, a different shade from every angle. It swells and crashes and rebuilds, like a living thing. And it stretches on and on, without end. It makes you feel small, in a way. But it also reminds you that whatever's nagging you probably isn't all that important."*

*"It sounds amazing," she said.*

*"It's better than amazing."*

*They rode in silence after that, until they reached the Southern Gate, the simple stone arch that marked the south end of Oren. As they approached it, Wren opened her eyes and twisted around in her seat to glance back at her home, glittering in the yellow light of morning. It looked tiny from there, so small she imagined she could put it in her pocket and take it with her. Instead, she said goodbye. She faced forward as they passed, without ceremony, into Palma.*

# IN THE FINGERPRINT OF GOD

According to legend, God once pressed his thumb into the earth, pointing to a place fit for kings. That place became known as Oren, a gaping crater in the landscape, with the palace smack in the center. When nobody else was within earshot, Father would say that a palace should be built on high ground, not in the belly of a valley, where it was vulnerable to invaders and floods and all manner of calamity. But the kings of Oren had never heeded that advice. Perhaps that was why Oren needed the Wall.

I followed Abi's springy mound of curls straight down into the fingerprint that day. I left behind Lollyhill's farms and mills and its single balloonist's workshop and traveled downhill through the Slope, where the working class of Oren lived. The Slope was a jumble of buildings as tilted as its name implied, where everything—even the people—looked ready to collapse. But eventually, the tight passages of the Slope opened onto the broad cobblestone lanes of Silk Valley, where you lived if fortune had plucked you out of the heap, dusted you off, and dressed you up.

Silk Valley is where Abi finally stopped walking, to my great relief. My legs were as wobbly as custard by then, and my lungs ached from the simple act of breathing. Abi, on the other hand, showed no sign of slowing down, like her feet were made of springs. I wondered why she'd chosen to pause here, on a pristine street where a girl in tattered clothes was almost certainly unwelcome. She was staring into the shop window of the dressmaker Jerrick Larue, the man famous for outfitting the queen in her finest gowns. Abi had apparently forgotten the urgent business of treason in the presence of some frocks, and with an absentminded smile on her lips, let her eyes pore over the elaborate creations on the dressmakers' forms. They were lovely, to be sure, but who had time for such frippery when a rebellion was being hatched and innocent people were being arrested?

A white man with a crooked nose and an impeccable suit leaned against the storefront puffing on a curved pipe. "Off with you!" he growled at Abi. He spoke with a thick Tuleran accent, which sounded to me like the words were caught in the back of his throat and had to be coughed up like phlegm. But to the rest of the world, it proved he was sophisticated. I knew he must be Mr. Larue himself. He sneered at Abi with bared teeth, and she sneered right back. But she also tore herself away from his window display.

Abi weaved for a few more blocks, and I followed, staying a few paces behind so she wouldn't spot me. Eventually, she plunged into the Market Day crowd, and hiding got a whole lot easier. I used to beg Mother to let me tag along on Market Day, to lose myself in the bright and buzzing labyrinth of stalls, knowing I'd convince Mother to buy me whatever exotic treat or toy caught my fancy. But that was almost four years ago. As the war dragged on, the number of vendors dwindled. No longer did delicacies from far-flung kingdoms line the stalls. But Orenites came anyway—

out of habit or nostalgia. And they still had to eat, even if beets were the only thing on the menu now.

"Prismena Reece!" someone called from behind me. I tensed and slowly turned. A paunchy white man with thick sideburns and even thicker spectacles stood behind a cart laden with dangling timepieces. Mr. Dudley, the watchmaker. His products whirred and ticked and chimed, each one singing its own mechanical tune. "I've got something for you," he said, beckoning me over.

Years earlier, Mr. Dudley had noticed me hovering by his stall, staring bug-eyed as he repaired an ancient timepiece. He'd waved me closer and let me bend my head over the tiny mechanism, explaining the different parts as he went about his work. He'd never received such interest from a child before, let alone a girl. It didn't take long for us to recognize our shared love of pulling things apart, learning their secrets, and putting them back together again. Watchmaking required Mr. Dudley to put the pieces back precisely as they had been, but we both preferred rearranging them into something new. When I got the idea to rig up a system to guide hot-air balloons with ropes and valves, giving pilots some freedom from the wind, Mr. Dudley helped me map out my idea with dimensions and schematics. And, at my urging, he proposed the idea to Father, who never would've abided it from his daughter's lips. But coming from Mr. Dudley, Father decreed that it was brilliant. That apparatus came to be known as Dudley Valves—a name which, I'll admit, stung at first. I didn't blame Mr. Dudley, though. Every time I passed through the market, he would fill my palms with pins, gears, hinges, and other castoffs of his profession that I'd add to my collection—even the occasional scrap of rubber.

But not today.

"I'm sorry," I called over my shoulder.

Abi had swerved into an alley, and I had to bump people out of my way to keep up. I trailed her down a corridor littered with trash and questionable puddles, a space so narrow I could reach out and touch the wall on either side. She slipped through an unmarked door, which instantly closed behind her. Arriving seconds later, I reached for the doorknob but stopped myself.

What was I thinking? That door would probably spit me into a den of criminals, and I was about to walk through it willingly. I pulled my fingers back as if the knob were molten. What a fool I'd been, following a stranger—a known traitor, no less—to a place that would almost certainly lead to more trouble. Chasing Abi had been a mistake. But it wasn't too late to correct it.

I turned to go. A long shadow passed over me.

"Well, well, well," said the man who had cast it. "What do we have here?" His silhouette blotted out the colors of the market behind him. His voice was a low rumble that echoed down the tight space. "What's a wee girl doin' all alone in a scary place like this? Ain't you heard only criminals creep around in dark alleys?" As he neared, his face came into focus. His oily white skin was crisscrossed with scars, his mouth a gaping black hole framed by nubby, empty gums.

Terror held me in place.

The man lumbered toward me on unsteady, spindly legs. "This 'ere alley is spoken for, girlie! It's mine! Get out!" He reached toward me, his gnarled fingers opening and closing on something invisible. In a moment, it would be my own skinny neck within their grasp. "Get out or pay!"

I yelped and scrambled for the doorknob. When my clutching hands finally found it, I burst through the mysterious door without another instant of hesitation. Whatever was waiting for me inside couldn't be worse than what had just lunged for me in that alley. Or so I hoped.

# A DEN OF TRAITORS

The air was thick with smoke and grease; it rang with the clamor of pots and pans and bubbling liquid. A tall black man in a sweat-stained apron moved around the kitchen with the grace of a dancer, brandishing a wooden spoon. When I hurtled inside, he froze midstir and spun around, spattering the walls with sauce. "What?" he bellowed.

"Um . . . is Abi here?" I asked, breathless and unable to come up with a good lie.

He heaved his big shoulders and rolled his eyes. "Another urchin," he muttered. He motioned to a door on the opposite end of the kitchen. "Halston's office is over there." Then he returned to the stove, channeling his irritation into aggressive whisking.

I gave the chef a wide berth as I tiptoed toward the office of someone named Halston. On the way, I passed a swinging door with a round window in the center that looked into a dimly lit pub. Having never set foot in such a place, where all manner of bad behavior was rumored to occur, I couldn't resist stealing a glance. A handful of men with drawn faces were hunched over dripping pints of beer. Others shoveled mounds of shepherd's pie into their mouths. Meanwhile, a pianist in the corner pounded out a jaunty tune that was strikingly out of place. It wasn't the rowdy den of vice I expected, and I have to admit I was a bit disappointed.

"Ahem!" grunted the chef, and I continued on my way.

I nudged the door to Halston's office open just a crack, revealing a sliver of peeling yellow wallpaper and a rickety table that held a single candle and a messy stack of papers. Beneath the table, a boy no older than three, with pale skin and a wild mane of black hair, played with an assortment of random items—a ball of yarn, a broken bracket, a handful of rocks.

"That sniveling rat-faced, lily-livered cur," yelled someone inside the room. Even though she was outside my line of sight, I recognized Abi's voice right away.

"We don't know for sure it was him," said another, calmer voice, this one belonging to a boy—presumably Halston.

"*I'm* sure it was him," said Abi. "I knew he'd crumble like a stale cookie. How else would the guards have known to inspect that flight? It can't be a coincidence that he got nabbed, and the next day our plans were foiled."

"C'mon, Abs," said the boy. "Guernsey has been delivering our messages for months. Why would he turn on us now?"

I gasped, then quickly clasped my hand over my open mouth. Had he just said *Guernsey*? Our clumsy pilot was in league with these scoundrels? And to think, Father was going to give him the workshop!

"He turned on us because his neck was on the line!" said Abi. "Because he's a rotten crud-covered cretin."

"Maybe you're right," said Halston, "but bad-mouthing Guernsey isn't going to get that box over the border. We need to get it delivered. Fast."

"Why don't we send it through the East Gate?" suggested Abi.

"No, they'll be expecting that," said Halston. "Especially when they find out their evidence is missing."

"That was brilliant, wasn't it?" asked Abi, her voice lilting with pride.

"What's our next move?" Halston wondered aloud, ignoring her.

"I don't know," said Abi, "but whatever you do, please don't make me follow some pampered kid all over creation again. I don't think I can handle another assignment like that."

I bristled at her description of me but held my tongue.

"I want to do more for the cause," she went on. "I can sneak into any place you please. Even the palace, I bet. And I can steal anything you can think of. You want the queen's crown? I can get it!"

"I know you can," said Halston. "You're the best deputy I've got. That's why I can't risk you getting caught. We've gotta be smart about this, Abs. This rebellion isn't a game, and it's not about sneaking around stealing things. It's about making the right move at the right time."

*Rebellion? I knew it!*

"Who's that?" chirped the little boy under the table. I'd been too busy eavesdropping to notice his eyes on me or his chubby finger pointing in my direction.

I tried to slink away, but the door swung open in a wide arc, putting me face to face with the rebels. Abi, her mouth hanging open, stood beside a boy of about eighteen. He looked familiar—with tan skin, serious brown eyes, and a pair of deep-set dimples—but before I could place him in my memory, he grabbed me by the wrist and pulled me into the room. In his other hand, he held a short but sharp-looking blade, which he thrust toward my neck.

"Wait!" cried Abi. "That's her—the balloonist's daughter, Prismena."

"Oh," said Halston, releasing me. He let the knife clatter onto the table, as if embarrassed that he'd threatened me with it. I got the impression he didn't have the heart to actually use it. Abi, on the other hand . . .

"Don't you know better than to sneak up on people like that?" she said.

"Excuse me if I'm not used to walking in on a bunch of *traitors* planning a rebellion!" I said, stumbling to the other side of the room, where the little boy gazed up at me in amusement. As I steadied myself against the table, my eyes swept over the paper on top of the stack and noted a handful of striking words. Perhaps incriminating words: *Guernsey; Tulera; chocolate; hot-air balloon.*

"What are you doing here?" asked Halston.

"She's spying!" cried Abi, shooting me an evil eye. "She's trying to figure out our plans so she can snitch. She flat-out told me she was going to turn me in for planting that box."

"I'm not a snitch!" I said. "You're just mad that I trailed you here. So much for knowing everything. You don't even know who's behind you!"

"She's gonna rat us out," said Abi. "We can't let her go. We should tie her up."

"You try it and I'll . . ." I lurched forward, not really sure what I'd do if she tried it.

"You'll what?" asked Abi, puffing up her chest.

Halston stepped between us. "Nobody's tying anybody up,"

he said. "If she says she's not a snitch, she's not a snitch. Besides, if Guernsey is out of commission, we might need her help."

"No, sir," I said, with a firm shake of my head. "I'm not a snitch, but I'm no rebel, either. I don't want any part of your so-called cause, whatever that is."

"I see the apple doesn't fall far from the tree," Halston mumbled.

"What?"

"Nothing," he said.

"I just want my mother's scarf back, and I want you to get my father out of jail. Then I'll be on my way, thank you very much."

"Oh, is that all?" snarked Abi. "Can we get you the king's knickers while we're at it? Tie her up, Hal!"

"Enough!" said Halston. "You don't have to help us, Prismena. Just don't tell anyone what happened today. Can we trust you to do that?"

"Sure," I said. "As soon as you get Father out of jail, I'll never mention it again."

"She's going to ruin everything," said Abi.

"Ugh," moaned Halston, cradling his head in his palms. "We didn't get the package delivered, and now this."

"All you have to do," I said, "is march up to the Royal Guard and tell them the truth—that my father didn't smuggle that chocolate. That he's innocent. It will only take a few minutes of your time."

"Ha!" Abi blurted out. "She wants us to 'march up to the Royal Guard'! I told you she was nuts."

"You got my father into this," I cried. "You have to get him out!"

"No, *you* got your father into this," Abi shot back. "You're the one who didn't tell him about your little 'collection.' Miss Goody Gumdrop is a liar and a sneak!"

"I am not!"

"Are too!"

"Ladies," snapped Halston. "Please keep it down! You're going to attract the Royal Guard!"

"She started it," huffed Abi. I glared at her.

"Prismena does have a point," said Halston. "It *is* our fault that Mr. Reece is in jail. And if he's still there on Savior's Day . . ."

"What?" I asked. "What happens on Savior's Day?"

Halston and Abi shared a meaningful look.

"What happens on Savior's Day?" I asked again, more urgently. "Is it the Palmerians? And their weapon?"

"The Palmerians are the least of your problems," said Halston. "Listen—"

A thundering crash from the next room made us all jump. The piano music suddenly stopped, replaced by a barrage of other sounds: The scrape of chair legs being dragged across a wooden floor. The thud of heavy objects falling. And voices.

"Where is he?" someone insisted. "Where's the scoundrel?"

"Nobody in here but good upstanding citizens!" said someone else.

"Tell me where he's at, or I'll knock yer teeth down yer throat!"

"I'd like to see you try!"

The chef poked his flushed, sweaty face through the door. Behind him, glass shattered. "Gruber, what's going on?" asked Halston.

"We've got company," said the chef. "Get rid of these kids. Now!"

# THE BACON TAX

Halston cursed as the commotion grew louder and more pitched. Above the grunts and crashes—and a sharp splintering sound I hoped was wood—a single voice declared: "By order of King Michael . . ."

Halston flung open his office door. The kitchen stood empty now, with pots boiling over and burnt strips of bacon spewing putrid black smoke. "You have to go," he said, nudging Abi and me back the way we'd come. "Get far away from here. And find a way to deliver that candy. I'm counting on you, Abs."

"Aren't you coming with us?" asked Abi.

"No," said Halston, cramming the stack of papers into a satchel slung across his body. "I've got to take care of some things first. I'll send for you when it's safe to meet."

Abi nodded while I stood there dumbstruck.

"And one more thing . . ." Halston lifted the little boy from beneath the table and thrust him at Abi. "Look after my nephew."

"Wh-what?" stammered Abi, but Halston had already shut the door, leaving us alone in the kitchen. Abi held the boy at arm's length and regarded him with bewilderment, as if Halston had handed her a leprechaun. I shared her shock—Abigail Smeade was the last person I'd trust with a small child. She'd probably recruit the poor kid into a life of crime. Abi finally rolled her eyes and settled the dazed child on her hip. "C'mon. We have to get out of here before that fight moves into the kitchen."

Just then, the swinging door burst open, propelled by an airborne chair that passed only inches from our heads. The little boy wailed and buried his face in Abi's shirt. I stole a glance into the pub, where stools and tables had been toppled to form a makeshift barricade. The same men who'd been slouched over their beers were now locked in an epic battle with the Royal Guard, fists and knees and bottles flying. The pub was finally living up to my expectations, at least.

We burst into the alley, where the man with the scarred face was slumped by the door. He roused when it swung open. "You're back!" he snarled at me, his tongue flapping against his gums. "Did'n' I tell ya this was my alley?" His breathing was loud and ragged as he stood there, blocking our way.

This time, I had no escape. I couldn't go back inside, and I couldn't get past him. So I did the only reasonable thing left. I screamed. I screamed and screamed at the top of my lungs until something jabbed me deep in the gut and knocked the wind out of me. I doubled over, sure I'd been stabbed or hit with a blunt object.

In fact, it was Abi's surprisingly sharp elbow.

"What in blazes are you doing?" she hissed. "Do you want to bring the whole army out here?" She turned to our captor. "I'm sorry, Simon, she's new here. She doesn't know what's what. *Of course* this is your alley, and we've brought you the tax. Here you go." She plunged her hand deep into the pocket of her breeches and removed a greasy strip of bacon. The man gave Abi a toothless smile as he took it. He stepped aside and, with a wave of his arm, allowed us safe passage down the corridor. I stared in disbelief.

"You really don't know anything," whispered Abi.

We broke from the alley and emerged back into the Market Day crowd, which promptly and mercifully swallowed us up. I took one of the little boy's hands, Abi took the other, and we pretended we weren't fleeing from a brawl inside a seedy pub. After all, what could be more ordinary than a group of siblings running errands at the market? But my pulse was thrumming wildly, my head whirring. I glanced back at the establishment we'd just left, where a metal sign hanging above the door creaked ominously. THE DEAD MAN'S TROUGH.

I shuddered, and Abi tugged at me to keep me moving.

# FINGERS CROSSED

When we'd wandered far enough from the Dead Man's Trough, we stopped pretending to be a family. We dropped one another's hands.

"All right, Goody Gumdrop," said Abi. "What's your next move?"

"If you aren't going to help me get my father out of jail, I'm going to do it myself," I said, with more confidence than I felt. I set my sights on the palace gates in the center of the market and began pushing through the crowd in that direction. Abi stayed on my tail.

"You don't really think you can convince the Royal Guard to unlock the prison and let your father walk away scot-free, do you?" she asked. The little boy, whose name I'd found out was Cole, grumbled as she dragged him along.

"Of course I do. Father's a law-abiding citizen. He pays his taxes and fills out all the forms required by the Ministry. One small box of candy doesn't outweigh a lifetime of good behavior. I'm sure the king's soldiers are reasonable people."

"I hate to break it to you," said Abi, "but 'reasonable people' don't become henchmen for the king."

"Well, I wouldn't expect a thief to understand," I said.

"Oh, I forgot," said Abi. "Gumdrop only steals from her own father." She stroked the scarf in her hair.

"Give that back," I snarled. "You've got no need for it now."

"You bet I do," said Abi. "I need to make sure you don't sell us out. You know too much about our plans."

"Really?" I said sarcastically. "It sounds to me like you haven't got a plan."

"Hmph" was her response, and I knew I'd won that round.

I continued past the Market Day stalls until I stood in front of the iron gate surrounding the soaring stone facade of the palace. Before King Michael's reign, the citizens of Oren could walk right up to the front door of the royal residence and rub the ancient lion-shaped knocker for good luck, their fingers leaving an oily sheen on its brass nose. But when King Michael took the throne, he announced that luck was an illusion and Oren needed solid things, like walls and fences, to stay safe and happy. Now the Royal Guard stood watch in front of an impassable gate that opened only to admit the carriages of the rich and well connected, swallowing them up in its gaping golden jaws.

"Cole and I will be waiting right over here," said Abi, setting the boy down on a wall across from the palace. "No funny stuff."

With Abi's eyes on my back, I approached the gate. The palace grounds contained not just the royal residence but stables, two separate kitchens, the homes of noblemen and advisors—practically an entire village. Most importantly, it housed the prison. My heart rose at the thought of Father's nearness, then sank again when I remembered how out of reach he was.

Two guards stood stonelike in front of the gate. They wore an elaborate livery: brass-buttoned purple jackets, black pantaloons, and black velvet capes. Their copper helmets and breastplates gleamed in the late afternoon sun, as did the razor-sharp tips of their spears. They stared with blank expressions into the distance.

"Er, excuse me, sir," I said to the nearest one, holding my voice steady with great effort.

He didn't answer. Or move. Not even a flick of his eyes to see who had spoken.

"I'm sorry to bother you," I continued, "but I'd like to speak to someone about a prisoner. My father is a balloonist in Lollyhill—the only balloonist, in fact, other than the royal balloonist. He was arrested today for having unauthorized inventory in his vessel, but it was an innocent mistake. If you check your records, you'll see that my father has never broken the law in his life. I know the Ministry of Balloons keeps meticulous records, and—"

"Girl," said the guard, and I started, as if a statue had spoken. "The next trial date for inmates of the Royal Prison is in ten days, before the Savior's Day celebration. Doling out justice always puts the king in a festive mood. He will ensure that your father, like all the citizens of Oren, receives a fair and speedy trial."

The other guard made a sound in the back of his throat, like a snort.

"I am very grateful," I said. "But surely something can be done sooner in a case like this. As I said, he's innocent."

"If you'd like to petition the warden for release of a prisoner before trial," said the guard, "you have to submit an official affidavit stating your case."

"Oh," I said, brightening. "I'd like to submit one, please."

"To submit an affidavit, first you must request the official royal form."

"Okay. How do I request the form?"

"The king's secretary distributes the forms."

"Can I speak to him?"

"Only by appointment."

"How do I make an appointment?"

"You simply fill out the form requesting an appointment with the royal secretary."

"Let me guess . . ."

"The royal secretary distributes those, too."

This time the other guard failed to stifle his laughter, which burst from his mouth in a single loud honk.

"Your best bet is to bring your evidence to trial on Savior's Day," the first guard continued. "You've got evidence, don't you?"

"Yes," I said. "I saw someone put the illegal box in his balloon. With my own eyes. I'll tell that to the king. I'll swear it."

"Hmm," said the guard, frowning. "Is that all you've got? That'll make it your word against the arresting officer's. And you're the prisoner's daughter—not exactly an unbiased witness. What you need is hard evidence—documents and the like. Have you got any?"

I thought about the stack of papers in Halston's office, the ones he'd hastily shoved into his satchel, and the words I'd picked out from them: *Guernsey; Tulera; chocolate; hot-air balloon.* Surely those documents would reveal the rebellion's scheme to take advantage of an innocent balloonist. But how could I get my hands on them? I shook my head.

"If you don't have evidence, then I suggest you talk to the big guy," said the guard. "The one in the sky, I mean. Because you've got a better chance with divine intervention."

"Yeah, girlie, it's time you started prayin'," added his colleague, with shaking shoulders.

"What happens if my father is found guilty?" I asked, panic creeping into my voice.

"Don't worry," said the first guard. "Smuggling is a minor offense. He'll only get a few years. Five at the most."

"Five *years*? In prison?" I said. "But my father is a good man! He doesn't belong in there!"

"We've got so many good men locked up in there it's a wonder the place hasn't floated up to heaven by now!" said the second guard, doubling over with fresh peals of laughter.

Then, just as quickly, he straightened up and grew serious. "Please clear the road."

A carriage was approaching, grander than any vehicle I'd ever seen up close. I scrambled out of its way. Through the open window, I recognized Mr. Larue, the dressmaker. He caught me looking at him and yanked his curtain closed with a frown. Then the guards pulled open the golden gates with a loud metal shriek and let the mean old snob inside.

I sucked in a deep breath and held in the tears threatening to pour out of me. I couldn't fall apart just yet. Not while I still had a chance to save Father. I needed hard evidence, and there was only one way to get it, even if it was going to be highly unpleasant. I turned around, prepared to come face to face with Abi's smug grin.

Instead, I found Abi flanked by a trio of small admirers: Cole and a set of twin girls about his age with identical freckles, pigtails, and corduroy pinafores. They wore perfect pink bows in their hair and patent leather shoes without a single scuff on them. They were gaping at Abi's strange clothing, and she was teaching them how to make their stiff corduroy dresses twirl. A great big smile lit up her face.

Until a woman in a prim linen dress brought an abrupt end to the twirling lesson. "Phyllis! Florence!" she yelled. She stamped her foot and nearly spilled the vegetables in her basket. "Get over here now!" The girls stopped spinning, and their shoulders sank as they shuffled to their mother's side. "What did I tell you about children like that?" she hissed, giving Cole and Abi a withering look. "They're filthy! Let's go."

Abi blinked a few times like an animal caught in bright lights. I kept waiting for her to curse or sneer, as she had with Mr. Larue. Instead, she took Cole by the hand and pulled him close. Her face crumpled a little, as though she might cry, but then she noticed me watching and set her jaw. She marched over to me with Cole in tow, her expression steely again.

"Well?" she demanded. "How'd it go?"

I didn't want to admit that she'd been right, so I skipped over that part altogether. I took a deep breath and said what I knew I had to say, as much as it pained me. "I can get your candy over the Wall."

"What was that?" asked Abi, leaning in and cupping her ear as if she hadn't heard me.

"I *said* I can get your candy over the Wall."

"Oh yeah?"

"Yes," I said. I didn't actually have a plan, but I'd come up with something later, if it came to that. Hopefully, I could get the evidence I needed long before I had to engage in any more illegal activities.

"Why are you suddenly willing to help?" she asked skeptically.

"Because . . . I need *your* help. You said you could break in anywhere. Does that include the jail?"

"Of course it does."

"If I deliver your candy, can you help me get Father out of there?"

"You bet your skinny butt I can," said Abi.

"Do we have a deal, then?" I stuck out my palm, to seal the bargain with a handshake. But I kept my other hand behind my back with my fingers tightly crossed, which everyone knows makes a promise null and void.

Abi studied me like she was weighing her options, but I knew she didn't have any left, either. Halston was counting on her to get that candy delivered. "All right," she said. "Deal." She clasped my hand so tightly I could still feel the squeeze of her fingers for several seconds after she let go.

"This doesn't mean I'm part of your rebellion," I added. "This is strictly business."

"Fine by me."

"And I'll take my scarf now."

Abi sucked in air through her teeth. "I'm afraid I can't do that, Gumdrop. I still need some insurance. As soon as you get the candy delivered, you can have it back."

"What insurance do *I* have?" I said. "How do I know you're going to fulfill your end of the bargain?"

"You have my word," she said.

"Oh, good," I muttered. "The word of a thief."

"Take it or leave it," she said. And with a resigned groan, I agreed to take it.

# THE MYSTERIOUS MATTER OF THE WREN

"The first thing we need to do is lose the dead weight," said Abi, cutting her eyes toward Cole. He didn't seem to notice. He was too busy picking up handfuls of dirt and stuffing them into his pockets, for no good reason as far as I could tell.

"But Halston told you to look after him," I said. "Isn't Halston, like, your boss or something?"

"I don't have a boss," Abi snapped. "I work for Halston when I please, and I don't work for Halston when I don't please. Besides, I didn't join the rebellion to be a babysitter for a grubby little kid. Halston doesn't appreciate what I can do."

"I know how that is," I said under my breath. "But we still can't leave the kid by the side of the road."

"Obviously," said Abi, rolling her eyes.

"Why don't we take him home?" I looked down at the boy. "Where do you live, Cole?"

He stared up at me as though I were speaking Tuleran.

"Where are your parents?" I asked, crouching beside him.

He still didn't answer.

"Do you live close to the market?"

No response.

"Does your uncle Halston have a girlfriend?" asked Abi.

"Abi," I cried. "Can you please focus?"

"It might give us a clue," she said with a shrug. "You never know."

"I'm huuuuuungry!" the boy finally whimpered.

"I guess he's coming with us," said Abi. "Cole, as soon as we get to Prissy's house, we'll feed you, all right? But you've gotta keep up."

Cole brightened.

I did the opposite.

"Excuse me? Did you say we're going to *my* house? I can't bring traitors into my home while my father is in jail for treason!"

"All right, genius, then where do you suggest we go with a hungry three-year-old? All that food in your kitchen is going to spoil if nobody eats it."

"How do you know what's in my kitchen?"

"I followed you around for three days, remember?"

"Ugh."

"And you've got real beds there, too. With straw mattresses. We're going to need a place to sleep tonight if we don't hear from Halston." The sun was already dipping behind the horizon, turning the sky a dusky orange. After the day I'd had, the thought of my bed *did* sound good, even if it meant dealing with two uninvited houseguests.

"Why don't we go to *your* house?" I said, though we'd already started walking toward Lollyhill. Cole bounded ahead of us, stopping every now and then to pick up a shiny rock or grab the tail of a passing dog.

"Ain't got one," said Abi, with a measure of pride.

I gasped. "You don't have a house? But where are your parents?"

"Ain't got those, either."

"How is that even possible?"

"Parents are overrated, Gumdrop. You'll see."

"But if you haven't got a home, where do you—?"

"Stop right there!" said a baritone voice.

Cole had scampered way ahead of us, to the intersection where the Royal Road cut through the market. Now he stood, small and trembling, in front of a royal guardsman.

"Wh-wh-? B-b-" I tried to formulate the words to ask the man why he'd stopped us, but all that came out of my mouth were a string of incoherent sounds. Had he followed us from the Dead Man's Trough? Did he know about the smuggled chocolates? Or worse, about the rebellion?

"Look!" squealed Abi. She pointed at the road behind him, where a dozen more soldiers in full regalia, with stern faces and gleaming weapons, were blocking the way. In the middle of all that military bravado was a carriage, ornate and shimmering gold, the stuff of fairy tales. It made Jerrick Larue's fancy carriage look like a rickety old wagon. But it was leaning at an awkward angle, with one of its wheels butted against a giant boulder. Several of its spokes had snapped like toothpicks.

The carriage door swung open, and the crowd almost cheered. But the people stiffened when a delicate silver slipper landed on the top step and they realized it wasn't their beloved King Michael emerging. It was Queen Catherine, the barely tolerated. She didn't smile or wave at her subjects as she descended, and they greeted her with an equally icy silence. Only Abi seemed excited to see her.

"That dress!" murmured Abi, tiptoeing closer. "Look at the

detail on the hem. And that coat. Exquisite!" The queen wore a flowing purple dress and a matching velvet bolero. Her pantaloons winked under her hem when she stepped down the stair. Her skin was caked in pale-white powder, her lips were painted deep red, and a gem-studded barrette sparkled in her jet-black hair. She was certainly more pleasant to the eye than mealy King Michael, but in a cold, unyielding way, like a diamond.

Some of the soldiers set to work on the wheel, sweating through their thick military jackets, while another group created a barricade around the queen, even though the crowd was distinctly uninterested in her. Except Cole. I don't know whether he was restless or if the queen's shiny jewelry caught his eye, but he surged forward, toward the monarch and her guards. The soldiers instinctively reached for their weapons, but it was the queen's reaction that sent Cole reeling backward. Her eyes flicked up from the ground and skimmed over the boy—clad in rags, filthy and uncombed—and she gagged as though about to be sick. She pressed an embroidered handkerchief to her lips and turned away in disgust. She might as well have struck him. He recoiled and buried his head in my skirt.

The soldiers soon repaired the carriage, and the queen quickly disappeared again behind its darkened windows. The wheels groaned into motion, and the procession marched out of the market with great ceremony. The gap in the crowd closed behind it, and everyone returned to buying and selling as though nothing had happened. But something *had* happened. A crestfallen little boy clung fiercely to my legs as that golden carriage rumbled to the palace gates.

"It's all right," I said, kneeling beside Cole and wiping the matted hair from his forehead. "We'll get you washed up in Lollyhill. Then you'll look like a proper gentleman, and that mean lady won't even recognize you." Cole dutifully nodded, but I could tell he didn't believe me.

"Besides," added Abi, "she's as cuckoo as a clock." She crossed her eyes and stuck her tongue out the side of her mouth to demonstrate, which earned a peal of giggles from Cole and a grateful smile from me. I rose and reached for Cole's hand. That's when I noticed that something was balled up in his fist.

"What's that?" I asked.

"Mine!" he said, pulling his hand away and clasping it to his chest.

"I'm not going to take it from you," I said. "I only want to see it."

He released his fingers reluctantly, one by one, revealing the small brown object in his palm.

"Is that a bird?" asked Abi, peering down.

"No," said Cole, his fingers curling protectively over it again. "It's a wr- . . . a wr—"

"A wren!" I cried. "It's a peach pit in the shape of a wren. And it's *mine*! Where'd you get that?"

"No!" said the boy, shaking his head so hard his shaggy hair whipped around his face. "It's mine!"

"My mother brought that back from Palma years ago. It used to sit on our mantel, until . . ." I bit my lip, trying not to think about Mother's things and how they'd been sold and scattered.

"Did you say a wren?" asked Abi.

Cole and I both nodded.

"How strange," she murmured.

"Of course it's strange," I said. "This boy I've never seen before in my life has my mother's souvenir!"

"Yeah, that too."

"What do you mean, 'that too'? What else is strange about it?"

"It's probably nothing," said Abi, "but the leader of the rebellion is called the Wren."

"I thought Halston was leading the rebellion."

"No, Halston's a grunt like me," said Abi. "A more important grunt, but still a grunt. You don't think people who lead rebellions go around shouting it from the rooftops, do you? Nobody's seen the Wren in real life, except Halston. We don't even know his real name. He's just . . . the Wren."

After that, I agreed to let Cole keep the peach pit, if only to prevent a meltdown in the middle of the crowded market. We trudged up the Slope and into Lollyhill, but the ground was no longer solid under my feet. Even the sky refused to stay put, stubbornly swirling around and around. It reminded me again of being with Mother in Fletcher's field—how sometimes after a balloon launch I'd fling my arms open and twirl until I fell down dizzy in the grass. Then, even after the ground caught me, everything would keep spinning, as if I'd set the world in motion. The balloon above me would become two balloons, or four, or six, bobbing along like bath bubbles. That's how I felt that day in the market. Only this time, Mother wasn't there to pick me up and lead me home.

Until that moment, the events of the day had seemed arbitrary, as though I were a leaf being batted around by the wind. But I was beginning to wonder if everything that had happened was more than a coincidence. Maybe—just maybe—I'd been lumped together with Abi and Cole and Halston for a reason. Maybe the wren's appearance in my living room and now in Cole's pocket, and its connection to the rebellion was some sort of . . . sign.

Or maybe it was merely a lost trinket.

That was the more likely explanation.

Wasn't it?

# EXILED IN PALMA

*In the early days of Wren's exile, Palma struck her as incurably foreign, and part of her resented it simply because it wasn't Oren. She bristled at the accents, the jarring flavors of the food, and the strange customs (she nearly socked the first person who tried to greet her with a kiss). But her resistance was just a symptom of a deep and crippling homesickness. As the days became months, Palma became her home, and she came to think of it only with abiding gratitude.*

*The newlyweds settled in a small house on the property of Mr. Hillman, the kind farmer who drove them over the border. Jaxson worked alongside him on the farm, growing things they couldn't get back home: peaches freshly plucked from the tree; a nut called a pecan, which Wren could eat by the fistful or bake into a pie; sweet kiwifruits that sprang from snaking vines. Meanwhile, Wren found work tutoring the son of a local nobleman. She had to give her father credit for bucking one tradition, at least, by teaching her to read and write.*

*Wren hadn't sent word to her father to tell him where she'd gone, or that she was safe. It pained her to sever ties with him so completely, but she couldn't risk having him ride into Palma to drag her back home. And he would've been well within his legal rights to do so, even though Wren was a grown woman, and a married one at that.*

*Since she couldn't trade letters with her family, Wren sought reports of home wherever she could, though it was hard to come by in her tucked-away patch of Palma. She heard that the princess had been kidnapped, that King Reginald had died, and that Lord Michael had ascended to the throne. She learned that her homeland was in turmoil and that Oren and Palma were on the verge of war. This news tore Wren's heart in two.*

*Occasionally, Mr. Hillman would sell their produce to vendors in Oren, and Wren would travel with him as far as the border so she could steal a glimpse of her homeland from the hillside. On one visit, they saw men clearing trees from the land on either side of the Southern Gate. On the next visit, huge stones extracted from the mountainsides were being fitted, one on top of the other, along the border. The last time Wren went to the gate, an impenetrable wall one hundred feet tall sliced the land in two, concealing Oren completely. In place of the simple archway that had marked the Southern Gate for decades, a locked door blocked the way, with its new name etched into the rock: SAVIOR'S GATE.*

*A line of Palmerian wagons stretched for miles, waiting to get into Oren, but nearly all of them were turned away. Including Mr. Hillman's. Most of the peaches in his cart spoiled before they could be eaten.*

# THE GROWN-UPS ARE PLOTTING

When my vision came into focus the next morning, a ruddy, chubby-cheeked face was hovering over me. It took me several confusing seconds to recall who Cole was and what he was doing in my bedroom. Then memories of the previous day walloped me like a sucker punch—Father's arrest, the rebellion, the bar fight, the alley monster, the Mad Queen, and, of course, Cole and his peach pit. I grunted and pulled the sheets over my head to block it all out, but the weight of Cole's stare bore through the covers. I sighed and heaved myself onto my elbows. Then a rustling in the living room reminded me that Abi was also loose in my house, almost certainly causing trouble. I leaped out of bed.

She sat on the living room floor, surrounded by thread, sewing shears, and pieces of fabric. She was focused so intently on something in her lap that she didn't look up when I stumbled into the room. "What are you doing?" I said. "Did this stuff come from Father's workshop?"

"Yep," she said. "That place is incredible. Look." She rose, letting assorted junk clatter to the floor. Cole made a dash for the shears, which I nimbly scooped up and held out of his reach. Meanwhile, Abi spun around so I could see her clothes from every angle. She'd patched her tattered breeches with scraps from all the balloons in the shop. There was *The Flame, Tiger Lily, Saint Ursula, Goldilocks*—a colorful hodgepodge on top of the brown cambric. "Well . . . ?"

"But you only had holes on the knees," I pointed out.

"Yeah, I got a bit carried away. Do you like it?"

I did, if I was being honest, but I was too livid to admit it. "Father's gonna kill me! He's very particular about his workshop. Goodness gracious, Abi."

"Relax, would you, Gumdrop? I'll put everything back where I found it."

"I've had just about enough of you doing whatever you like, with no regard for the consequences. You're like a . . . a walking tornado, destroying everything in your path. I, for one, will not—"

"I'm hungry!" Cole blurted out, completely oblivious to my rant. In my short time as one of Cole's babysitters, I'd realized that he had only two states of being: hungry and bored.

"I'll fix us some porridge," I sighed, trudging to the kitchen. "Please don't break anything while I'm gone." This warning was directed at both of them. They gave me sheepish shrugs.

"Killjoy," Abi muttered as I left the room. Cole giggled.

Moments later, we were seated at the kitchen table around steaming bowls of porridge. I'd even topped Cole's helping with a crooked smiley face made out of blueberries.

"Now let's get down to business," said Abi through a mouthful of porridge. "What's the plan to get those chocolates into Palma?"

I made a show of swallowing my food and washing it down with a gulp of water before I answered. "I've been giving it serious thought," I said. "I have lots of ideas, but none of them are *just right.* I know how important this mission is, and I don't want to rush into it." I hoped she couldn't tell that I was stalling, trying to buy time until we could see Halston again and I could get my hands on his satchel.

"That's all well and good," said Abi, "but we're on a deadline here. So I'm gonna need you to . . . you know . . . rush into it a little. Can't we just hop into one of those balloons out there?"

"No way," I said, firmly shaking my head.

"Why not? It's the obvious solution. That blue one is all strung up and ready to go. It's practically begging us to use it."

"For one thing, my father will have my hide . . ."

"He sounds like a very violent man," Abi said under her breath.

"More importantly, we don't have a pilot."

Abi lifted her eyebrows. "Really?"

"Really," I said. "I've never flown a balloon before."

"But I thought you were a balloon expert."

"You keep saying that, but you're the only one who thinks so. My father never lets me man the balloons. He doesn't think I'm ready. I'm not sure he'll ever think I'm ready."

"Well, your dad's not here," said Abi. "This is your chance. Don't you want to fly one of those things?"

I gazed out the kitchen window, to where *Percival* cast a blue-tinted shadow over the landscape. I imagined piloting him: the coarse texture of the ropes, the pull of the wind, the whoosh of the fire. All of it under my command, responding to my every movement.

Yes, I did want to fly one of those things.

"We can't take a balloon," I said, without actually answering Abi's question. "The Royal Guard would spot us in the sky, and we'd end up in prison with Father. There has to be another way."

"I'm bored," Cole announced. He'd eaten some of his food and apparently smashed the rest of it. The blueberry smiley face had been reduced to a few purple smears on his cheeks.

"Hush," said Abi. "The grown-ups are plotting."

"You're not grown-ups!" giggled Cole, as though she'd made a hilarious joke.

"As far as you're concerned, we are," said Abi. She turned back to me to continue our conversation, but Cole would not be so easily ignored. He scooped up a congealed glob of porridge with his spoon, tilted it back at an angle, and flung it in Abi's direction. It sailed through the air and landed with a plop in her mass of curls.

Cole cackled with glee. I covered my mouth and tried not to burst into laughter, too. Abi glared at both of us, then slowly rose from the table and left the house to rinse the porridge out of her hair at the well.

"You shouldn't have done that," I said to Cole, grabbing a rag to wipe up the mess. Cole only beamed at me, proud of his direct hit. "Grin all you want, but I wouldn't be surprised if she comes back and flings *you* across the ta—"

I stopped scrubbing and stared at the porridge splattered halfway across the kitchen. Cole cocked his head and stared at me, probably thinking I'd lost my mind as I gazed into the distance. But I hadn't lost anything. In fact, I'd *found* my idea. I knew exactly how to get that candy over the Wall.

But could I really go through with it? Was I really going to give the rebellion the means to betray the kingdom? On the other hand, if I didn't come up with some way to deliver the candy, Abi would eventually get suspicious and break off our deal. I had to stick with the plan, just for a little longer.

Besides, I had a *really* good idea.

I rushed out the front door, leaving a puzzled Cole in the kitchen and almost running into Abi on her way back inside. Her hair was wet, her curls limp and dripping. "Where are you going?" she called after me.

"You'll see!" I shouted back.

Ten minutes later, I returned, breathless and carrying my burlap sack. I dumped its contents on the floor, the things I'd kept hidden for so long now suddenly, startlingly on display in my living room. But a heap of contraband was nothing compared to the mess I'd gotten myself into so far. And what I was about to propose next.

"Wow," said Cole, seizing the flying machine. Abi picked up a strip of rubber and began measuring it around her waist, devising ways to incorporate it into one of her skirts. Meanwhile, I riffled through the rest of it until I found what I was looking for.

"What are you doing?" asked Abi, peering over my shoulder as Cole swooped the flying machine around the house.

"I'm building a machine," I said. "One so simple a three-year-old can understand it." I placed a thick stump of charcoal on the ground, then I balanced a thin strip of metal on top of it. I centered the metal piece so it rocked gently back and forth.

"A seesaw?" asked Abi.

"Close," I said. I adjusted the metal piece so it was no longer centered—so one end rested against the floor and the other was raised in the air. Then I banged my fist on the raised end, and the other side flipped up. "A catapult! It's the same concept Cole used when he flung his porridge at you, only on a much bigger scale."

"Do you really think we can build something like that?" she asked.

"Not by ourselves. But we could do it if we had help."

"Leave that to me," said Abi. "You come up with the design, and I'll find some builders."

"Really?"

Abi nodded. "Not bad, Gumdrop."

We were going to build a catapult big enough to toss things over the Wall, and nobody was there to tell me it was too dangerous or outlandish. Even though we'd be breaking more laws than I could count and Father would be furious, a smile rose to my lips and my body hummed with energy. I couldn't remember the last time I'd felt that way.

But a knock on the front door dampened my excitement. "Halston!" cried Abi, hopping up from the floor. I felt a rush of relief—and a twinge of shame—as I rose to greet him. Once I had the evidence from his satchel, this would all be over, like I wanted. I'd gotten so carried away with the prospect of turning my idea into something real that I'd almost lost sight of my goal—getting Father out of jail.

"Prismena Reece, open this door at once!"

A woman shouted through the keyhole, stopping Abi just short of throwing the door open. We both froze. My gaze slid across the room to Abi, hers to me. Neither of us budged or even breathed, in case a creaky floorboard might give us away. I clasped Cole by the arm to keep him from barreling toward this newest distraction.

"What do we do?" I whispered.

"Stay quiet," said Abi. "Pretend nobody's home."

Another knock, louder and more insistent than the first, punctured the silence.

"I know you're in there," said Ms. Stoneman. "And I expect a very good explanation for why you're not in school!"

# WHAT TO DO WITH A LYING TRUANT

"Hide," I whispered to Abi and Cole. "I'll get rid of her."

"No!" said Cole, stamping his foot right where he intended to stay—smack in the middle of the living room.

"Cole, you have to hide right now," I said. "It's important!" He shook his head. I could make excuses for my absence from school, but how was I going to explain the strange little boy in my house?

"Cole, please!"

"No!" He sucked in a big gulp of air, readying his lungs for an eruption. I shot Abi a panicked look, but she shrugged unhelpfully.

And then it hit me. "One," I said.

Cole held his breath for an instant, not sure how to react, but his eyes lit up when he realized what was happening. He gleefully scampered off to find a hiding spot for hide-and-hunt. Abi nodded at me with admiration as she trailed off after him.

Unfortunately, three-year-olds aren't as good at hiding as they think they are. Cole crawled under the kitchen table where we'd just had our porridge, leaving his tiny foot poking out from the tablecloth, which hung down to the floor. But it was the best I was going to get. I had to keep Ms. Stoneman from coming inside.

I slumped my shoulders and rubbed my eyes until they were red and raw. When I looked sufficiently miserable, I shuffled to the door and cracked it open. "Ms. Stoneman," I croaked. "What brings you here?"

"Don't play dumb with me, Miss Reece," she said. "It's an insult to me as your educator. Why aren't you in school?"

"I'm sick," I said, adding a sniffle for emphasis.

"Pishposh," she said. "I know what happened to your father yesterday, and it doesn't mean you can skip school. If anything, you need school more than ever. You need an example of obedience that you're clearly not getting at home. And no child should be left to her own devices. No good can come of it."

"I'll be in school tomorrow, Ms. Stoneman, I promise."

"Hmph," she grunted. "See to it that you're at your desk by first bell or—"

Cole coughed.

"What was that?" asked Ms. Stoneman, her puckered lips clumping into an even tighter O of disapproval. She rose onto her tiptoes and peered over my head into the house. "Is someone else here?"

"What?" I asked, feigning surprise. "I—I didn't hear anything. Nobody's here but me." To prove it, I opened the door wider, giving her a full view of the empty living room behind me.

"I don't believe you!" She wedged her elbow between me and the door and shoved past me into the house. She scanned the place with squinty eyes.

Before she could spot Cole's foot, with its toes impatiently wiggling, I called out, "Two!" The wayward foot quickly retreated into hiding with its owner.

"Excuse me?" snapped Ms. Stoneman, spinning around to face me. "Did you just say 'two'?"

"No, I said *'Achoo.'*" I smiled sheepishly at her. "Blasted cold!"

"What are you up to?" she asked, stepping in close and staring intently at me. I didn't flinch. She turned on her heel and walked into the kitchen.

"What's all this?" she asked, waving her arms at the dirty breakfast dishes caked in crusty porridge. "Why so many dishes for just one child?"

"Uh . . . they're from yesterday," I said. "I haven't gotten around to cleaning up yet."

"Hmph," she muttered, as if I were proving her point. "Living in filth."

She paced the length of the table, the same way she did in the classroom. Only now she was standing inches away from Cole's hiding place. The tablecloth bulged. Then a pudgy hand crept out from under it, heading right toward the shiny silver buckle on Ms. Stoneman's left shoe, which must've looked quite enticing to a curious toddler. "Three!" I shrieked.

Ms. Stoneman stomped her left foot, nearly smashing Cole's tiny fingers. He yanked his hand back under the table. "You are testing the limits of my patience," she cried, so flustered a few stray hairs escaped from her bun. "I don't know what you're playing at, Miss Reece, but it's settled. I can't leave you here alone." She shook her head in exasperation. "But what am I going to do with you? I suppose I could bring you home with me . . ." My heart momentarily stopped beating at these words. "But my cats don't take kindly to visitors. Hmm, what to do with a lying truant . . ." She tapped her index finger against her pursed lips as she thought. Then the tablecloth rustled again. This time, it brushed her ankles, and her eyes flared. "What. Was. That?" she growled.

"Um . . ." I groped for an answer as she sank into a crouch and slowly lifted the hem of the tablecloth.

*"Rats!"* I shouted. "We have rats!"

Ms. Stoneman released a shriek that could've shattered glass. She sprang to her feet and fled from the kitchen as quickly as her silver-buckled shoes would carry her. She skidded to a stop beside me, visibly shuddering, her face glowing red with fear and embarrassment. And then anger. She smoothed her hair, then clamped her hand down on my forearm. "I've had enough! You can't stay here one moment longer! I'm taking you to Kluwer House."

From an unknown hiding spot, I heard Abi gasp, but Ms. Stoneman was too busy dragging me toward the door to notice.

"You can't do that," I protested. "I don't belong in a children's home." I'd only seen such places from the outside, but that was all I cared to see. Children's homes were desolate and scary, full of the sorts of kids who could eat me alive. Kids like Abi, come to think of it.

"I don't see any parents here," said Ms. Stoneman. "It seems to me a children's home is precisely where you belong. Your father should've thought about your well-being *before* he violated the law."

"Can I at least get my toothbrush?" I asked, hoping to escape

Ms. Stoneman's grip and make a run for it. But she shook her head and gave me a tight-lipped grin, as if she knew exactly what I had in mind. She roughly prodded me out of the house.

Before I made it off the porch, I called over my shoulder, "Four!" which earned me a shove down the steps.

I traveled with my schoolmistress-turned-jailer down the dusty road from Lollyhill to the Slope. As we walked, Ms. Stoneman delivered an extended monologue on the ingratitude of my generation, blaming me for every act of defiance a student had ever committed in her classroom. But her voice faded into the background. All I could think about was Father. I'd lost my one chance to rescue him, and now there was no hope for either of us.

"Here we are," Ms. Stoneman said at the gate of a rickety house. The crooked walls buckled beneath the weight of a crumbling roof, and the windows were boarded up with slats of wood. It looked like something Cole might have built with blocks, except his house would've been sturdier. And more welcoming.

"Are you sure this is it?" I asked.

"Shh," hissed Ms. Stoneman. "You've got some nerve turning up your nose. Remember, if the Kluwers take you in, you will be their guest."

She marched me to the front door and pounded on it. It creaked open, revealing what I first mistook for a living skeleton. I recoiled from the man's pitch-black eyes, set deep in his skull, and the skin stretched tight over his jutting cheekbones. His bald head was framed by tufts of black hair springing up above his ears. With a swift flick of his thumb, he popped open the shell of a pistachio and tossed the bright-green nut into his mouth. He flung the empty shell pieces over his shoulder.

"Ah, Ms. Stoneman," he said, green specks dotting his teeth. "How kind of ya to grace my stoop agin. What've we got here?"

"This girl," said Ms. Stoneman, shoving me forward, "is recently relieved of her father. He was forcibly removed by the Royal Guard, and now she is entirely on her own."

"Ah, I see. A sad fate indeed." He tried to appear sympathetic, but it only twisted his features so he looked more terrifying than before.

"Can you offer her your hospitality?" asked Ms. Stoneman.

"What for-tu-di-nous timing," said Mr. Kluwer, "We just had a bed open up. We'd be delighted to host the dear girl."

"My father will come for me," I blurted out, even though I had little hope of that actually happening.

"Of course he will," said the man, turning his hollowed-out eyes on me.

"How will he find me?" I asked.

"We'll make sure he knows where to find ya," said Mr. Kluwer, clutching my shoulders with cold, bony fingers. "Just tell us where you live. We'd love to pay a visit." Again, that devious smile twisted his face, and he pulled me over the threshold.

"Just remember . . . ," said Ms. Stoneman. "Gratitude!"

Then the door slammed shut on her crumpled smile. I'd never been so sad to see it go.

# WELCOME TO KLUWER HOUSE

The foreboding exterior of Kluwer House aptly prepared me for what I found inside—a jumble of dreary rooms, a complete lack of sunlight, and a carpet of pistachio shells. Each room was crowded with children, from toddlers to teenagers, all somber and smelly and coated with grime. They stared at me with fierce eyes as I entered, and I wanted to scream that there had been a mistake. That I didn't belong here. But who would've listened?

The master of the house turned me over to its mistress, since boys and girls stayed in separate "wings." Mrs. Kluwer made up for her husband's lack of hair with a shock of brassy yellow frizz haloing her withered face. She shared her husband's bony physique, but Mrs. Kluwer was stooped, her movements labored. It didn't help that she wore a utility belt loaded with curious instruments whose purpose was unclear but ominous. As she led me through the girls' wing, she sighed every few steps, weary from the exertion of walking. When we reached the final room, she pivoted and leaned in to me closer than was comfortable. With two fingers, she peeled one of her eyelids back. Her bulging, naked eye rolled around wildly.

"Now be honest," she said. "It looks weird, don't it?"

"Um . . ." Of course her exposed eyeball looked weird, but I shook my head, in case it was a trick question.

She released her stretched skin and sighed. "Well, it looks weird to me. Ain't white enough. I told the doctor, but the man's a quack. What does he know? I s'pose it's another cross I have to bear. I got so many these days I plumb lost count. Here's your bed." She pointed to two burlap sacks laid out on the dirt floor, with strips of newspaper spilling from their torn seams. "Dinner at sundown, and one trip to the outhouse," she said. "Make it count." Then she hobbled from the room, still grumbling to herself about various aches and pains.

I fell onto my side on my itchy "mattress," with my knees pulled up to my nose. The other girls sat cross-legged on their sacks, in groups of two and three, playing makeshift games. They spoke in hushed voices, and even during their play, they didn't smile or laugh. Caked-on dirt concealed their faces like masks, making it impossible to tell them apart. I wondered how long it would take for me to look like them. To *become* one of them.

Father's trial was in nine days, and now I had no way to reverse the awful thing I'd done. I thought about our hot-air balloons that seemed to defy the natural laws and about the machine I'd dreamed up to shoot candy over an impassable wall. But balloons and gadgets wouldn't do me any good here. I found myself wondering what Abi would do in my position. Surely she'd know how to escape from a place like this.

But I wasn't Abi. I was trapped. And because of me, Father was, too.

"You're new here," someone said. A pair of feet appeared in my line of sight, with one pinky toe poking through a hole in torn stockings. The feet belonged to a girl with a round, pink face framed by bursts of choppy blond hair that looked like she'd cut it herself with a dull knife. "First night's always the hardest," she said.

I didn't answer.

"I'm Roz," she said. She looked several years younger than me, but she carried herself with the sort of confidence that made her seem older. Just like Abi.

"Prismena," I muttered.

"Can I give you some advice, Prismena?"

"Can I stop you?"

"You ain't here to make friends, and I respect that. But you oughta take free advice from someone who knows a thing or two. And I know lots more than two things."

She paused. If she was waiting for me to be impressed, she'd have to keep waiting.

"Don't trust the Kluwers," she said. "That sounds obvious, but it ain't. Mrs. K acts sick all the time, but she'd chase a kid clear across Oren just to drag him back to this armpit. And that's not the most important advice. . . ."

She paused again. I stayed silent.

"Never stick around one of these places for too long. If they figure out you ain't got nobody comin' for ya, they'll send you packin'. You gotta keep movin' to survive. You gotta be one step ahead of 'em."

"What are you talking about?" I said. "How am I supposed to keep moving when I'm trapped here?"

"That's what you gotta figure out. That's what I'm tryin' to tell ya."

"But I *want* the Kluwers to send me packing."

"Not the way they do it. They'll toss you over the Wall if you're lucky. If you're not, they'll send you to the palace to work for King Michael."

I groaned and rolled away from her. These kids could mock me all they liked, but I wasn't going to fall for their lies. Nobody was tossing kids over the Wall, and they certainly weren't taking kids like these to work for the king. "Just leave me alone."

"Suit yourself," said Roz. Her stockinged feet backed away.

"New kid?" asked another little girl standing near me. I didn't bother to turn around and look, but she sounded about seven or eight years old.

"Yep," said Roz.

"Lightweight," said the girl. I was too numb to be offended. Anyway, it was kids like these—namely, Abigail Smeade—who'd gotten me into this mess in the first place. They were the last people I cared to impress now.

Roz and her friend plopped down on a bare stretch of floor near my bed to play X's and O's. From the sound of it, I gathered they were etching the letters right into the planks of the wood floor with a blade—quite different from how we played it at Lollyhill Day School. I thought, with a pang of regret, that if I'd joined the other kids playing X's and O's after school the other day, instead of wandering off to Fletcher's field to admire that stupid scarf, I could've avoided all this. Then Father would have been home, filling out forms for the Ministry, and I'd have been there, too, doing homework or preparing dinner. I longed for such tedium as Roz wrenched a knife through the wood to make her mark.

"Do you think she's a Vine?" Roz asked her friend.

"With those arms?" said the girl. "No way. She's gotta be a Nettle." This time, I was too confused to be offended. What did those words mean? And what was wrong with my arms?

Soon, a group of younger girls made up a game where they had to leap over a troll without waking it. And guess who played the part of the troll? I let them win every time, not even flinching when their tattered skirts went whooshing over my head. Eventually they got tired of that game. Next, I heard the soft squeak of the floorboards as one of them tiptoed toward me. She brushed my arm softly, and everyone behind her tittered excitedly. They must have dared her to touch me. But I wouldn't give them the satisfaction of lashing out or even cracking my eyes open. I ground my teeth and curled up into a tight ball.

Even after the girl crept away, my skin still tingled where she'd touched me. Then the sensation moved up my arm, like a feather trailing along my skin, and my eyes fluttered open. I realized with horror that the dare hadn't been for her to *touch* me. I stared down at a large, lazy cockroach traveling up the bare skin of my arm, its long antennae waving around in the air.

I screamed, sprang to my feet, and tore across the room as though the floor were on fire, all the while swatting at my arm. At some point, the bug fell off, but I could still feel the tickle of its tiny feet on my skin and see its crunchy, iridescent body headed toward my face. A sea of burlap beds slipped and slid beneath me as I ran. I ignored the shouts of protest as I disrupted conversations and upended games. But my frantic sprint came to a sudden halt with a sharp whack to the back of my legs. I collapsed in a heap on the floor, and hot tears sprang to my eyes as the pain radiated through my lower body. I wasn't sure what had happened until I heard Mrs. Kluwer's voice behind me.

"Just 'cause you're new don't mean you can go around actin' like a banshee," she hissed. She held a black rod, thick and sturdy at one end, thin and pliant at the other—one of the barbaric instruments she carried on her belt. "We've got a place for kids like you, who like to cause a fuss. Called the Hole. I'll let ya guess what's down there." She ran a single fingertip up my arm, which made my skin crawl all over again. Then she cackled.

I stood slowly and limped back to my spot on the floor. The glares of the other girls followed me, burning as fiercely as the welts forming on the back of my legs.

"See," Roz's companion snickered. "I told you she was a lightweight."

# A COUPLE OF WRITHING BEASTS

I spent the rest of the afternoon curled up on the floor. I would've stayed there until nightfall, but Mrs. Kluwer swept into the room pounding on a metal pot with a wooden spoon—the Kluwer House equivalent of a dinner bell. My stomach retched at the thought of food, but I feared I'd meet the bottom of the mistress's boot if I didn't peel myself off the floor and line up with the others.

We crowded into a dining room with a big wooden table in the center. It wasn't quite long enough for all the backsides jostling for a seat, and I found myself pressed between a little girl with a phlegmy cough and a tall boy who kept banging me in the chin with his elbow. Mrs. Kluwer deposited small bowls of watery rice in front of each child, and the others instantly began shoveling it into their mouths. I peered down at the slop in front of me—unappetizing, to be sure, but at least it looked inoffensive. Until one of the grains of rice started to squirm and wriggle across the bowl on its own. At the sight of the tiny ricelike worm, that morning's porridge churned in my belly and started to make a return trip up my throat. I stood, hoping to avoid another scene, but a shrill "Sit down!" from across the room made me drop back onto the bench and swallow whatever was working its way back up. I pushed away my bowl, which was quickly claimed by the kid across from me, who plucked out the writhing larva, tossed it aside, and ate the rest.

After dinner, we were granted a visit to the outhouse. The smelly building stood a short distance from the main house, and Mrs. Kluwer walked us there in groups of four. She trailed behind us, thumping her rod against the palm of her hand to remind us of its presence and groaning with every step. We clutched threadbare washcloths, barely visible nubs of soap, and small handfuls of salt we'd use to scrub the grime from our teeth. Nobody got a toothbrush.

"Remember, ladies," croaked Mrs. Kluwer, "cleanliness is godliness. I swear it's the filth you kids bring into this house that keeps me laid so low. Heaven knows, I'd be fit as a fiddle if I had another line of work. But I've been called to help the children of this kingdom. So I carry on."

Nobody reacted to the woman's words of woe as the steady beat of her rod kept time with our footsteps. I walked beside Roz, whose hair poked out in all directions, like a starburst against the pink-and-purple-streaked sky. She tilted her head back and sipped a deep breath of the frosted evening air with the ghost of a smile on her lips. These brief trips outside must have been a rare pleasure for these kids. Or should I say, for *us* kids.

I thought about what Roz said, about not sticking around Kluwer House too long. The idea of being sent to the palace to work for King Michael was nonsense, of course, but I couldn't help wondering what my chances would be if I made a run for it. Despite Mrs. Kluwer's ailments, she had proven to be light on her feet and quick with her weapon of choice. Plus, the property was ringed by a fence, made of bundled sticks, at least seven feet high. Escape didn't seem likely.

Mrs. Kluwer had warned us to keep our eyes forward no matter what, but an abrupt thud behind us made us all spin around. A spidery black beast was writhing there on the ground, yelping pitifully, its long, gangly arms twisting in the air. It took me several seconds to realize that the beast was the mistress of the house, laid flat on her back. Her thrashing legs were tangled in the hem of her skirt, and her black boots struck madly at the sky. In that instant of confusion, I noticed that she wore fine silk pantaloons, with the unmistakable shimmer of expensive material. Just like the queen.

"C'mon!" cried someone peering out from behind a nearby tree.

I recognized Abi's crooked white teeth, bright against the darkening night. An unexpected grin sprang to my lips at the sight of her. But what was she doing here? Had she been caught, too? In her hand, she held one end of a thin wire—the same wire that must have tripped Mrs. Kluwer, who was still struggling to regain her footing.

"Let's go!" urged Abi, waving me on.

I hesitated for an instant, imagining the wrath of the Kluwers if they caught me. I remembered the bite of the rod against my skin and the threat of whatever slithering creatures lived inside the pitch-black Hole.

"My back!" moaned Mrs. Kluwer, lolling helplessly in the grass. "Someone save me!"

"Come. On," insisted Abi, stepping toward me.

Roz and the other girls ran toward the fence, which now had a small hole sawed into it. I snapped out of my daze and joined them, while Mrs. Kluwer groaned piteously. Abi's face hardened, and suddenly she sprinted past me toward the wailing woman. She picked up the black rod, which had rolled away from Mrs. Kluwer's bony hand, and chucked it as hard as she could into the woods beside the outhouse. Then she gave the old woman a kick in the rump for good measure.

We crawled to freedom on our hands and knees through the hole in the fence. On the other side, the escapees dispersed, scattering in different directions with joyous whoops.

"Follow me," said Abi, grabbing my hand before I could even brush off the dirt. We sprinted, hurtling through the avenues, alleys, and backyards of the Slope. Blood chugged through my body, drowning out any other sound. I had no idea where Abi was leading me, but the only thing that mattered was putting miles between me and Kluwer House.

When we emerged from the Slope into the open spaces of Lollyhill, we finally slowed down, and the effort of our uphill run caught up with us. My heart became a hammer, taking steady whacks at my rib cage.

As soon as I had enough air in my lungs, I said, "Thank you, Abi."

"Did you see her?" Abi panted in reply. "She was wiggling around like a bug!"

"Seriously," I said. "You saved me."

"Of course I did," she said with a shrug. "It's my job. I can't deliver that candy with you inside Kluwer House, now can I?"

"I guess not. Well, thanks for . . . doing your job."

"It was spectacular, wasn't it? The way she came crashing down?"

"Yeah," I muttered.

"I had to borrow some tools from the workshop," Abi said, as she led me down the dirt path beside Fletcher's Mill. "Before you get upset, let me remind you that I did it to rescue you from the Kluwers. I used your dad's handsaw to cut through the fence, and I used a piece of catgut to trip the old hag. I tied one end to a tree and held the other end in my hand. Just before she passed by I pulled it tight—*fwing!*—so that it caught her ankles."

"Good thinking," I said.

We hopped over the fence onto the Fletchers' property. There, nestled in a little red wagon, Cole happily gnawed on a hunk of peanut brittle. I recognized the wagon as my own, the one I'd once used to cart my dolls across our fields when I was a little kid. When Cole saw me, he beamed and started chanting, "Prissy, Prissy, Prissy!"

"Hi, Cole," I said. Then my legs collapsed beneath me, and I sank into the soft grass. Abi did the same, and Cole tossed his head back in laughter, thoroughly entertained by this new game where we all pretended to be rag dolls.

# A NIGHT AT THE MILL

Abi and I stayed plastered to the ground long enough to watch the pinks and purples in the sky give way to a curtain of dark blue and a scattering of stars. Cole, meanwhile, clambered out of the wagon and sprinted through the open fields, chasing fireflies and giggling with nerves every time he got close to one.

"It'll be pitch-dark soon," said Abi. "We need a place to camp tonight."

"We can't go back to my house," I said. "The Kluwers will definitely come looking for me there. We can stay here." I pointed to a stone building over the ridge, with a giant waterwheel attached to its side. The wheel churned slowly, propelled by a gushing creek. "That's Fletcher's Mill. The owners are . . . neighbors of ours." It wasn't ideal, but my legs were throbbing after the lashing from Mrs. Kluwer and the run to Lollyhill. I wouldn't make it much farther.

"Perfect," said Abi.

"We have to leave before sunrise," I added. "Mr. Fletcher is the old-fashioned type who rises and falls with the sun. If he finds us, I'm not sure how I'll explain this."

The truth was, Mr. Fletcher wouldn't take kindly to a Reece on his property, no matter the reason. Years ago, the Fletchers had been our closest friends as well as our nearest neighbors. When Mrs. Fletcher got sick, Mother didn't think twice before rushing to the old woman's bedside. In fact, Mother refused to budge, even when Father urged her to come home and let the doctors handle it. And it turns out Father was right. Mother caught whatever it was that ailed Mrs. Fletcher. She was laid up at the Fletcher house for three days, so ill they wouldn't even let me visit. Mrs. Fletcher eventually recovered, but Mother didn't. And Father never forgave the Fletchers for her death.

I shoved those memories out of my head and heaved open the wide doors of the mill. Stepping inside that building always left me awestruck. The far wall was lined with rows of wooden looms linked together by an elaborate pulley system—one of my inspirations for the Dudley Valves. When the wheel turned outside, it pulled the ropes suspended from the ceiling, which set the looms into motion, using the force of water to turn raw wool into delicate yarn. Because of the sharp autumn wind, the whole place was seething with movement when we walked in, like a crew of ghosts was diligently weaving in the otherwise empty space. On the other end of the building, fluffy lamb pelts were stacked high, along with spools of finished yarn as tall as Cole.

"Wow!" said Abi. She bounded across the room with a lit candle fluttering in her hand, and reached out to one of the bouncing looms. Cole ran at top speed to dive into a pile of pelts.

"Stop," I yelled, and they both froze. "We have to leave everything exactly as we found it."

"Killjoy," sighed Abi.

*"Baa,"* bleated Cole, petting one of the pelts as though it were alive.

"If you won't let us play, we might as well eat," said Abi. She unveiled the food she'd swiped from the pantry of my house. The stale bread and pocked oranges were as decadent as a royal feast as we stuffed them greedily into our mouths.

After we'd eaten our fill, we spread out a piece of balloon canvas—a remnant of bright-orange *Tiger Lily*—to shield us from the cold, damp ground. Then we heaped lamb pelts on top—an exception, Abi pointed out, to my rule against touching anything. It was worth it. The fluffy matted wool was more comfortable than my own bed. I leaned back and took in a square of stars through the small window at the top of the building. The rush of the creek and the jingle-jangle of the pulleys sounded like a lullaby, comforting and constant, even if it *was* being performed by ghosts. I guess if I had to be suddenly orphaned and homeless, there were worse places to do it. Abi settled in beside me.

"You've stayed at Kluwer House before, haven't you?" I asked her as we watched Cole repeatedly send my little red wagon crashing into mountains of wool—an activity I decided to allow in order to keep him occupied.

Abi bristled at the question. "What makes you think that?"

"Because you knew exactly how to rescue me."

"I told you, I used my head. It wasn't that hard to figure out that you'd eventually have to go to the outhouse."

"But how'd you know precisely what to take from the workshop?"

"Look—just because we're working together doesn't mean we need to trade life stories, okay? It doesn't make us friends or anything."

"Fine," I said. "I was only trying to make conversation. Don't forget, *you're* the one who dragged *me* into this mess. I was minding my own business when you hopped out of that stupid tree."

"How about we both mind our own business from now on?" she said. "Agreed?"

"Agreed," I snapped. We both grew silent and let the mill do the talking.

"Look!" said Cole, running over and, mercifully, cutting the tension. He held out a floppy rag doll, which had been lovingly crafted with button eyes and even a tiny pair of overalls.

"Where'd you find that?" I asked.

"Over there," he said, pointing to a corner of the mill. "Can I keep it?"

"No, Cole, you have to leave it here," I said. "But you can sleep with it tonight."

Cole pouted, but at the mention of sleep, he rubbed his eyes and yawned with his whole body. I lifted him into the wagon and covered him with a pelt, tucking in the edges to protect him from the nip of the air.

"Do the colors!" he said.

"The colors?" I asked. "What's that?"

*"Pink to heal you,"* crooned Abi, crawling over to peek into the wagon.

*"Red to fight!"* added Cole.

*"Green to keep you warm at night,"* they sang together.

As they finished the nursery rhyme, an image flashed behind my eyes. Of Mother sitting beside my bed, singing that song. The same one I had seen carved into tree trunks. Why hadn't I remembered it before now? What did it mean?

"Now tell me a story," said Cole.

"Your turn," Abi said to me. She lay back on our makeshift bed with her hands clasped behind her head.

"Um, okay. I'll tell you one Father used to tell me." I rested my head on the cold lip of the wagon. "Once upon a time, there was a brave knight called . . . Sir Cole." The real Cole murmured with pride. "One day, a giant a hundred feet tall stomped into Oren, crushing buildings and trees, and terrorizing all the townspeople."

"Eating them?" asked Cole, with fear in his wide eyes.

"No," I said. "The giant didn't want to eat them. He was looking for a new pet. He thought the tiny people were adorable, and he wanted one for his very own. Brave Sir Cole walked right up to the giant and volunteered so nobody else in town would have to live with the mean, stinky monster. The giant scooped up Sir Cole, put him in his pocket, and carried him home, which was in a foul-smelling bog far, far away."

"Oh no," said Cole.

"Don't worry," I said. "Sir Cole had a plan. On his first night in the bog, he asked the giant why he lived all alone. The giant pouted and said he hadn't met the right giantess. 'I have an idea,' said Sir Cole. 'Take a bath! But not in the bog, like you usually do. Take a proper bath. With soap.' The giant had never heard of such a thing. So Sir Cole helped the giant find fresh water and heavy-duty soap, and the giant took his very first bath. Guess what happened then?"

"What?" asked Cole.

"The giant's bath created huge bubbles, bigger than a house. Bubbles even bigger than the palace of Oren! But they were lighter than air, too. So when the giant wasn't looking, Sir Cole hopped inside a bubble and floated away. The giant leaped out of the water to catch his pet, but the bubble had drifted up so high that even the giant couldn't reach it. Sir Cole floated all over the world in his bubble, and when he finally arrived back in Oren, he popped it with his sword and landed safely back home!"

"Hooray," said Cole, his eyelids fighting valiantly against the weight of sleep. "Was the giant mad?"

"Not at all," I said. "The giant smelled so good after his bath—like candy canes and lavender—that he soon met a nice giantess. They lived happily ever after. And Sir Cole did, too."

I peered into the wagon to see Cole's reaction to this happy ending, but he'd already drifted into sleep. His eyelashes rested softly against his flushed cheeks, and his pink lips were wrapped around his thumb. Abi, too, was snoring soundly.

The rhythm of Abi and Cole's breathing merged into the cadence of the mill, like two new instruments joining a symphony. I lay down and listened, wondering again how any of us had wound up here. Would Cole remember any of this when he returned to his normal life, whatever that was? And what about Abi? What would happen to her when I found the evidence of Father's innocence and turned it over to the king? She'd hate me for exposing the rebellion, but like she said, it's not like we were friends or anything. Surely she'd find a way to slip past any trouble I caused her. Surely she wouldn't end up back in a place like Kluwer House.

Would she?

I chased these questions around and around in my head, unable to hold on to any answers, until the song of the mill finally lulled me to sleep, too.

# A MEAGER PATCH OF HAPPINESS

*The Orenite troops rolled in like storm clouds, darkening Wren's sun-drenched existence in Palma. The first time she saw the familiar purple coats of the Royal Guard on a Palmerian street, her heart fluttered in her chest like a moth trapped under glass. If Orenite soldiers were here, then the rumors were true. Oren was at war with Palma.*

*Soon Wren's young pupil went into hiding with his family. Mr. Hillman fell ill and took to bed, while Jaxson continued to work the farm on his own. But the pecans he produced were shriveled and black, the peaches hard and tasteless. Some people suspected the Orenites of poisoning the crops, but Wren believed the land was aching as much as the people, that the roots of war had sunk deep into the soil. Food became scarce, with nothing coming over the border, and what little they had, they were forced to share with the soldiers marching in daily. Oren had destroyed Palma's ships and balloons. They were captives in their own land.*

*In the presence of her countrymen, Wren held her tongue, lest they recognize her accent and deem her a traitor to Oren. Or worse, drag her back home. She watched, helpless and mute, as the soldiers spat at Palmerian peasants in the market, calling them "dogs" and treating them as such. It made her heart ache and her blood boil. But what could she do against the force of the Oren army?*

*The Palmerians resisted at first. A handful of skirmishes took place at the border, near the Southern Gate, which Wren refused to call Savior's Gate. The Palmerians fought bravely but were roundly defeated. Of course they were. They'd never expected such aggression from a neighbor they'd trusted for so long.*

*But somehow, even in the midst of all that devastation, Jaxson and Wren eked out a meager patch of happiness. They invited the neighbors into their home, though their guests could scarcely fit between its four walls. Wren wore her favorite silk scarf—the only luxurious thing she owned—pairing it with her threadbare cotton dress. She pulled together what remained in the cupboard and invented something she called sweet beet cake, which everyone politely ate until it stained their lips deep red. Mr. Hillman gathered enough strength to play his pipe, and they all danced, bumping into one another in the crowded space. Jaxson regaled them with stories about his days in the market. He told them about a man who pretended to turn water into wine by dyeing it with nukka berries, famous for moving the bowels (a sham which ended quite badly for him), about the time a little girl tied the butcher's shoelaces together and stole a lamb shank, about the whole market trembling when he fell. These stories made them laugh and smile, as though they really had something to celebrate.*

*And as Wren cradled her growing belly, she believed that maybe they did.*

# RETURN OF THE KLUWERS

I woke with a start, just as the violet glow of dawn began seeping behind my eyelids. If the sun was up, so was Mr. Fletcher, already tending his sheep and his fields. If we lingered in the mill, he'd soon find us and ask questions I wasn't prepared to answer. I shook Abi out of a heavy sleep.

"Five more minutes," she mumbled, rolling over and rubbing her eyes.

"We don't have five minutes." I lifted one end of our bed and tugged, turning her out onto the cold dirt beneath.

"Fine," she whined, groggily stumbling to her feet. "How come *he* gets to sleep in?" She motioned to Cole, still snug in the cushioned wagon and making soft *num-num* sounds.

"Because he's still a three-year-old when he wakes up."

"Good point," said Abi. "Let him sleep."

Abi and I gathered our things and erased all evidence of our night at Fletcher's Mill. As we folded the tarp, we heard a lone voice outside. And by the sound of it, its owner was heading in our direction. "If I'd a been there, I'd a caught 'em all, every last one," it said.

"It's Mr. Fletcher," I whispered. "Hide!" Abi grabbed the

wagon's metal handle and pulled it to the corner of the room, slow enough that the rusted wheels wouldn't squeak. Cole didn't wake up; in fact, he burrowed deeper into the pelts, soothed by the movement. Abi stowed him behind a tower of spools, and then the two of us crouched behind a loom and held our breath.

"Pshaw," cackled a female voice. "I'd like to've seen you try!" With a pang, I realized it wasn't Mr. Fletcher bearing down on us but the Kluwers, hunting for last night's escapees. Hunting for *me.*

"Do you realize how much you cost us, woman? Twenty-five cents for each girl. Four girls. That's almost . . . That's . . . That's a lot of money!" said Mr. Kluwer. He pushed open the door to the mill, and they stepped inside. A chill wind accompanied them, and my skin rippled with goose bumps.

"If you'd stop yer whinin' and start lookin', maybe we'd find 'em and get our money back," said Mrs. Kluwer. "Ever think a that?"

"It's a fine thing you're not in charge a the boys," said Mr. Kluwer. "We'd be broke!"

That comment was followed by the fleshy *thunk* of his wife's palm landing squarely on the side of his head. Mr. Kluwer gingerly rubbed the spot where he'd been smacked, while Mrs. Kluwer looked around and released a long whistle.

"Will ya get a load a this?" she said. "Whatta place! What is all this?" She approached the jerking machine that concealed Abi and me. We huddled closer together behind it.

"C'mon, woman, we're not here to sightsee," said her husband. "Nobody's here. Let's go."

Mrs. Kluwer grumbled but backed away from us. The two of them started toward the door, bickering all the while. As their footsteps began to recede, Abi and I exhaled with relief, grateful that the dotty old Kluwers were more intent on fighting with each other than on finding the runaways. But then something rattled behind the tower of spools.

We heard a whimper, then the sharp intake of breath that always came before Cole's wailing—a pattern I'd come to know well. Abi and I exchanged panicked glances. We scrambled out from behind the loom as quickly as we could, but it was too late. Cole let out a full-throated howl, which echoed off the high ceiling, bounced out the tall windows, and drifted into the open fields.

Proving once again how swiftly they could move with the right motivation, the Kluwers reappeared in an instant, descending on us with their arms outstretched like two grinning ghouls.

"Thought you could hide from us, did ya?" panted Mrs. Kluwer, her frizz streaming wildly around her reddened face.

"Thought we was fools, did ya?" wheezed Mr. Kluwer.

"There's been a mistake," I said, stepping forward. "I'm not an orphan. I've got a father. Elmore Reece, the balloonist. We live up the road. I don't belong in a children's home."

"Some father you've got," said Mr. Kluwer with a chuckle. "Ms. Stoneman said he was carted off by the Royal Guard."

"Who's the little sweetie?" asked Mrs. Kluwer, craning toward Cole.

Abi wrapped her arms protectively around the boy and turned him away from the woman's leering gaze.

"He'll fetch a pretty penny," Mrs. Kluwer whispered loudly to her husband.

"If you try to take us, I'll scream!" said Abi.

"Scream all you'd like," said Mr. Kluwer. "Nobody around here cares about the likes a you. In fact, they pay us real handsome to get you trash off the streets. So go on and scream."

Mrs. Kluwer lunged at me, pinning my arms to my sides with a surprisingly solid grip. At the same time, Mr. Kluwer leaped for Abi and Cole. Cole kicked at him vigorously, but soon Mr. Kluwer's long arms circled both of them.

"Let me go," I cried, trying to wriggle out of Mrs. Kluwer's iron grasp.

In the commotion, none of us noticed the grizzled old man who had joined us in the mill. Until he spoke.

# MR. FLETCHER LAYS DOWN THE LAW

"What's the problem?" asked Mr. Fletcher. His words were as slow as syrup, his demeanor as calm as a cow chewing cud. His face was etched with wrinkles, and feathery wisps of gray hair sprang from his balding head. All that, combined with his dirty overalls and rusty pitchfork, made him the very embodiment of a Lollyhill farmer.

Mr. and Mrs. Kluwer smiled, showing off their long yellow teeth, but they didn't loosen their grips on us. "There's no problem," said Mr. Kluwer, struggling to maintain his composure as he was throttled by Cole's tiny shoes and Abi's fists. "These hooligans ran away from our children's home last night, and we found 'em hiding out in your mill."

"Ah," said Mr. Fletcher, scratching at the salt-and-pepper whiskers on his chin. "That's concerning indeed."

"We'll just collect our charges and be out of your way, sir," added Mrs. Kluwer, suddenly all polite and genteel.

"Very good," said Mr. Fletcher absently. "Sounds like everything is in order, then."

Mrs. Kluwer's lips twisted into a triumphant grin. She stepped forward, dragging me along with her, and gave Mr. Fletcher a curtsy that looked more like an awkward stumble, with her arms and legs akimbo.

"There's just one thing," said Mr. Fletcher, fixing his ice-blue eyes on the half-bent Mrs. Kluwer. "That one there is the Reece girl. She's the balloonist's daughter."

"W-well, we don't know the details of the girl's situation," stammered Mrs. Kluwer, "but she was left in our care only yesterday."

"*I* know her situation," said Mr. Fletcher. "Her father is a good man. A good neighbor. And he wouldn't like his girl locked up in a children's home while he's away." I could scarcely believe such flattering words about Father were coming out of Mr. Fletcher's mouth.

"With all due respect," said Mr. Kluwer, "the child cannot be left on her own."

"Then she can stay here," said Mr. Fletcher. "I'll look after her."

The Kluwers locked eyes, and Mrs. Kluwer's lips hardened into a frown. "Fine," she spat, shoving me roughly toward Mr. Fletcher. "We'll take the others, then."

"Very good," said Mr. Fletcher.

"No!" cried Abi. "When my parents find out about this, they'll—"

"Hush!" growled Mr. Kluwer.

"I'll just need you to provide the proper paperwork," said Mr. Fletcher, still unfazed by the bizarre scene unfolding in his mill.

"Excuse me?" yelped Mrs. Kluwer, her not-white-enough eyes bulging from her face.

"If these children belong with you," said Mr. Fletcher, "I

presume you can provide me with a document of some kind, proving your claim."

"We've been charged with clearing the unwanteds out of this area," said Mr. Kluwer. "That activity is for the public good and doesn't require paperwork of any kind. Everyone knows that."

"Not me," said Mr. Fletcher with a shrug. "I don't pretend to be well versed on the laws, being a simple miller and all. But it seems to me, if you're gonna lock these children away against their will, there should be some official documentation."

"This is ridiculous," snarled Mrs. Kluwer, dropping any pretense of manners.

Mr. Fletcher took a step forward, twirling his pitchfork as he went. "I am twenty minutes behind in my work this morning. Kindly unhand the children and come back with the paperwork. Then we can conclude this most unpleasant business."

His tone left no room for argument, and the Kluwers didn't dare offer any. They pushed Cole and Abi to the ground and, with a glare at the old man, stalked out of the building, mumbling complaints and promises to return.

When they'd gone, I ran to Mr. Fletcher. "Thank you," I said. "My father is—"

"Don't tell me," he said. "The less I know, the better. Those vultures will be back soon, with the Royal Guard in tow. You can't stay here."

We nodded. Then Cole cautiously crept up to Mr. Fletcher, holding out the rag doll he'd found the night before. When Mr. Fletcher's eyes landed on it, he flinched—a subtle, almost imperceptible twitch. But I saw it, plain as day.

"Oh," he said. "That belonged to a child who's long gone. You can keep it."

Cole beamed and squeezed the stuffed toy to his chest. I studied the old man's face for some clue about the long-gone child. The Fletchers never had any kids of their own, as far as I knew. But his face wasn't giving anything away.

"I'll leave some biscuits and bacon by the hitching post," said Mr. Fletcher. "Eat, and then go hide somewhere. And stay hid, you hear?"

"Yes, sir," we said.

He sighed heavily and turned to leave. From the doorway of the mill, I watched him, stamping the blunt end of his pitchfork into the dirt as he walked toward the braying sheep in the distance. My legs itched to chase after him, as I might once have done, but I knew with a sinking heart that I could no longer do that. We were on our own once again. Mr. Fletcher didn't look back.

# MRS. MULBERRY'S HAUNTED MUSIC SCHOOL

Abi's long-legged gait kept her several paces ahead of Cole and me as we trudged once more into the heart of the kingdom. She zigzagged down hidden paths and cut through claustrophobic alleyways, leading us into parts of Oren I never knew existed. By the time we reached the Slope, she'd taken so many rights and lefts, I was thoroughly lost.

"Where are we going?" I asked.

"To get you some builders!" she called over her shoulder. "You'll see."

We entered a shabby neighborhood of houses, three and four stories tall, crammed so close together they formed a tottering, mismatched wall of their own. Some of them had swaying shingles out front advertising tailors, carpenters, and rope makers. We stopped in front of a ramshackle building with a bright-green door and a hand-lettered sign in the window that read MRS. MULBERRY'S MUSIC SCHOOL.

"Here we are," said Abi.

"What are we doing here?" I asked. "Getting piano lessons?"

"Not quite." Abi bypassed the green front door and snuck around to a back entrance, which she rapped on in a specific pattern—*knock-knock-pause-knock-pause-knock*. After a moment, it swung open, and a girl in a maid's uniform—a frilly white apron over a long black dress, with layers of petticoats underneath—stood inside.

"Whoa," I said. "Fancy."

"Not really," said Abi, waving us inside. "This is Marybeth. She's a housemaid at the palace."

"I empty chamber pots and sweep the fireplace," said Marybeth. "Hardly fancy." Marybeth was a few years older than me—around Halston's age. She had curly brown hair and an overbite that made her look a bit like a rabbit.

"How do you move around in that skirt?" I asked.

"Slowly," said Marybeth with a wink.

"What are you doing here?" Abi asked her.

"The chef sent me out for eggs," said Marybeth, "and I took a little detour. I miss this old place."

"What *is* this old place?" I asked. We'd entered a dusty living room with a full-sized piano in the corner and a small, crumbling sofa in the center. Musical instruments were piled on or propped against every piece of furniture.

"Welcome to Mulberry House," said Abi with a proud grin. "The *real* children's home."

"Really? What's with all the instruments?"

"Mrs. Mulberry gives music lessons here three days a week," said Abi. "The rest of the time, it's all ours."

"She lets you use her house?"

"No, but she hasn't lived here since her husband, Roger, died," said Marybeth. "Her children whisked her off to their fancy homes in Silk Valley, but she refuses to sell this place. She insists on teaching her lessons here so Roger can hear."

"Mrs. Mulberry isn't exactly the charitable type," said Abi. "No way she'd let us crash here if she knew. She's really mean."

"She looks like a wicked witch," said Marybeth. "She's older than time and has hideous warts all over her skin."

"And whenever a kid misses a note, she swats their wrists with a drumstick."

"And she smells like sour milk."

"And she coughs into her students' hair while they're playing."

"But that's not the worst thing . . ."

"Not even close . . ."

I gulped. "What's the worst thing?"

Cole's eyes grew as wide as saucers. Abi and Marybeth shared a conspiratorial look.

"Mrs. Mulberry's house is haunted," whispered Abi.

I guffawed and rolled my eyes, but Cole whimpered and latched onto me. "You're joking, right?" I said.

"It's true," said Marybeth. "Roger's ghost wanders around upstairs, listening to the music lessons. Her students can hear him up there, rattling around and moaning."

"That's nonsense," I said to Cole. But I had to admit, the place *did* give me the shivers. Old photographs of serious, dead-eyed people lined the walls. Yellowed lace curtains fluttered in the windows, pushed by a nonexistent breeze. Even the clocks had stopped, stuck in time, with nobody around to wind them. I decided then and there I didn't want to spend any more time than necessary at Mulberry House.

"Let's show them the living quarters," said Marybeth, moving toward the staircase.

Cole shook his head.

"I'll protect you," I whispered into his ear.

I lifted Cole onto my hip and followed the girls up a narrow staircase to the second floor, where an eruption of chatter and movement shattered the frozen quiet of the floor below. Like at Kluwer House, a hive of small rooms was teeming with children of all ages, sprawled on crude beds. But that was where the similarities ended. The faces at Mulberry House were lively instead of stoic, the voices unrestrained instead of hushed. Drawings and newspaper clippings were pinned to the walls. Colorful fabric strung into bunting decorated the ceiling. Baby dolls and stuffed bears littered the floor. I could tell at a glance that these children intended to stay here. This place was really a home.

"Hey, Abs, who're your friends?" someone called from across the room.

"This is Prismena," Abi announced, "and the little guy is Cole." Children emerged from every corner and crevice, shouting introductions and greetings, offering handshakes. Cole spun in place to take it all in, a stunned smile on his face.

"It's you!" called a girl with short, choppy hair. "You made it."

"Roz!" I cried, happy to see her even though our first meeting hadn't exactly been friendly.

"I met Prissy at Kluwer House," said Roz. At the mention of the K-word, the crowd issued a chorus of boos.

"Sorry about how I acted yesterday," I said to Roz. "I wasn't exactly myself."

"It's all right," she said with a shrug. "Being at Kluwer House does that to people."

"But *I* broke them out," said Abi, stepping into the center of the room. "I knocked Mrs. Kluwer right on her skinny butt!"

The kids cheered and whooped.

"How'd you meet Abs?" someone called out to me.

"We met in Lollyhill," I said, not keen to share the details of my first humiliating encounter with Abi. "That's where I live."

"Where you *live*?" repeated Roz, her brow wrinkled in confusion. "I didn't know there was a children's home in Lollyhill."

"I don't mean in a children's home," I said. "It's where I live with my father."

The boisterous children grew suddenly quiet. The tone of the room shifted, like I'd said something wrong.

"Are you tellin' me . . . you've got parents?" said Roz, in a tone that made it sound like an accusation.

"Yes," I said, my voice shrill in the thickening silence.

Roz turned on Abi. "You brought *tourists* here? What were you thinking?" Roz was at least three inches shorter than Abi, but Abi shrank back.

"Relax," she said. "Her dad got tossed in jail, and she has nowhere else to go. She's not a snitch or anything. I can vouch for her."

Abi shot me a warning glare, and I squirmed. I shuddered to think of how Abi and Roz would react if they knew I was only sticking around to get my hands on Halston's satchel.

"I hope you're right," said Roz. Then she asked me, "So, what'd you bring for the pot?"

"The *what*?"

"Ugh," she groaned. "Tourists." She pointed to a mountain of items—clothes, toys, candy—piled high in the center of the room. I'd figured it was the natural mess of a house without parents, but Roz explained, "If you want to stay at Mulberry House, you've gotta put all your worldly possessions into the pot. Food, clothes, everything. Then you take what you need when you need it. So . . . what've you got?"

I went through the motions of digging through my pockets, even though I knew they were empty. We'd abandoned our wagon and our tools at the mill, and we'd ravenously eaten all of Mrs. Fletcher's food within minutes of receiving it. Only Cole had anything left. He reluctantly placed his new doll on top of the pot, but he concealed his carved peach pit in his tiny fist.

"The boy can stay," said Roz. She focused her hard stare on me, and I bit my lip.

"Here," said Marybeth, striding to the center of the room. She removed three fuzzy brown balls from the pockets of her apron and dropped them onto the pile. "This contribution is made on behalf of my new friend, Prismena. It's called kiwifruit. It's green inside, believe it or not. And delicious. The palace imports them from . . . Well, I'm not really sure where they import them from, but they're incredible."

Marybeth looked over at me and smiled. I mouthed, *Thanks.*

"Good, that's settled," said Abi, though Roz didn't appear to think so. "Now on to more pressing matters. Prissy and I are working on a top-secret mission for the Wren, and we've come for recruits. We need the bravest, strongest, cleverest kids we can find. Is there anyone like that here?"

All at once, the kids clamored for Abi's attention, raising their hands and shouting "Me! Me! Me!" Even Cole waved his hand in Abi's face, begging to be picked.

"Hold on," Abi shouted, hushing them with a raised palm. "Before you volunteer, I must warn you that this mission will be very dangerous. You might have to face the Royal Guard! You might have to duel with King Michael! You might even wind up in the clutches of the Mad Queen!" Her voice was pitched with excitement. And when she cried, "Who's with me?" every voice rang out in the affirmative, their faces glowing with anticipation.

"What a good-looking band of soldiers," Abi said. "Now get out there and fill your bellies. You're going to need your strength for the task ahead. Then meet us in Between as soon as you can. Two miles south of the East Gate. Now . . . *go*!"

With pounding feet and hoots of excitement, the children of Mulberry House bounded down the stairs and swarmed into the streets of Oren. Abi hung back and picked through the pot as the room emptied. When she found a bright-red crepe skirt, she let her patched riding breeches drop to the ground, much to Cole's amusement.

I gasped. "Abi! What are you doing?"

"Wardrobe change," she said, shimmying her new skirt up over her undergarments. "Don't you get bored wearing the same thing all the time?"

"Not really," I said, self-consciously smoothing my coarse brown dress. "Abi, where are those kids going to 'fill their bellies'?"

"The market, of course."

"Do they have money?"

"Do they look like they have money?" said Abi. "Some of

them will barter, but most of them will take what they need . . . if you catch my drift."

My eyes widened. "You mean they'll *steal* it?"

"They've gotta eat," she said.

"Oh. And why did Roz call me a 'tourist'? What does that mean?"

Abi sighed. "You still don't get it. In this kingdom, there's 'us' and there's 'them,' and you're . . . well, you're 'them,' Prissy."

"No, I'm not!" I cried, irked for reasons I couldn't quite put my finger on. "The Royal Guard is after me! The Kluwers are after me. And my father is in jail for treason. How could I possibly be 'them'?"

"Because you *have* a father! He'll probably be released any day now, and everything will go back to normal for you. You'll sleep in your big house, you'll eat three meals a day, and you'll tell everyone at school about the neat adventure you had with a bunch of plucky orphans. But that won't happen for us. This is it for us—scavenging and stealing and hustling. All those things you turn up your nose at."

"I'm not turning up my nose," I said, lowering my chin to prove it. "I just didn't realize places like this existed."

"Of course you didn't," said Abi. "Why would you?" She picked up a large purple coat from the pile at her feet. It had two rows of shiny brass buttons down the front, like the ones worn by the Royal Guard. "We get all sorts of uniforms in the pot," she said. "Know why?"

I shook my head.

"Because a bunch of these kids are the children of soldiers who died in the war. Everyone knows the story of King Michael, the Savior of Oren. But nobody talks about what the war really cost."

"Abi . . . Was your dad a soldier?" I asked softly.

Her mouth pressed into a hard line, and she dropped her gaze. I could tell I'd guessed right.

"I—I'm so sorry," I said.

"I'm fine."

"If it weren't for the beastly Palmerians—"

"It's not that simple."

"But there must be someone who can help," I said.

"Who?" snapped Abi. "The guards at the jail? Remember how well that worked out for you?"

"There must be something you can do!"

"There *is* something I can do," she said. "And I'm doing it. It's the 'so-called *cause*' you don't want any part of."

I didn't have a response. Abi tossed the blazer back onto the pile and adjusted Mother's scarf, which still shimmered in her curls. Then she extracted Cole from the pot, where he'd burrowed deep inside, pretending to be a bunny.

As the three of us headed to the exit, one boy remained in the room, sitting cross-legged with a rusty metal chain on his lap and an inscrutable smile on his face.

"Look what I found," he said to Abi, jiggling the chain. "Marsha Peterson is going to flip!"

"You're awful," said Abi.

"What's he going to do with that?" I whispered as we took the stairs to street level.

"It's almost time for Marsha Peterson's violin lesson," she explained. "And he's going to make sure this house stays haunted."

# GOING HOME

*Wren's son didn't cry when he entered the world. He only whimpered, like he already knew the danger of being too loud. As Oren's army laid siege to their little corner of Palma, Jaxson, Wren, and their baby, Tobias, huddled together, not knowing when—or if—it would end. They locked the doors and closed the curtains while the war raged on around them. Whole days went by without Wren feeling the warmth of the sun on her skin. Her son's smile filled their little house with light, but she longed to drench him in the real thing, to show him oceans and hilltops and hot-air balloons. Instead, her eyes grew accustomed to the dark.*

*And she was afraid. With every howl of wind, every rattle outside, she tensed and covered Toby in blankets as if he were something stolen. And in a way, he was.*

*"What if we'd never come here?" she blurted out one night.*

*"What?" said Jaxson. "Wren, you don't mean that—"*

*"What made us think we deserved happiness more than anyone else? Look what we've done, Jaxson! Our son may never know anything but war!" The words had been heavy stones on her heart for weeks, ever since Toby was born. She'd been crippled by guilt and*

*doubt, and suddenly it was tumbling out. But saying it aloud didn't make it easier to bear.*

*"This is all going to end soon," said Jaxson, taking her hand. "King Michael will grow tired of this war, if we simply wait."*

*"People are dying while we wait. Every day, people are dying."*

*"I know," said Jaxson. He grew quiet, no doubt remembering the Palmerians they'd known who hadn't survived. And wondering how their families in Oren were faring.*

*"We can go back," said Wren. "If we tell the soldiers we're Orenite citizens, they'll take us home. Or . . . or we can sneak over the border. The Hillmans have a balloon hidden in their shed—"*

*"The Palmerians gave us a home," said Jaxson. "They let us be a family. We can't abandon them now."*

*"On the other side of that Wall, we—"*

*"On the other side of that Wall, there is no 'we.' And if we had stayed, there would be no him." Jaxson pointed to the gurgling child on the bed.*

*"I—I just never thought it would get this bad," she said, and hot tears flooded her eyes. "I never thought it would hurt this much. I love you, but—"*

*"Enough of this talk," said Jaxson, pressing a finger to her lips. "You're tired. You're homesick. That's all."*

*It wasn't all.*

*"I'm so sorry," she said, collapsing into her husband's arms. Sobs racked her body as she apologized over and over for the things she'd done and the things she was about to do. "I'm so sorry."*

*Jaxson fell asleep, curled around his son, but Wren stayed awake. She waited until their breathing was heavy and deep, and then she rose quietly from their bed. When she reached the doorway, she paused but didn't look back. She knew if she did, she'd lose her resolve. Instead, she scrawled a note.* I'm sorry, *it said. "I have to do this. I love you."*

*She thought about her last night in Oren, tiptoeing out of her father's house. Had it hurt this much? She could hardly remember that life anymore. Would she forget this one, too? She steeled herself before stepping out into the chilly night.*

*It wasn't difficult to find what she was looking for on the streets of Palma. The Orenite soldiers packed the pubs and inns, swigging pints of ale and resting their muddy boots on tabletops. At first, they ignored her, probably assuming she was another Palmerian beggar. When at last she found a soldier willing to listen, she could barely push the words out of her throat. He had to lean in close to hear her.*

*"I'm from Oren," she said. "I want to go home."*

# TREASON IN THE EASTERN WOODS

The eastern woods didn't have a name—not an official one, anyway. People simply called it Between, the stretch of uninhabited land that separated Lollyhill from the Wall, filled with nothing but trees and streams and wild creatures. That's where the bravest, strongest, cleverest kids in Oren congregated that fine autumn day to fling candy over the Wall.

I'd never ventured into those woods before, even though they butted up against our land. Father never would've allowed it—not that I would've asked permission to go there. Between wasn't exactly a welcoming place, unless you were a critter. But on that day, I braved it. I tramped through the fallen leaves, my face battered by branches and my progress tracked by pairs of eyes I could feel but couldn't see.

We headed south, to the section of the Wall that separated Oren from Palma. "I thought we were delivering the candy to *Tulera,*" I said, ducking to avoid a whack from a low-hanging branch.

"Change of plans," said Abi, charging ahead. "When we had Guernsey, we were going to send it to Tulera, and our allies would get it to Palma. But now that we've got you, we can cut out the middleman." She grinned at me, and my stomach dropped. In my eagerness to build the catapult, I'd almost lost sight of what it would be used for.

"Now that I'm officially part of this . . . thing"—I refused to admit out loud that I was part of the rebellion—"will you tell me what the message on the candy wrappers means? What's going to happen on Savior's Day?" As I asked these questions, I tucked one hand behind my back and crossed my fingers again, just in case.

"Not yet, Gumdrop. Maybe after the candy is delivered." She eyed me skeptically. "*Maybe.* Here we are!" We emerged in a small clearing, where a break in the trees gave us an unobstructed view of the Wall. I'd seen it up close plenty of times on Savior's Day, when it was draped in banners and overshadowed by the festivities. But out here, in the quiet woods, it looked stark and imposing, as though it were striving to block out the sky. I felt tiny in its presence.

"Whoa!" gasped Cole, who seemed even tinier.

Behind us, something rustled in the bushes. Something bigger than a fox or a raccoon, judging by the disturbance it caused. "What's that?" I yelped, huddling closer to Abi and Cole. They shook their heads and laughed at me.

Luckily, Abi's recruits soon poured into the clearing to join us, chattering, roughhousing, and—I hoped—scaring off the wild beasts of the wood. Abi took charge, climbing onto the thick trunk of a fallen tree and announcing our mission: to build a catapult so large it could deliver a package over the Wall, without the Royal Guard being any the wiser. She summoned me to join her and told everyone the catapult had been my idea, which prompted a round of applause that made my cheeks go pink. Then she roused them with a speech that soon had everyone eager to do strenuous labor. I had to admit, I was impressed.

Abi set to work divvying up the tasks and bossing people around, which suited her perfectly. I'd whisper into her ear what needed to be done, and she'd bark it out at a volume ten times louder. In this manner, we directed the kids of Mulberry House to gather felled timber and massive boulders from across the forest. Even Cole "helped," dragging bundles of sticks from one place to another. They weren't strictly necessary for the machine, but nobody would've dreamed of telling him that.

Once we had the materials we needed, we pieced them together according to the specifications I'd doodled on the back of Father's official paperwork for the Ministry of Balloons. It was backbreaking work, but hardly anyone complained. In fact, the children joked and made a game of it, competing to see who could lift the most or build the fastest. By the time the last piece was fitted into place, the sun had peaked in the sky, and we were all dripping with sweat.

At last, we stood back to admire what we'd made. The finished machine was a giant version of the tiny catapult I'd built in my living room—a long beam attached at a single point to a heavy wooden frame. One end of the beam was attached to a sling, which would hold our cargo. A massive boulder was strapped to the other end. I compared it to my drawing, measuring and remeasuring every piece. Finally, I determined that it was just right, even if it did wobble precariously every time the wind blew.

"Is that thing really going to fling our chocolates over the Wall?" Abi asked, squinting at the catapult skeptically.

"Uh . . . yes?" I said, chewing my lip.

"If you say so," she said. "Load her up!"

Everyone cheered as the cargo was carried into the center of the crowd.

"What is it?" someone asked.

A boy reached into the box and held up one of the shiny packages for everyone to see. "Candy?" he said. The children hushed and looked to Abi for an explanation. I could practically hear their stomachs rumbling.

*"For the cause!"* cried Abi.

Without a pause, they hollered back: *"For the cause!"* I still didn't understand the cause these kids were so riled up about, but apparently it outranked hunger.

"Here we go," said Abi, giving me a wink. My heart was thumping, my stomach twisting up in knots. After all this, what if it didn't work?

Then again, what if it *did* work?

Five of the strongest kids hoisted the boulder up with ropes, which lowered the sling to the ground. Then the children set to work loading it with the first bundles of candy.

*"Fire!"* shouted Abi.

The ropes were released, and the boulder crashed to the ground with a thud that made the ground tremble. The beam swung in an arc at breakneck speed, whipping the sling into the air. The machine creaked and jerked but held together—barely. Then bundles of candy hurtled out of the sling, straight toward the Wall.

Up, up, up. Speeding toward it.

And then, narrowly, sailing over it.

It worked! My invention had worked, and for a few jubilant

moments, I forgot that I'd broken the law, disobeyed Father, and participated in a rebellion—again. The Between erupted with hoots and hollers, and we all stumbled backward through the woods for a better glimpse of the candy falling into Palma.

The packages should have kept their speed and thumped straight into the ground on the other side of the Wall. The chocolate should have wound up squashed, but the message would have been delivered.

Instead, the bundles paused in midair, caught there by something tied to them. "Abi?" I asked, spinning to face her. "What did you do?"

"I know, I know," she said, her cheeks rosy with excitement. "I have to stop stealing your father's stuff. But once a thief, always a thief, I guess."

She'd attached a small square of silk to each bundle of candy, and like miniature balloons, they drifted gently into Palma, dotting the sky with color.

"Actually," I said. "It's okay. In fact, it's a great idea. I only wish I'd thought of it myself."

# A BLOOD-RED SMILE

A little girl sprinted into the clearing with such speed she almost careened right past all of us and ran smack into the Wall. Luckily, she skidded to a stop when she spotted Abi. "I . . . have . . . a message," she wheezed. She bent over double to catch her breath. When she straightened up, her eyes landed on me and widened. "Are you *her*?" she asked. "Are you the balloonist's daughter?"

"Um . . . yeah."

"Wow," she breathed, as if Father were some kind of celebrity. A long time ago, Oren's balloons had been world-renowned, and the balloonists who made them had been respected craftsmen. But after the war started, the Royal Armory had taken over most of the forges to make weapons. It's true that Father was the last of a dying breed, but that didn't make him famous. Far from it, in fact.

"What's the message?" demanded Abi, recalling the girl to her mission.

"Oh yeah," she said, still heaving. "It's from Halston."

*"Really?"* cried Abi. "Where is he? Where has he been?"

"He got stuck at the pub. Royal Guard everywhere. Gruber

stashed him. In the whiskey cellar. He wants to meet. In Lollyhill. At the balloonist's workshop. Now."

*"Now?* We have to go!" She shoved the rest of us out of the way as she charged into the brush. "C'mon!" she shouted to me.

"But what about the Kluwers?" I called after her. "And Ms. Stoneman? And the Royal Guard? That place could be swarming with people who want to catch me!"

"Halston's there," said Abi. "So that's where we're going."

Sighing, I swung Cole onto my hip, though my arms were still shaky from carrying boulders, and I plunged into the forest to keep up with Abi—a task that was becoming all too familiar. Just like her, I'd been waiting anxiously for Halston's arrival, but now that it was here, a growing sense of dread crept over me—one that made no sense. Once I got what I needed from him, I could put an end to this whole miserable business. I should've been elated or, at the very least, relieved. Why wasn't I?

When my house finally came into view, my heart lurched toward it. It was hard to believe that Ms. Stoneman had dragged me away from the place only yesterday. It felt like an eternity ago. So much had changed, but the quiet stones gave no indication that anything was different. They looked so ordinary, in fact, that I began to wonder if I'd imagined the whole thing. But the wriggling child in my arms was proof that I hadn't.

"Are we going home?" asked Cole, rubbing his eyes with exhaustion. The poor kid must have been missing his parents and his uncle. He must've been wondering how he'd wound up on the run with two perfect strangers, being whisked madly from place to place. I could certainly relate.

"We're going to *my* home," I told him. "But we're meeting your uncle Halston there so he can bring you back to *your* home."

"Oh," he said. "I'm hungry."

"Of course you are," I said, playfully squeezing his chubby arm.

Meanwhile, Abi barreled ahead of us toward the workshop. When she reached the doorway, she came to a sudden stop, caught her breath, and smoothed Mother's scarf. Then she sauntered inside, cool as a kumquat. I arrived just behind her, panting and spent from having lugged a three-year-old the whole way.

Inside, Halston was casually pacing the room, whistling as he perused Father's vast collection of tools. And there, sitting unattended by the forge, was his satchel. I released Cole and planted myself next to it.

"It's about time!" said Abi, marching up to Halston. "I heard you've been up to your neck in whiskey, while I've being doing all the hard work."

"Ha!" said Halston. Then he brushed past her to squat beside Cole. "Hey, little man. Have the girls been taking good care of you?"

Cole mumbled something indistinct and inched closer to me.

I inched closer to the satchel.

"I'm sorry we got separated," Halston said. "But everything is back on course now."

Cole grunted.

"How about a bath?" said Halston, no doubt catching a whiff of the boy's pungent smell. "I can take you to a place with hot water."

"No!" said Cole, stamping his foot. "I don't want a bath! I want food!"

"Okay, I'll get you food."

"I want *Prissy* to get me food."

Halston sighed and rocked back on his heels. "I see you have a fan," he said to me. "And I see you and Abi haven't killed each other yet. Tell me, what have you been up to?"

"Completing the mission, that's what!" said Abi, stepping in front of Cole and back into Halston's line of sight. "We chucked those chocolates into Palma just like you asked. South of the East Gate."

"Brilliant," said Halston, smiling so wide it dimpled his cheeks. "Our allies are sure to find them there."

"Prissy designed a giant catapult, and I bundled the chocolates in balloon scraps so they'd stand out. They won't be missed."

"Well done!"

"We did have a few hiccups, though. Prissy got picked up by the Kluwers, so I had to break her out. Then they tracked us down, but we escaped again. Then we went to Mulberry House for—"

"Good," said Halston distractedly. "I'm glad it all worked out. And most importantly, you brought Cole back to me safe and sound. Thanks, Abs."

"Yeah, yeah," she muttered. "You're welcome."

She was mumbling something under her breath about being a glorified babysitter when Halston suddenly hushed her and cocked his head to the side.

"What?" insisted Abi.

"Shh," he hissed.

And then I heard the faint but distinct clip-clop of approaching hooves. I sucked in my breath and looked to Halston.

"Expecting anyone?" Abi whispered to him. Outside, a horse neighed, and a bridle jingled. Someone was coming.

"Stay here," he said. He padded to the partially open door, and Abi stayed at his heels, ignoring his instructions. He peeked out, his hand poised on the knife in his belt. But then his face lit with recognition. He relaxed, and I did the same. I turned back to more pressing matters.

As Halston and Abi busied themselves with the new arrival, Cole and I were left alone by the forge. Halston's satchel was gaping open at my feet, practically inviting me to riffle through it. This was the chance I'd been waiting for, but I only had seconds to get what I needed. I crouched beside the bag and began pawing through the crumpled documents inside. I didn't have time to figure out what was what, so I decided to take everything. Surely something in this stack would prove Father's innocence and pin the crimes of the rebellion where they belonged: on Guernsey and Halston and . . . Abi.

I hesitated. Maybe Abi and the other kids from Mulberry House *were* criminals, technically, but if I turned them in, I'd be sentencing them to Kluwer House. Or jail. Or worse.

But if I had to choose between them and Father, was that really a choice at all?

It was too much to sift through in the time I had left. As long as I had the evidence, I could decide what to do with it later. Cole gazed at me doubtfully as I removed the papers from the satchel.

"Prissy?"

I jumped at the sound of Abi's voice, scattering the documents across the floor. She had returned and was staring at me, her brow creased in confusion. But confusion was quickly veering into anger. "What are you doing?"

"Abi, I . . . um . . . Nothing." I clumsily gathered the papers and stuffed them back into Halston's satchel, crumpling them even more. She stomped toward me. But just as she was about to let me have it, Halston strode into the workshop. And he wasn't alone.

A slim figure in a long, dark cape swept into the room with him. A cavernous hood concealed the wearer's face in shadow. Like the cloaked images of Death I'd seen in old books, the visitor moved with an unnatural lightness, seeming to float rather than walk. When a pale-white hand reached out of the wide velvet sleeve and pushed the hood back, I gasped without meaning to. A blanket of jet-black hair tumbled down, and the woman's green eyes shone in the dim light of the workshop. She was beautiful. But dangerous, like the flames in the forge.

"I got your message," she said to Halston. "Are these the young traitors you told me about?"

"Yes," said Halston, his head bowed.

Abi and I stumbled backward. Cole cowered behind our legs.

"And the boy?"

Halston reached behind us and lifted Cole by the scruff of his shirt. His limbs flailed as he cried out and reached for me. Halston presented him to the Mad Queen of Oren like an offering.

Her blood-red lips spread into a smile.

# AN AUDIENCE WITH THE MAD QUEEN

"How could you?" Abi cried, glowering at Halston. She ran at him, swinging her fists, but he held her off with an outstretched arm. Instead, she pelted him with every awful word ever invented—and a few I think she made up right on the spot.

"Are you quite finished?" he asked, unmoved.

"Was this your plan all along?" Abi screeched. "To hand us over to these . . . these tyrants?" She nearly spat at the queen when she said it. "You can't get rid of us all! You can't keep us quiet! You think we're weak and unwanted, but together we're stronger than you!"

"Enough!" growled Halston, his hand again moving to the knife lashed to his belt. Abi looked up at him with hate in her eyes, her chest heaving, but she stopped raving.

The queen crouched down in front of Cole, studying him curiously. She'd probably never been so close to someone so filthy before. She reached out to him, and he swatted her hand away. She winced. She'd probably never been pushed away like a plate of beets before, either.

"Do you know who I am?" the queen asked Cole. Her voice had a rasp to it, a rawness I didn't expect to hear there. Cole shook his head, a defiant frown plumping his bottom lip. "I'm the queen," she said. "I'm the ruler of this whole kingdom. Including you."

The boy's eyes darted back and forth, between the intimidating stranger and Abi and me. He seemed to understand now that she was important and that crossing her would get him into trouble. His little body started to tremble, and a tiny bulb of snot crept out of one nostril, but he didn't cry or scream. He didn't even pull away this time when the queen placed her palm on his cheek, her milky-white hand a stark contrast to his ruddy complexion. He whimpered only two words: "Prissy. Abi." We both started toward him, but Halston restrained us.

"It's okay," said the queen, settling back on her heels. "He may go to them."

Cole threw himself at us. We wrapped our arms around him and sank our noses into his oily hair, pungent with dirt and sweat. The queen watched with the same expression she'd worn at the market when Cole had approached her. Scornful. Squeamish. Like she might be sick.

The three of us stood before the queen like petitioners on Judgment Day as she rose, a specter in purple velvet, pacing in front of Father's wall of brightly colored balloon tarps. For a long moment, she seemed lost in her own thoughts. When she finally spoke, it was again to Cole. She pointed to the object in his fist. "What have you got there? May I see it?" It was an order, not a request.

Cole slowly placed his peach pit in her open palm. She held it up with two fingers, turning it over and over. "I knew a man once who made carvings like this," she said. "He'd suck the pulp from the peaches and whittle away at the pits with a sharp little penknife. It's not easy working with something so small, and he had the scars on his fingers to show for it. But then he'd hold up a perfect replica of a monkey or an owl or a dragon, and it would all seem worth it."

"A dragon?" Cole said softly.

"Yes," said the queen. "A dragon, a unicorn, a mermaid. That man could turn a peach pit into anything you can imagine."

She smiled and was transformed. For an instant, she became a beaming pink-cheeked woman—not a haughty queen. A strip of light cut through a small window and stretched across her face, from her forehead to the bridge of her nose. Her eyes, up close and splashed with sun, were red-rimmed and puffy. Her purple riding dress—velvet like her cloak—was spotted with dried mud along the hem.

"When the crops began to die," the queen continued, "the only peaches left were withered and not fit to eat. That man would peel off their sour flesh and turn them into something wonderful. I asked him why he bothered, and he told me no gift should be wasted, not even rotting peaches. He'd pass the carvings out to children who didn't have any toys or any . . . anything." Her voice hitched at the back of her throat, like lace caught on a nail.

Halston stepped toward her, but she waved him off. Cole blinked at her like a startled rabbit. Why was she telling us a story about rotting peaches? Was she as mad as everyone said? Was she losing the last of her senses, right there in my father's workshop?

"I shouldn't have come," she said, bowing her head. "I've put us all in danger . . ."

"Don't say that," said Halston. "Of course you had to come."

When she looked up, her face was streaked with tears.

"Tell him," said Halston, his tone firm and gentle at the same time.

The queen nodded like an obedient child. She sucked in a ragged breath. She reached up and pushed her hair behind her ear, causing her barrette—encrusted with jewels in the shape of her royal monogram—to clatter to the ground. And there it was—a divot in her earlobe, as if a small animal had taken a bite of her. The reason she always wore her hair down, according to Abi.

"You see, the man in the story . . . ," she said, drawing out the words as if trying to delay the end of the sentence. "The man in the story . . . is your father."

The queen's face was tense and expectant. But Cole stood there unaffected, his eyes blank.

"I've been searching for you for a long time," she said. She was paler than when she'd started, and her voice strained with the effort to keep from shaking. She reached out to Cole again, and he didn't flinch. She pushed back his unruly hair. Hiding behind that wild mane was a tiny ear with a dented earlobe. "I'm your mother."

# THE DEATH OF WREN

*To think, it all started with rebellion on a much smaller scale. Catherine was a young, headstrong princess then, defying her father at every turn. He told her to be more like the other ladies in court, those chattering twits who spent all day preening and gossiping. So how did she respond? By dressing like a peasant and sneaking to the market, of course. She didn't expect to fall in love. Not just with Jaxson, but with the others, too. The ones who toiled and struggled and didn't live in castles. She longed to be one of them.*

*Catherine was willing to give up her throne, and everything that came with it, for an ordinary life. By royal proclamation, she was betrothed to Lord Michael, a decision she'd argued against in a series of violent rows with her father, King Reginald. Her fate in Oren was sealed, so she had no choice but to flee, with no intention of returning. But Michael had other plans. He claimed that he'd married her before she left, so when King Reginald died, Michael crowned himself king. But his veins didn't carry royal blood, and he knew Catherine and her progeny could undermine his claim to the throne. Unless he made his lies the truth. When he learned that she'd run off to Palma, he laid waste to the entire kingdom for the sole purpose of bringing her back. And all for the sake of a crown he already wore.*

*Meanwhile, from her sanctuary in Palma, Catherine—now Wren—watched friends die and starve and struggle, all because of her. She convinced herself that Michael would give up eventually. But she was wrong. The guilt gnawed at her.*

*When Toby was born, Wren couldn't bear the thought of a life spent cowering. She couldn't stomach raising her son in a war zone, when she was the one person who could put an end to it. So one night, as her husband and son slept, she turned herself in to the Royal Guard. She would submit to Michael, so her family could be free. It was a deal with the devil, but what else could she do?*

*That night, her subjects became her captors, even though they addressed her as their queen. They tied her hands and loaded her into a golden carriage bound for Oren. As gutted as she was to be returning to the palace and marrying her worst enemy, she was glad she was leaving so soon. The farther she got from Palma, the safer Jaxson and Toby would be. She closed the curtains and stared straight ahead, seeing nothing. But when the wheels stopped rumbling, she knew they hadn't reached Oren yet. She expected to find herself at the gate of a prison or the edge of a deep pit. Either would've been fine with her.*

*But when she realized they'd stopped in front of her own little house in Palma, with the fields of their farm stretching out behind it, bile rose up in her throat. The officer in charge—a stalky gray-haired man named General Sorkin—came to her door and offered his arm, to help her disembark from the carriage. A laughable pretense of deference, which she refused. At the same time, two soldiers emerged from the house with Jaxson between them, bowed over and begging.*

*"Do you know this man?" General Sorkin asked her, thumping a pointy-tipped mace against his palm.*

*"I've never seen him before," said Wren. But she was no actress. The anguish was plain on her face.*

*"He's a traitor," said General Sorkin. "He kidnapped the queen."*

*"He didn't kidnap me," she said, her voice cracking. "I don't know him."*

*"Then you won't mind if we punish him for his crimes." General Sorkin strolled over to Jaxson. He calmly raised his mace and brought it down hard on Jaxson's left knee. Jaxson wailed and toppled over in pain.*

*"No!" she screamed. She could pretend no longer. "Stop this at once! On the queen's orders!"*

*"The king told us you would say that," said General Sorkin. "King trumps queen."*

*The soldiers heaved Jaxson back to standing, and Wren locked eyes with him. "I'm sorry," she whispered. "I'm so sorry." General Sorkin pulled his sword from its scabbard and lifted its deadly point to Jaxson's chest.*

*Jaxson didn't speak. He raised his eyes as a shadow passed overhead, barely visible against the black sky. Then he looked at her and managed a smile. And she realized what he'd done.*

*When he woke in the night and found Wren's note, he brought Toby next door and begged the Hillmans to fly him to safety in their balloon. Jaxson knew that Michael wouldn't stop even after he'd found Wren. Michael would keep searching and waging war until he found the man she ran off with. But there was still a chance to save Toby. After all, Michael didn't know the boy existed. Jaxson had stayed behind so their son could live.*

*The blade ran through Jaxson's chest with sickening ease. His white shirt blossomed red, and his eyes flared wide with shock before they went blank. Wren crumpled where she stood, clawing at the dirt and shouting to the heavens.*

*The soldiers hauled her limp body back to the carriage, but they left Jaxson where he lay. Wren sat beside the window again, this time with the curtain open. She had just one glimmer of hope bearing her up: that her son had survived. She watched the neighbor's balloon skim over the tallest trees.*

*The carriage inadvertently followed it as it rose higher and higher, drifting over the Wall into Oren. "He's going home," she thought. Even though they couldn't be together, she took comfort in the fact that she and her son would be in the same kingdom.*

*But that comfort was fleeting. The balloon jerked suddenly, as though pierced by something, and began to lose altitude. Wren didn't see it hit the ground, but the flames leaped as high as the Wall. She cried out, a long and desperate wail, releasing every emotion she had left in her.*

*And then she was empty. And quiet.*

*She didn't scream or resist after that. What did it matter that she was about to marry a monster? Who cared if she had to sit before a court of sycophants and endure their pleasantries? What difference did it make if every last person in her own kingdom hated her?*

*Catherine would arrive in Oren to take the throne. Wren was already dead. She perished that night, along with her husband and her son.*

*Or so she believed.*

# PLANS AND PROMISES

After the queen told us the tale of her life—about falling in love, fleeing her homeland, and losing her family—I stood stock-still in the center of the workshop. My eyes, wet with tears, swept over the vast space in disbelief. Everything was as it had been before: the rainbow of tarps, the dried grass of the baskets, the gaping black maw of the forge. But how could it possibly be the same? The queen's story—Wren's story—had upended it all.

"The *Wren* is the *queen*?" Abi squealed, dabbing at her own damp eyes. "The *queen* is the *Wren*? How could you leave out that minor detail, Hal?"

"People who lead rebellions don't go around shouting it from the rooftops," Halston reminded her. "Especially when they're part of the royal family."

"Catherine," I whispered, my gaze shifting back and forth from the queen to the beady-eyed bird in Cole's hand. "Cath-*wren*."

"Yes," said the queen. "It's a nickname my father gave me when I was small."

"Is Cole really your nephew?" Abi asked Halston.

"Yes," he said, blinking back tears. "Jaxson is . . . was . . . my brother. When the queen returned to Oren, I discovered what had happened to him. I also learned that the balloon carrying my nephew had crashed. But a child's body was never found in the wreckage. Catherine and I held out hope that he was alive, even though we didn't have any evidence. We spent years searching for him. A few weeks ago, one of my scouts found Cole, in Between. But I couldn't be sure it was really Toby—not until I brought him back to his mother."

"I haven't seen my son since that day," said the queen, without taking her eyes off the boy. Cole still squirmed under her gaze. "The day I left Palma. The day . . ." Her voice snagged, and she bit her lip.

"King Michael is a murderer," Abi growled. "He can't get away with this!"

"The king's atrocities go far beyond the murder of one man," said Halston. "He's already gotten away with far worse."

"He stole the crown," the queen said. "He told the Royal Council that we were married *before* I went to Palma, which made him next in line for the throne that was rightfully mine. But as long as I was missing, his position would never be secure. So he came for me and cast Palma as the villain in his story. He started a war for his own political gain and blamed it on the very victims who suffered at his hand."

"He's a monster!" said Abi. "Why are we waiting until Savior's Day to bring him down? Let's tell everyone the truth about him now. Nobody could possibly defend him once they find out what he's done."

"It's not that simple," said the queen. "Michael has done an excellent job convincing people that he's a hero and I'm a madwoman. I'm constantly surrounded by people who are either loyal to him or terrified of him. The moment I open my mouth to speak against him, I'll be struck down. It will not serve our cause to go shouting in the streets that King Michael is a villain. We must deliver our message strategically. On Savior's Day."

"How?" asked Abi. "What's the plan?"

The queen's eyebrows rose.

"It's okay," said Halston. "We can trust Abi. She's one of my best men." He winked at her, which caused her cheeks to bloom red.

"On Savior's Day, all of Oren will be gathered together at the Wall," said the queen. "I will have a brief opportunity to speak to the citizens of this kingdom directly, to tell them *my* truth about what Michael has done. They may not believe me. They may continue to think me mad. But I intend to speak honestly, which is all I can do."

"Well, I intend to do more than speak," said Halston. He picked up a metal pipe from the forge and brandished it like a sword as he spoke. "Once the queen says her piece, we'll send the signal to our troops, which will start the rebellion. It will mark the beginning of the end of King Michael's reign. We may not have a trained army or fancy weapons, but the men and women who have vowed to fight with us are loyal and passionate—farmers, laborers, tradesmen—many of whom knew my brother and loved him. On Savior's Day, we will make our stand. And King Michael will know that his crimes will not go unpunished."

"What's the signal?" I asked.

"As a matter of fact," said Halston, pointing with the metal bar at the tarps lined up behind him, "it's a hot-air balloon. A yellow one."

*"Goldilocks,"* I said. I gazed up at the unused envelopes stacked

on the shelves and pointed to the buttery-yellow one rolled up tight. "There she is."

"She's beautiful," said Abi.

"You should see her in the sky," I said.

"Does this mean we can borrow *Goldilocks*?" asked Halston. "We were relying on Guernsey to take care of the balloon for us, but he's . . . unavailable at the moment."

"O-of course," I said, with no actual authority to offer up one of Father's balloons. "What will happen when she flies?"

"We attack," said Halston, thrusting the metal pipe. "The only advantage we have over the Royal Guard is the element of surprise. We don't stand a chance unless we carry out a precise, coordinated attack. If everything comes together at the right moment, it'll work like . . . like . . ."

"Like a machine," I said.

"Exactly," said Halston. "All the different pieces acting as one."

"There's just one thing I don't understand," said Abi to the queen. "If you're on top of the Wall, surrounded by Orenite soldiers, how will you escape after you've made your speech?"

"I won't," said Queen Catherine flatly. "I don't plan to make it off the Wall. Not alive, anyway."

At once, our voices rang out in protest, but the queen shook her head. "The decision is mine, and it has been made. I'll hear no more about it. Once I've done my part, Halston will take over, using weapons with more immediate impact than words. I am not a headstrong princess anymore. If given the chance, I will rule Oren as is my birthright. But if I don't get the chance, I will leave the rebellion in Halston's capable hands, in hopes that one day he'll restore my son to the throne."

"But, Your Majesty," said Halston, "the cause is toothless without its leader. The cause needs the Wren. The cause needs *you.*"

The queen took a deep breath. Then she spoke with steel in her voice. "Ever since I learned my son might be alive, I've been biding my time. If I acted too hastily—if I died or was locked away before I could reveal the truth—Michael's treason would go unpunished and Toby's true identity would be lost forever. So I waited to seek my revenge against the king. I waited to restore the rightful ruler to Oren. And I waited to tell my story. But now that the prince has been found, I will wait no longer. I will speak on Savior's Day."

"Yes, Your Majesty," said Halston.

"Um, Your Majesty," I croaked, surprised to hear my own voice addressing the queen of Oren. "I—I might have an idea."

"You might?" she asked with arched eyebrows.

"I mean, I *do.* I do have an idea." I cleared my throat. "We can rescue you. My father is one of the most—no, *the* most skilled balloonist in Oren. He can pilot *Goldilocks* to Savior's Gate. He can send the signal *and* save you, at the same time."

"Prissy, your father is in prison," Halston said softly.

"Not for much longer," I said, my eyes darting over to Abi. She looked away.

Halston sighed. "That's not the only problem. We've asked your father for help more than once. He wants no part of the rebellion. He even threatened to turn us in. We can't count on him in this."

"But surely you didn't tell him everything," I said. "If he knew about the king . . . if he understood, I know he'd help."

"Prissy . . ."

"I'll convince him."

"You're being naïve . . ."

"If he won't agree, I'll do it myself!"

My words echoed off the walls of the workshop's wide-open space. Abi gasped, and everyone else was stunned into silence.

"Can you fly a hot-air balloon?" asked the queen, in a tone that betrayed her disbelief.

"Yes," I said, hurrying the answer out of my mouth before I could change my mind. "I can."

"Then I will not refuse your offer," she said. "But I am prepared to give my life on Savior's Day. Now I must go, as much as it pains me. I've already stayed too long. The king will grow suspicious." She reached out to Cole again and touched his cheek, carefully, as if he were made of smoke and her fingers might make him dissolve back into thin air. Then she pulled her hood up to conceal her face once more.

As she headed for the door, I stepped toward her, emboldened now. "Excuse me," I said. "My father . . . he's a good man, a law-abiding man. Is there any way you can help him?"

"No," she said. "I have no power within the palace walls. There's nothing I can do for him. You must give him the help he needs." Her tone was sharp-edged, as it had been when she'd arrived. She was already slipping into that other persona—the aloof, unpopular monarch. But her eyes told me she was truly sorry, and I believed them.

Then the queen of Oren swept out of the workshop in a flourish of velvet.

# HONOR AMONG THIEVES

"Queen Mama! Queen Mama!" chanted Cole. Though he'd cowered in her presence, he bounded around the workshop after she left, overjoyed at the prospect of a mother—and a queen, no less! Thankfully, he didn't seem to understand all the talk of kidnapping, murder, and war. Nor did he know that he was the rightful prince of Oren, next in line to be king.

"What will happen to Cole now?" I asked Halston. "I mean . . . Toby. His Majesty."

"Don't call him that!" snapped Halston. "As far as anyone knows, he's an orphaned boy named Cole. He's coming with me to the Thousand Spokes Inn, where he'll be met by the queen's lady-in-waiting, Greta. She's going to take Cole to the royal estate at Bellamy, where the king and queen spend the winter. Greta will claim Cole is her nephew who's been left in her care, the son of a recently deceased sister. That way, he'll remain close to the queen, without giving away his identity."

"Is Greta one of us?" asked Abi. "Can we trust her?"

"Yes. Greta has been with Queen Catherine since she was a princess. It was Greta who arranged for the queen to meet us here today. She can be trusted."

"I don't want to go!" said Cole, his buoyant mood deflating.

I crouched beside him. "You're going to a wonderful place called Bellamy, where you'll eat the most scrumptious food and sleep in a big soft bed. And your mama will be there soon. You're going to have a grand adventure!"

"Will you come, too?" he asked me.

"Not right now," I said. "But I'll visit you soon." The words rang false in my ears. I'd probably never see Cole again after today, unless he was on a platform and I in a crowd. But I'd be his subject then, not his babysitter.

"Will Abi come?"

"Sorry, kid," said Abi, tousling his hair. She removed something from a hidden pocket of her skirt and handed it to him. "But here's something to remember me by." Cole smiled and stuck the jagged piece of peanut brittle into his mouth, sucking on it like a pacifier. It seemed to soothe him as Halston led him outside and lifted him onto the horse. Then Halston mounted behind him and gathered the reins to leave.

"Wait!" cried Abi, casting a dark look at me before darting back into the workshop. She emerged with Halston's bulging satchel in her arms. She hoisted it up to him.

"Thanks," said Halston. "You girls keep a low profile until you hear from me, got it? We don't need any undue attention before Savior's Day."

"But what about Father?" I said. "We've got to get him out of jail before the trial!"

Halston sighed. "I'm truly sorry we got your father into trouble, Prissy, but we can't do anything reckless right now—certainly not a jailbreak. Not with Savior's Day right around the corner."

"But we need his help with *Goldilocks,*" I said. "With rescuing the queen from the Wall!"

"You said it yourself, Prissy—*you* can fly the balloon for us. We're counting on you, not your father."

I couldn't respond. My throat seized up, and my eyes filled with tears. To have gotten this far and still have no way to save Father . . .

"Hold on!" said Abi, grabbing the reins of Halston's horse. "I made Prismena a promise. I told her I'd help get her father out of jail if she got those candies over the Wall. And *I* never break a promise." She cut her eyes to me, and my cheeks burned. I was being shamed as a liar by Abigail Smeade, of all people. "Besides, we can't leave him in that place. Or Guernsey, either. It's too dangerous."

"What do you mean, it's 'too dangerous'?" I asked.

Halston and Abi locked eyes. "We have to tell her," said Abi.

Halston sighed. Then he nodded.

"King Michael has a huge stockpile of something called Black Powder," said Abi. "It's unstable and very dangerous."

"But Black Powder is a myth," I said. "People who have nothing else to brag about will invent something to make themselves sound impressive. The Palmerians . . ." I let my words trail off when I realized whom I'd borrowed my words from. I was parroting Ms. Stoneman.

"That's exactly what King Michael wants us to think," said Halston. "He doesn't want anyone to know Black Powder exists. Not until he can unleash it himself."

"So . . . what are you saying?"

"King Michael's got barrels of the stuff," he said. "We

don't know what he's using it for, but we know he's building something—some sort of weapon. And he's doing it on the palace grounds. In the cellar . . . beneath the prison."

A wave of nausea crashed over me. Of course King Michael was building a highly explosive, deadly weapon below the prison. What did he care if he blew a bunch of inmates sky-high? "I have to get Father out of there." I gulped, swallowing the bitter taste creeping up my throat.

"We can't be rash about this," said Halston.

"Don't tell me not to be rash," I snapped. "My father is in prison for treason, *and* he's sitting on top of a weapon powerful enough to turn the whole building into rubble. If there's an accident or . . . or if he's still in there when the rebellion begins and he's deemed a traitor, he'll never make it out. It'll be much worse than a stupid prison sentence. He'll be . . ." I faltered, unable to say it out loud. "I have to rescue him before Savior's Day."

Halston sighed again. "Very well," he said. "Just don't get caught. I'll need you on Savior's Day."

"We won't get caught," said Abi. "Who do you think you're talking to?"

I managed a weak smile at her, but she didn't smile back.

"We have to go," said Halston. "I've got to deliver Cole to his . . . aunt."

Cole looked down at us and mumbled a garbled goodbye, trying not to let the hunk of peanut brittle slip out of his mouth. Abi and I waved as they rode off. We stood there, staring after them, until the horse disappeared from view and the dirt it had kicked up settled back down. Then Abi spun around and glared at me. I had some explaining to do.

# NO REST FOR THE REBELLION

"Well?" Abi demanded, crossing her arms and tapping her foot impatiently. "What were you doing with Halston's papers?"

"I can explain," I squeaked.

"You were going to rat us out, weren't you?"

"No! Well . . . m-maybe. I don't know. I hadn't decided yet."

"I *knew* it! I can't believe I was actually starting to trust you!"

"I just needed to keep my options open."

"I *told* you I'd get your father out of jail!"

"I didn't think you really meant it," I said.

"I may be a thief, but I'm no liar," Abi shot back. "We shook on it!"

I cringed, recalling my crossed fingers. "I'm sorry, Abi."

She narrowed her eyes at me.

"Now that I know what the rebellion is fighting for, I'd never do anything to stand in the way."

"Do you swear?"

"I swear!"

"Does this mean you want to be part of the so-called cause now?"

"I guess I do," I said sheepishly.

Abi sucked in her cheeks. She rocked from foot to foot. "All right," she said finally. "I'll keep my end of the bargain and help rescue your father. Even though you don't deserve it."

"Thank you, Abi," I cried, bolting toward her with my arms outstretched.

"Don't even think about it," she said, backing away, "or you'll make me change my mind."

"Got it," I said, dropping my arms to my sides. "So . . . now what?"

"We'll stay here tonight, rest, and figure out how we're going to get your father out of jail. If the Kluwers or Ms. Stoneman or anyone else comes poking around, we'll hide. Then in the morning, we'll head back to Mulberry House and get whatever supplies and recruits we need to save your old man."

"I like the sound of rest," I said, plopping down on the front porch steps. "I'm beat."

"Me too," said Abi, sitting down beside me and stretching her skinny legs out in front of her. "I think we walked the length of the Wall today."

"And we built a catapult."

"And we met the queen!"

"I can't believe Queen Catherine was in our workshop. Father will never believe it!"

"I can't believe you agreed to rescue her in a hot-air balloon on Savior's Day. I didn't know you had it in you, Gumdrop."

"Neither did I," I said, gazing up at *Percival,* still hanging limp from the masts. "I'm still not sure I can pull it off."

"C'mon, Prissy, you know hot-air balloons like I know the cut of the queen's last Savior's Day dress—which was an empire-waist gown with a sweetheart neckline, in case you were wondering. You can do this."

"Sure, I know all about balloons when they're on the ground. I understand how they work. But it's entirely different when they're in the sky."

We both sighed and stared at the big balloon towering over us.

"I've got it!" said Abi, kicking my foot with hers. "Get up."

"But we just sat down," I groaned.

"We've got more to do. Come with me."

I reluctantly pulled myself off the porch steps. "Is rebellion always this exhausting?"

"Yes," she said. "We can sleep *after* we've defeated evil." She marched toward *Percival*. "*You* are going to fly on Savior's Day," she called over her shoulder, "so it's time you got some practice."

"*What?*" I screeched as it dawned on me what she had in mind. "We can't, Abi. Halston told us to lie low, remember?"

"He also said he was counting on you to fly the queen to safety. How are you going to do that without taking at least one solo flight first?" She climbed onto the platform and into *Percival*'s basket.

"I don't think this a good idea," I said.

"I've never let that stop me before. Besides, we'll keep the balloon tethered. We won't actually go anywhere."

I hesitated, but Abi didn't. In one quick movement, she flicked her wrist and lit a match. Then she rose onto her tiptoes and tossed it into the brazier swinging over her head.

"*Abi?* What did you just do?"

She smirked. Above her, a tiny orange flame latched onto a

clump of hay and started to grow, lapping up the old rags and other kindling Father had stuffed into the brazier two days ago in preparation for flight. Billows of smoke, thick and black, began rising into *Percival*'s belly.

"Argh," I cried, and took off at a sprint to the well. I returned lugging a sloshing bucket of water against my hip, which I awkwardly heaved into the basket. I nudged Abi aside and raised it over my head to douse the flames—drenching both of us in the process.

"Wait!" cried Abi. She'd craned her neck back, her eyes wide as saucers, as the envelope inflated above her. "Just a few more minutes."

I lowered the bucket and stared up, too, as *Percival*'s slack fabric grew taut and round. Watching a balloon take shape was breathtaking, no matter how many times you'd seen it. Before long, *Percival* stood upright, fully inflated and starting to pull away from the ground. It had been months since I'd been in a balloon, and I was suddenly overcome by the desire to take off—to feel the shifts in the air as the balloon climbed, to see the world from a great distance. And Abi did have a point: we wouldn't technically be breaking any laws. *Flying* a balloon required a permit from the Ministry, but *hovering* in one did not.

"Stay here," I told her. I hopped out of the basket again and ran to the back of my house. In the left-hand corner of the wall, I pried a stone loose and reached into the small, damp hole behind it. I removed a clunky item wrapped in linen, then replaced the missing stone and sprinted back to the balloon, where I proudly presented the object to Abi.

"What on earth is that?" she asked. The device consisted of two metal tubes bound together with leather straps, with round pieces of glass fitted to the ends of each tube.

"They're called binoculars," I said. "Mr. Dudley invented them. They allow you to see across long distances."

"Um . . . Exactly how many secret stashes do you have?" she asked, peering at me curiously.

I shrugged. "Some things are just too good to give up."

"You surprise me, Prismena Reece. So does this mean you'll take me flying?" She bounced up and down excitedly, making the basket wobble.

"Only to the ends of the ropes," I said, pulling myself into the rising balloon. I had to shove aside some crates of produce as I climbed inside, leftovers from the foiled Tulera flight. "We'll hardly skim the treetops, so hopefully nobody will notice us. I'll do some drills, and then we're coming right back down. Got it?"

"Yes, captain!" said Abi. And I had to confess, I quite liked the sound of that.

We began to ascend faster as the fire grew, and it made me feel bleary and light-headed—but in a good way. Even if we were no more than a few feet off the ground, we were up in the air. We were above it all. We were *flying.*

# FLYING

The balloon jerked softly when it reached the ends of its tethers. I lifted the binoculars to my eyes and looked toward the center of Oren. Because of Lollyhill's natural elevation, I could see the entire tapestry of the kingdom to the west—the squashed jumble of the Slope, the wide avenues of Silk Valley, the teeming mayhem of Market Square. And the imposing fortress in the center of it all: the palace. I winced, reminded of Father's imprisonment, and passed the binoculars to Abi.

*"Whoa!"* she hollered when she brought them to her eyes. "This is incredible!" She zipped around the basket, taking in every possible view. When she looked toward Between, she brightened. "Can you bring us over there, closer to those trees?"

"I guess we'll find out," I said. "Let the practice begin."

I closed my eyes for a moment, picturing what Father would do next. I knew the balloon's ropes and pulleys like the contours of my own face, but I'd never been allowed to control them before. I gathered the necessary lines in my hands. They were rough and thick and resisted my grasp. I looked up and determined which valve I had to open to push us toward Between, then pulled down on the corresponding rope with all my might.

High above us, a square of fabric flapped open, releasing a stream of air. The balloon responded by pitching steeply in the other direction. Too steeply. The sudden shift knocked Abi to the floor and sent a pile of tomatoes bouncing around the bottom of the basket.

"Prissy?" Abi said, scrambling back onto her feet. "You've got this, right?"

"I've . . . got it," I grunted, yanking another rope to close the valve I'd just opened. But once again, I moved too quickly, pulled too hard, and the valve snapped shut with a *thwack*. The balloon reversed itself and bucked in the other direction, sending Abi tumbling to the other end of the basket.

"Maybe I had too much faith in you," she groaned, rolling on the floor and cradling her stomach.

"I've got it this time. I swear." I adjusted the ropes again, more gently, until the balloon leveled itself. I slumped with relief and wiped my brow, which by then was beaded with sweat. "Shall we try that again?"

"Do we have to?" asked Abi, who'd turned a sickly shade of green.

"I know what went wrong," I said. "I was too hasty. I've got to listen to what *Percy* is telling me from now on."

"Oh, great," muttered Abi, "she's talking to the balloon now."

This time, I opened the valve gradually, and a gentle stream of air nudged *Percival* to the east. I tended the fire and checked the fastenings. When I was satisfied that everything was in order, I leaned back and let my eyes drift shut as the wind caressed my skin and we bobbed softly at the level of Between's treetops.

"Nice job," said Abi, pulling herself up off the floor. "But next time, maybe skip the part where you shake us around like a rattle."

"I'll take that into consideration," I said. "It doesn't help that we have all this junk in here." I kicked a stray tomato.

"Speaking of 'junk,'" said Abi, "this food is never going to make it to Tulera now, and it'll rot if we leave it sitting here. Why don't we toss it?"

"Abi, that's littering! The Ministry strictly forbids dumping trash from hot-air balloons."

"Don't think of it as littering," said Abi. "Consider it a delivery."

"A delivery to whom?" I said. "The squirrels?"

"You'll see," said Abi. She picked up a big green apple from the spilled inventory and, before I could stop her, flung it as far as she could toward Between. It thumped to the ground at the edge of the woods. "Now watch."

As I held the binoculars to my eyes, I remembered the commotion that had spooked me when we were in the woods earlier, and I was grateful to be fifty feet up in a hot-air balloon. Sure enough, I spotted movement below. A dark shape emerged from behind a tree and headed slowly toward the fruit. The creature was about three feet tall, slightly stooped but walking on two legs. From my vantage point, I couldn't tell if it was covered in leathery skin or tufts of matted fur, but I could tell that it was dirty. It prodded the apple with its foot. Then it picked it up.

With hands.

"What is that thing?" I asked.

"It's a child," said Abi.

"A . . . *human* child?"

"Yes," said Abi, rolling her eyes. The child-beast looked up at our balloon. It smiled and waved, then took a big bite of the apple. "Now help," said Abi. She scooped up an assortment of fruits and vegetables from the bottom of the basket and shoved it into my arms. Together, we chucked Father's abandoned inventory out of the balloon, as more and more children crept out of the woods and pounced on what we dropped from the sky.

"They're filthy," I said. "What are they doing down there?"

"They live there."

"In Between? But why?"

"Because the other option is Kluwer House," said Abi. "And you've seen what that's like. Plus, anyone who stays at one of those homes too long gets sold to the Royal Guard."

"Really?" I said. "I thought Roz was messing with me about that."

"Nope," said Abi. "That's how King Michael keeps the 'unwanteds' off the streets of Oren. Kids who don't get claimed by an adult are either sent back over the Wall or taken to the palace to build the king's weapon."

"You mean King Michael's got *kids* working with Black Powder?"

"Yep," said Abi. "Kids nobody will ever miss."

"That's awful," I said. Below us, the children marveled at our balloon. The bigger ones waved; the smaller ones jumped up as if they might be able to reach us. "But you said King Michael sends kids *back* over the Wall. What do you mean, 'back'?"

"These kids are Palmerian," Abi said flatly.

I gasped. "I don't believe it. Are you sure?"

Abi nodded. I gaped down at the woods.

"I've never actually seen a Palmerian up close before," I said softly.

"How do you know?" said Abi. "Do you really think you could tell the difference?"

"I—I guess not. It's hard to see what they look like under all that dirt."

"Out here, they look as savage as King Michael says they are."

"How'd they wind up in Between?"

Abi tossed another apple with all her might, then explained: "There are two ways for Palmerian kids to get into Oren. Nettles stow away in wagons coming through the gates, and Vines climb over the Wall."

"So that's what those words mean," I said, recalling the confusing conversation between Roz and her friend at Kluwer House. "But are you seriously telling me that kids climb over the Wall?"

"Would I lie to you, Gumdrop?"

"Yes," I said. "Absolutely."

"Well, this is the honest truth. Palmerian parents send their kids over the Wall so they can have a better life."

"A better life," I repeated, watching dirt-caked kids snatch spoiling fruit off the ground. "Is this really where Cole lived before Halston found him?"

"Yep. He was a wildling, just like them."

"Poor kid."

"Not for long," said Abi, taking the binoculars from me. She pointed them to the north, toward the royal estate of Bellamy. "Pretty soon he'll be the richest kid in the kingdom. And speaking of Cole . . ."

"Yeah?"

"I think we have a little problem."

"What's that?" I asked.

Abi thrust the binoculars back at me. I looked north and spotted a shimmering gold vehicle in the distance, leaving the Thousand Spokes Inn. It was moving swiftly along an empty country road. "Is that the royal carriage?" I asked.

"Yes," she said. "Unless you know someone else who owns one made of solid gold."

"So what's the problem?"

"It's going in the wrong direction, you dolt. It's not heading to Bellamy. It's taking Cole straight to the palace!"

# THE CAPTAIN TAKES CHARGE

"What do we do?" I cried. With every passing second, Cole was moving closer to the palace. He was probably bouncing happily on the cushioned seats and admiring the carriage's sparkly interior, with no idea that he was galloping right into the arms of the one person who most wanted to hurt him. Meanwhile, Halston and the queen were both blissfully unaware of what was about to befall the newfound prince. Only Abi and I knew what was happening, and we were hovering high above it in a hot-air balloon.

The basket pitched, and from the corner of my eye, I saw something falling. At first, I thought Abi had dropped another piece of cargo, but then I realized with stomach-clenching clarity what it was—one of *Percival*'s tethers snaking madly to the ground.

"Abi," I yelled, turning on her as violently as I could manage without rocking the basket. "What are you doing? Are you trying to get us arrested? Or killed?"

"Of course not," she said. "But Cole—"

"No," I cried, panic and fear and anger filling me up until I felt like I might burst. "No! You don't get to come aboard *my* balloon and release the tethers without permission. You're not in charge here, Abi! This is *my* vessel! *I* am the captain!"

"Then start acting like it!" she snapped. We stood still and stared at each other as the balloon bobbed at an awkward tilt. Without our voices, all the other sounds around us seemed to become unnaturally loud: the whistle of the wind, the creaking of the basket, the blood thrumming in my ears.

Then I calmly moved to the side of the basket, bent over its ledge, and screamed into the sky.

*"Arrrrgh!"* My voice carried over the fields of Lollyhill. Over all of Oren in the distance. I screamed until my cheeks were red and my throat was raw. And when I'd finished screaming, I straightened up, smoothed my dress, and cleared my throat. "All right," I said. "Let's save Cole."

Abi nodded. On my order, she released the remaining tethers.

Father always said a balloonist doesn't use his hands or his eyes—a balloonist flies with his whole body. I never knew what he meant until that day. I loosed a rope, bit by bit. Only this time, I did it with my eyes closed. I paid attention to the pattern of the fibers sliding against my palms and the way the balloon reacted to every inch I gave. I noticed the air as it swirled around me, changing direction and speed. I listened to the pitch of the wind, the way it slapped the fabric. I noted each bulge and billow of the envelope. The balloon was a machine, but flying it was a dance. You had to feel it. And suddenly I felt it.

"You're doing it!" shrieked Abi, and my eyes fluttered open. Her cheeks were pink with wind and glee. We'd traveled several miles north and were moving steadily, heading toward a patch of open field about a mile ahead of the speeding carriage. We were going to catch it.

"Don't get too excited," I said. "That was the easy part. I still have to bring this thing down."

"You can do that, right?"

"One way or another," I mumbled.

Despite my warning, Abi did get too excited. She jumped up and down, making her bright-red skirt flutter. And making the basket wobble. I stumbled and lost my grip. The rope I'd been holding whipped through my hands so quickly the friction burned my palms. The attached valve flung open. The air rushed out. We began to drop.

Fast.

The wind battered us, lashing my hair so violently I thought it would be torn out by the roots. Tears stung my eyes and blotted out my vision. I thrust my hands in front of me, blindly groping for the loose rope. When my hands closed on it at last, I pulled the valve shut again, slowing our descent. But it was too late to change course.

"Duck!" I cried. Abi and I dove to the bottom of the basket and curled up like snails. But nothing could've prepared us for impact. When we hit the ground, my bones jammed into one another. My head bobbed around like my neck was on a spring. The basket tipped, rolling us out like a pair of dice. Sky, grass, trees, and *Percival*'s navy-blue bubble whirled together into one chaotic blur. When the spinning finally stopped, Abi and I came to rest in the grass, splayed out like starfish—bruised and beaten, but still breathing.

"Abi," I groaned, "are you okay?"

"Uhhh."

"Me too."

*Percival* had taken a licking, as well, but he quickly buoyed himself back up and began to rise again, apparently content to drop us off and be on his way. Even though my head was woozy and my body had been pummeled, I leaped to my feet.

*"Percy,"* I cried, scrabbling for his ropes.

"Let him go!" called Abi.

Regal, reliable *Percival.* Mother had named him, had loved him. I couldn't let him drift into oblivion. I kept running after him, even as his ropes slipped farther out of my reach.

"You'll never catch him," Abi implored me. "And even if you do, you can't hold him down. You'll fall and break your neck!"

With a resigned groan, I stopped chasing the balloon. I doubled over in the field to catch my breath. I felt like I'd been run up and down on a washboard and hung out to dry. But Abi had already taken off, sprinting toward Cole. So I gathered what little energy I had left and followed. Mending myself and mourning *Percival* would both have to wait.

# THE COST OF LOYALTY

"What's our plan?" I shouted to Abi as we ran.

"I have no idea!" she called over her shoulder.

The carriage came toward us at a steady clip, and we waved it down by jumping up and down in the middle of the road and ranting like a couple of maniacs. We must've been a sight—scraped and shaken, grimy with grass and dirt. The driver pulled back on the reins, and the horse reared, stopping just short of trampling us. Beside the driver, a burly soldier growled, "What's this nonsense about? Did you fall off that balloon?"

"Balloon?" said Abi. "What balloon?"

"The giant blue one right there," he said, pointing at the sky behind us.

"No," said Abi without turning around.

"Never mind. Whaddaya want?"

"We need your help," she said. "We were passing through the woods back there, taking a shortcut, when we saw a woman ride by on a wild horse. The animal must've gotten spooked, because it had a crazy look in its eye. And the lady riding him was terrified."

"Sorry, kid," said the driver. "We don't have time to rescue a damsel in distress. We're on royal business. We've got to get the queen's maid and her nephew to the palace, on the queen's orders. Now get outta the road."

"But it *was* the queen!" cried Abi. "She was the woman on the runaway horse!"

"The queen?" chuckled the soldier. "Alone in the eastern woods? That's preposterous."

"It's true," insisted Abi. "She saw it, too." She nudged me.

"I—I did," I stammered. "I saw it."

"Her Royal Highness is banged-up pretty bad," Abi said. "I think she might have a broken leg. She sent us to get help."

The driver made a move to climb down from his perch, but the soldier stopped him. "Why should we believe a couple of gutter rats like these?"

"Didn't the queen go riding today?" asked Abi.

The two men locked eyes but didn't answer.

"Besides, we've got proof," she blurted out. I shot her a confused look, but she stared straight ahead. I hoped she knew what she was doing.

"Let's have it, then," said the soldier.

"The queen knew nobody would believe us, so she gave us this." Abi removed a small glittering object from the pocket of her skirt.

"The queen's barrette!" gasped the driver. He jumped from his seat and leaned over the item in Abi's hand. "It's the real thing. That's the queen's monogram!"

"Of course it is," said Abi, snatching the barrette away from him and tucking it back into her pocket. "You'd better get to her soon, or King Michael will hear about your delay and blame you for anything that happens to her in the woods."

"What's going on?" called a soft voice from inside the carriage. A petite woman with a crown of braids woven into her blond hair poked her head out the window. She wore the black-and-white uniform of a household servant, but the epaulets on her shoulders indicated that she held a senior position among the staff.

"Miss Greta, the queen is in danger," said the driver. "We must go to her with haste. We'll return as soon as we can for you and your nephew."

*"What?"* said Greta, fear and mettle mingling in her voice. "You can't honestly intend to leave us here unguarded."

"I'm sorry, ma'am," said the soldier. "Stay put, and we'll be back in an instant." The two men dashed into the woods, in the direction of Abi's pointing finger.

"I can't believe they left me," said Greta, pouting like an unhappy child. "Vile servants!"

"Aren't you a servant?" asked Abi.

"I'm the queen's lady-in-waiting," said Greta, stepping out of the carriage. "Not that the likes of you would understand the difference." She didn't hide her disdain as her eyes roamed our filthy clothes and hair. "Who are you?"

"Friends of the queen," said Abi. "Which is apparently more than we can say for you."

"Let me see Cole," I demanded, rushing to the carriage door.

Greta stepped into my path. In her hand, she held a knife—small but sharp, and aimed squarely at my chest.

"What are you doing?" I cried.

"I'm doing my duty as a citizen of Oren," she said, "by stopping a traitor and handing over a false prince."

"The only traitor here is you," sneered Abi. "And that man who calls himself king."

"King Michael is the true king!" said Greta. "An honorable king who doesn't go running off to foreign lands with dirty commoners. A man who is loyal to those who are loyal to him."

"Oh, that explains it," said Abi. "Have you been trading information about the queen in exchange for rewards from the king? I bet handing over this little boy will earn you a title."

"Don't you dare judge me, you urchin."

"You'll be sentencing that child to his death," I cried. "How will you live with that?"

"Such is the cost of loyalty," said Greta. "Now get out of here, you disgusting cockroaches." She spat in the dirt at my feet and held her knife aloft, ready to strike.

A muffled whimper came from the carriage, and I peered around the glowering maid. There was Cole, his hands bound and a crude gag stuffed into his mouth. Without a second's hesitation, I ran toward him.

Greta lunged at me, her blade glinting in the setting sun.

# BLOOD IN A GILDED CARRIAGE

Greta knocked me flat on my back, then fell on top of me. I tried to shove her off, but she clung to me, jabbing with her knife—thankfully, without hitting her mark. I'd like to think I could've easily whupped her if the last few days hadn't left me sore and depleted. But the truth was, Greta was feistier than she looked. For a mousy housemaid, she wasn't easily shrugged off.

A blur of red streaked toward us at full tilt. Abi, her skirt fanning out behind her, threw her weight at Greta, pushing her off me and knocking the knife out of her hands. They both landed on the ground and began rolling around and around, each one taking a brief turn on top.

"Go!" cried Abi, struggling to restrain Greta. "Get Cole!"

When I pulled myself off the ground, a stinging pain shot up my left arm, and I realized Greta hadn't missed her mark after all. Blood soaked the left sleeve of my dress, which now hung in tatters. At the sight of those blooming red stains, my legs went as limp as pasta noodles and my head lolled back on my neck. I stumbled toward the carriage and collapsed against it, pressing my forehead to its cool exterior. I took long, deep breaths, willing myself not to faint. Then I glimpsed Cole's pleading eyes through the open door and, with gritted teeth, forced myself upright and took wobbly steps toward him.

I removed the gag from Cole's mouth and untied the twine from his wrists. He sucked in a big gulp of air and instantly began to wail, spewing out all the pent-up fear and pain he'd been holding in. "Prissy," he moaned. I clasped him in a brief hug, all the while smearing the lavish interior of the carriage with blood. Then I lifted him out of there with my good arm.

Outside, Abi was still struggling with Greta. Abi was bigger and stronger, but Greta was ruthless, baring her teeth and sinking them into Abi's shoulder, making Abi squeal in pain.

And making her mad in the process. With a grunt, Abi finally overpowered Greta, pinning her to the ground. I handed Abi the twine I'd removed from Cole's wrists, and Abi tied Greta's arms in complicated knots. When the queen's lady-in-waiting could no longer budge, the three of us considered our thrashing, cursing captive.

"Not such a high-and-mighty lady's maid now, are ya?" gloated Abi, panting. "Now, what to do with you . . ."

"If I might make a suggestion," I said. "Regarding the knot. A pulkker would be more secure with this type of twine."

"Let me handle this," said Abi. "Being a gutter rat has taught me a thing or two. Now, we can't leave her here because those men will be back any minute. And if Greta returns to the palace, she'll tell the king everything. She's seen Cole—and us. She knows too much."

"So what do we do with her?" I asked, glaring at the snarling woman and pressing on my wounded arm to stanch the bleeding.

"We have to get rid of her," said Abi darkly.

*"What?"* I gasped. "I know I've crossed a few lines lately, but I can't—" I lowered my voice so Cole wouldn't hear me. "I can't murder someone!"

"I don't mean kill her!" cried Abi. "Lordy, Prissy, do you really think I'm that bad? We're going to hide her deep in the woods until we can figure out what to do with her."

"Oh," I said. "I knew that." A jolt of pain shot up my left arm, and I winced.

"We've got to take care of that wound," said Abi. "You're no good to anyone without two working arms."

"You'll never get away with this!" shouted Greta. "King Michael's men will squish you like the bugs you are!"

"Shut up!" yelled Abi. "The queen is going to punish you for what you did. If the wolves don't get to you first." Abi retrieved Greta's knife from the ground and roughly pulled her to her feet. She pressed the blade—still slick with my blood—into the small of Greta's back and nudged her toward the woods.

"It doesn't matter," Greta spat. "It's too late. The king already knows everything. It's only a matter of time before he finds that little boy and . . ."

As Greta spouted a string of threats, I doubled back to the carriage and found the wad of fabric she'd used to quiet Cole. I stuffed it deep into her mouth to sop up her venom, narrowly avoiding her gnashing teeth.

# DASHING THE SMILE FROM HER LIPS

*Catherine's son was alive.*

*She'd touched his dirt-smeared skin and tousled his tangled hair. If she hadn't, she would've sworn he was a ghost, a vision she'd conjured up after years of wishing him into existence. But he was real. He was alive. And she couldn't dash the smile from her lips.*

*Not even when Michael stormed into the stables while she was brushing her horse's heaving flank. She'd galloped home as fast as she could go, but it hadn't been fast enough. "Where have you been?" demanded the king.*

*"Riding," said Catherine without looking up.*

*"Your guards said they lost you at Lollyhill," he said with ire in his voice.*

*"It seems your men can't keep up with me," she replied.*

*"Look at me when I'm speaking to you," he roared, swatting the brush out of her hand. The horse flinched and shuffled away. "You are to stay with your guards at all times. I'll not have the queen of Oren riding into the woods like a commoner. It's for your own protection."*

*"Ah, it's my well-being you're worried about, is it?" She held his gaze.*

*"Careful, woman. You're bordering on impudence." He stepped closer, the swell of his chest almost bumping hers. "I'll not have it."*

*"Forgive me, my lord. I wouldn't dream of offending my esteemed husband and king." She said the right words, but infused them with grit and defiance and a touch of laughter at his expense. They hit their target, and the king's face screwed up tight and bloomed bright red. He reared back and raised his arm to strike her. One blow from him and she'd be upended, no matter how hard she dug her heels into the stable's dust. "You'll bruise me," she warned, without a trace of fear.*

*He didn't complete the swing. Savior's Day was approaching, and he needed her beside him, unblemished. The posters promised as much.*

*"You're right," he said, "I'd be devastated if anything were to befall the queen of Oren before the big day. I wouldn't want any accidents marring that stunning royal cheek. I think the safest course is to keep you confined to your quarters for the next week."*

*"You can't be serious," said Catherine. "The incompetence of your guards is not* my *fault."*

*"It's settled."*

*"You can't put the queen on house arrest. It's unheard of!" Catherine's protests had little to do with boredom or the need for fresh air. If she couldn't leave her rooms, she wouldn't be able to visit her son at Bellamy. She'd be cut off from the rebellion. What's more, these might well be her last days in the palace, her last chance to uncover proof of Michael's guilt.*

*"Don't fret," said the king, smiling like he knew he'd won, "you'll reemerge on Savior's Day. And what a grand day it will be. I've got quite a surprise in store for our prosperous kingdom—one you'll particularly enjoy."*

*"What are you talking about?" asked Catherine. "What surprise?"*

*"Oh, I don't want to spoil it for you, my dear. You'll find out on Savior's Day, just like everyone else. Indeed, it will bring me great pleasure to see the look on your face when I share this news." His eyes glittered like he was already imagining it. Which, of course, meant it was something unspeakable.*

*Catherine didn't know what she was up against, but she knew she had to do everything in her power to prove to Oren that Michael was a false king—before he revealed his "surprise" on Savior's Day.*

*But first, she'd have to escape from her own locked room.*

# EVERYTHING YOU NEED IS IN THE POT

The cold liquid ran down my arm and trickled into the long gash there. "Ouch," I screamed, jerking away from Abi. If she had stuck a lit match into my open wound, it probably would've burned less. "What is that stuff?"

"It's alcohol," Abi said. "It keeps wounds clean, believe it or not."

"Where'd you get it?"

"From the pot, obviously. Everything you could possibly need is in the pot. Medicine, toys, satin gloves with pudding stains on the elbows." At that, she reached over and snatched a pair of pudding-stained gloves and stuffed them into her pocket.

We were sitting cross-legged in one of the bedrooms of Mulberry House, where Abi was tending to my injury and a group of little girls was taking turns braiding Cole's floppy hair. "Now hold still!" ordered Abi.

"No," I snapped. "Quit it!"

"Fine," she said. "But if your arm gets infected, it'll turn green with pus. Your fingers will get black and stiff, like burnt matchsticks, until you can't use them anymore. Then the infection will travel up to your armpit, and you'll have to cut the whole thing clean off."

"That's not true."

"Maybe not," she said. "If you want to take that risk, suit yourself." She stoppered the bottle of alcohol and stood to leave.

"Wait!" I said. "Don't go."

"I knew you'd come to your senses." She plopped back down beside me and set about soaking a rag in the vile liquid. "You'll thank me when you're a famous balloonist one day. You'll need two good hands to pull all those ropes."

"Until Father finds out I lost *Percy,*" I said. "Then he'll never let me set foot in a basket again."

"Oh, he'll come around," said Abi. "Especially when he finds out *Percival* was sacrificed to carry out a daring rescue."

"Father isn't exactly keen on his daughter getting involved in daring rescues," I said. "But while we're on the subject . . ." Abi chose that moment to press the alcohol-soaked rag onto my arm, and I squealed. "What's the plan to get him out of jail?" I asked through clenched teeth.

"Great question," said Abi. "First, we need a way to get inside the palace, which means getting past the guards at the gate. Then we have to break into the prison building, past yet another guard. Then we have to steal the warden's key and open your father's cell. Finally, if we can do all that without getting caught, we have to sneak back out of the palace with an escaped prisoner in tow."

"Are you kidding me? That's impossible!"

"Not impossible," said Abi. "Just highly improbable. Pulling off an operation like this would normally require months of planning and a whole team of accomplices."

"We don't have months," I reminded her. "Savior's Day is next week."

"I know," said Abi, drying my arm with a fresh towel. The bleeding had stopped and the bright-red gash was deepening to maroon. "But we have Marybeth."

"The chambermaid? How can she help us?"

"She's our man on the inside," said Abi. "She can give us the lay of the land, show us where the palace is vulnerable. Now hold still. It's time to patch you up." She held up a long shiny needle trailing a length of thin wire.

"What's that for?" I asked.

"You need stitches," said Abi. "Obviously."

"No way!"

"Stop being a baby. I've done this loads of times. The kids in here are always busting themselves open."

"My arm is actually feeling better already," I said, crawling backward like a crab to get away from her. "It's practically healed."

"Prismena, get over here!" Abi cried as I shimmied into the middle of the pot.

"Abigail Smeade, you filthy liar!" called a little boy. His angry voice rang through the halls of Mulberry House, accompanied by the tromping of several pairs of small feet. A ragtag bunch of kids with frowns on their faces burst into the room, and I silently thanked them for distracting Abi from the needle in her hand.

"What are you doing here?" she asked them. "Why'd you leave your post?"

"We went to the spot, just like you told us," said the eldest boy, "and nobody was there."

"You promised we'd get a captive!" said one of the other boys.

"You said we could tickle her with feathers," moaned the youngest, with a limp feather dangling from his tiny hand.

"What do you mean she wasn't there? You ding-dongs must've gone to the wrong place. We left her there, tied up good!"

"With this?" said the oldest boy. He dropped a long piece of twine at Abi's feet. The very one she'd used to bind Greta to a tree. I *knew* we should've used a pulkker knot.

"Oh," mumbled Abi, the color draining from her face. "I—I'll make it up to you boys, all right? I'll steal some extra chocolate on Market Day." The boys conferred and agreed that extra chocolate would make up for the missing prisoner. They stomped out of the room.

Abi and I stared at the twine on the floor with fear in our eyes, as if it were a snake that might spring to life and bite us.

Greta had escaped, and soon King Michael would know for certain that the queen's son had been found. He'd know that an orphan boy named Cole with long dark hair and a crimp in his ear could unravel his claim to the throne. He'd even know the rebels had met at Father's workshop in Lollyhill. All of us were in more danger than ever before. Including Father.

"What do you think you're doing?" screeched Roz, next in line to stomp into the room with her hands on her hips. I was still nestled in the pot. "You're bleedin' all over everything!"

"Sorry," I said. I tried to pick myself up, but the effort sent hot waves of pain through my arm. I fell back again, this time landing on the hard brass buttons of a coat. I winced.

"If you think tossin' *yourself* in the pot counts as a contribution, you're wrong," said Roz. "Did you bring somethin' with you this time?"

"Um . . ." In all the excitement of lost princes and crashing balloons, I'd completely forgotten about my contribution. I looked over to Abi, who shrugged.

"Not yet," she told Roz. "But she'll have something soon. I promise."

"I've heard that before," huffed Roz, stomping out of the room. As soon as she was gone, Abi instinctively reached for her pocket, feeling for the outline of the queen's barrette.

When she caught me noticing, she snapped, "What?"

"I guess not *everything* you need is in the pot," I said, with one raised eyebrow.

"Hush up and keep still," she said, brandishing her needle yet again.

"Wait a minute," I said, leaping to my feet. "That's it!"

"What's it?"

"We can hide stuff in our clothes!"

"Huh?"

I fished for the coat I'd recently sat on and held it up for Abi to see. It was the uniform of a royal guardsman. And along with it, as small and bright as those brass buttons, came the first spark of an idea.

# A FEW BRUISES FOR THE CAUSE

Forty-eight hours after the spark was lit, my idea had grown into a full-blown plan to break Father out of jail. As dusk settled on Oren, Abi and I sat side by side in a darkened doorway outside the palace, waiting.

"Do you think it'll work?" I asked, for the tenth or perhaps the twentieth time. My hand crept to the wound on my arm, but Abi smacked it down. She'd agreed not to give me stitches, but she wouldn't tolerate scratching.

"It'll work," she said.

"It *has* to work," I said, as if I could make it true just by saying so.

"Of course it'll work," said Abi. "Probably."

"Probably?"

"Look at the bright side—if it doesn't work, at least you already know someone else in prison."

"Ugh."

A cart rumbled toward us and rolled to a stop beside our doorway. The driver squinted down at us. She wore a housemaid's uniform and had a familiar overbite. She smiled and hopped out of her seat. "Are you ready?" asked Marybeth.

"Do you think it'll work?" I asked her, hoping for a more reassuring second opinion.

"Beats me," she said. She untied her lacy white bonnet and tossed it at me. "We've got to hurry. Quincy is guarding the servants' gate right now. He's as blind as a bat and as dumb as a rug. Jensen has the next shift, and once he takes over, you're toast. You'll never make it past him." She pulled off her apron and then, without so much as blushing, unbuttoned the length of her dress, stepped out of it, and kicked it toward me. "Make sure to pull the cap down low, to hide your face. Never look anyone in the eye. And always mumble 'Yes, ma'am' and 'Yes, sir.' The trick is to be as invisible as possible."

I nodded, scrambling into Marybeth's clothes.

"Take the cart straight to the kitchen. Do you remember where it is?"

I nodded again. Abi had drawn a map of the palace grounds on the wall of Mulberry House, using a piece of charcoal. I'd studied it until I could reproduce it from memory.

"If anyone asks, you went to the market to get provisions for the servants. They'd never send a housemaid to buy food for the royal family. The chef takes care of that himself. Got it?" I peered at the contents of the cart: bruised fruit, overripe vegetables, and graying strips of meat. Definitely *not* fit for a king.

"Got it."

"And don't forget to find—"

"The skull-shaped key," I said. I could've recited the plan in my sleep. But carrying it out would be another story.

Meanwhile, Abi flitted around me with her needle and thread. Marybeth's clothes were at least two sizes too big for me, so she made some necessary nips and tucks. Then she added a few embellishments, specifically for the mission.

"What are you going to wear?" I asked Marybeth, who was clad only in the petticoats she wore under her uniform.

She took one look at my discarded brown dress, stained and pungent after several days of wear, and wrinkled her nose. "I'll manage. Now . . ." She held out the lash she'd recently used on her horse. "Go on."

"What am I supposed to do with that?"

"Hit me," said Marybeth. "And hurry." She shoved the whip into my hand and turned to the side, offering up her exposed arm. "Just a couple whacks should do."

"You want me to *hit* you? I—I couldn't possibly . . ."

"You have to," said Marybeth. "I can't give you my uniform without a good alibi, or King Michael will put me in the stocks. Go on now. A few blows right here, on the fleshy part of my arm."

I gripped the lash, and Marybeth squeezed her eyes shut. I lifted it over my head. I'm not sure which of us was more nervous. "Why are you doing this?" I asked, with the whip frozen in midair. "You've only met me once. Why are you helping me?"

"For the cause," said Marybeth, cracking her eyes open. "What are a few bruises for the cause?"

"Oh," I said.

"Besides, Abi told me you're the balloonist's daughter. Is it true?"

"Yes. So?"

"Enough blabbering," barked Abi, bursting in between Marybeth and me. "If you want something done right, you have to do it yourself." She swung her fist and slugged Marybeth—hard—on

her exposed arm. Marybeth yelped. Abi recoiled and punched her again in the same spot.

"All right, enough!" whimpered Marybeth, her jaw clenched with pain.

"Give us an hour before you go back to the palace," said Abi. "And tell them you were robbed by bandits with their faces covered up. They attacked you and stole your cart."

"I know the drill," said Marybeth, gently touching her injuries.

"And just for good measure . . ." Abi slapped Marybeth across the face with an open palm. "Bruises on the face will get the most sympathy. Good luck."

I leaned down to the housemaid hunched over in the street and whispered, "Thank you."

Marybeth moaned in reply and hobbled over to sit in the doorway we'd abandoned.

"She'll be fine," said Abi. "Trust me, it's better coming from us than one of the king's goons. Now . . . are you ready?"

"I think I'm going to puke."

"Are you sure you can do this, Gumdrop? I'll go in if you think you're gonna crack."

"I can do this," I told Abi. And myself. "I've got to. Father would let the building collapse around him before he'd let someone else break him out of jail. I'm the only one who can convince him to leave."

"All right," she said. She adjusted my cap and the folds of my dress. "Whatever you do, don't breathe a word about the rebellion. No matter what. Even if they catch you. And torture you. And threaten everyone you know and love. Got it?"

"Did anyone ever tell you you're not very good at pep talks?"

She flashed a smile that showed off all those crooked teeth. "You'll be great. I'll be waiting for you right outside the gate. Good luck!"

My mind and my body felt numb as I drove Marybeth's cart to the servants' entrance. It was less grand and golden than the front entrance but still intimidating. It was guarded by a single soldier, who I prayed was blind-as-a-bat, dumb-as-a-rug Quincy. "Welcome back, Miss Marybeth!" he said. "How's the haul today?"

"Good, sir," I muttered, breathing a sigh of relief. I kept my eyes down, as instructed.

"Excellent! I can't wait to see what the chef makes of it. We'd better get it into the icebox before it gets spoiled. Unless it already is, eh?" He chuckled amiably as he unclasped a key from his belt and unlocked the gate. With a grunt, he swung it open to allow me through. As soon as the horse clip-clopped over the threshold, a rush of relief flooded my body. Maybe—just maybe—I could pull this off.

"Hey, wait!" yelled Quincy. "Stop right there!"

My newfound confidence fled as quickly as it had appeared. I tensed and prepared to be yanked out of the cart by the scruff of my stolen uniform and tossed in a prison cell. If I thought the rats at Kluwer House were bad, I could only imagine what they were like in the royal jail. Probably the size of dogs. With the boldness of cats.

"Sir?" I mumbled, pulling the reins. "Is something wrong?"

"Yes," he said, marching to my cart. "You dropped this."

Quincy placed a small, smooth object into my palm. Cole

had loaned me his peach pit, on the strict condition that I bring it back to him unharmed. He'd assured me, as he reluctantly parted with it, that it was good luck. And so far, it seemed to be working. Quincy tipped his cap and, with a wave of his arm, welcomed me into the palace.

There was no turning back now.

# THE BEST-LAID PLANS

The royal chef rushed around like a frantic chicken, with none of Gruber's brawny elegance. He whipped eggs for a custard and dropped balls of dough into hot oil, all while barking instructions at me. He warned me not to spill the prisoners' gruel, or it'd come out of my allotment, like last time. He warned me not to give anyone seconds, no matter how much they begged. And he warned me, above all, not to dawdle. After each warning, I nodded, not that the cook spared me a glance. It was no wonder he failed to notice that the maid who normally delivered the meals had transformed into an entirely different person.

The dish served to prisoners consisted of all the palace scraps, mashed together into a lumpy gray gruel. It wobbled on the plates as I unsteadily walked the stone path from the kitchen to the prison yard. It didn't help that my skirt was loaded with secret compartments and pockets, brimming with the items I'd need to get Father and me out of there alive.

The palace was impressive from the outside, but it was even more breathtaking within the gates, especially in the smoky pink light of the setting sun. Soaring buildings in honey-colored stone surrounded gurgling fountains, charming statues, and magical gardens laden with roses and butterflies. But one building blighted the landscape—a windowless structure whose stones were green with mold and whose timbers were black from rot. The prison itself served as an ugly reminder of what was inside.

I set the tray on a stone bench and removed a small bag of pecans from one of the hidden pockets in my voluminous dress. Pecans were a delicacy these days, grown only in Palma, but Marybeth had managed to snag a few from the royal pantry. Apparently, the warden had a particular weakness for them. I set them on my tray and approached the prison.

The door was defended by a stock-still soldier. When I arrived with my plates of gruel, he gagged but didn't question me. Like the others, he barely noticed me—another housemaid. He unlocked the heavy wooden door and let me pass. The door slammed shut behind me, and the lock clicked into place. I had no choice but to keep moving forward.

The prison and its occupants were the responsibility of the warden, a heavyset man with a mustache as thick as a ferret resting on his upper lip. As Marybeth had described, he was sitting on a chair in the prison's entryway, his head tipping forward as he dozed off. The bang of the door startled him, and he grunted at me, annoyed that I'd disturbed his nap. I kept my eyes pinned to the floor, which was strewn with sawdust to soak up liquids I didn't even want to think about. I lifted my gaze briefly, long enough to seek out the precise location of the keys that would set my father free. They were hanging right there, an arm's length away, on a large iron hook. All I had to do now was steal them.

I'd practiced the next part over and over with Abi: Offer the warden the pecans. Create a distraction by dropping the bag and spilling them all over the floor. When the warden bent down to help me retrieve them, lift his key ring from its hook and replace it with the replica in my pocket, strung with random bits and bobs from the pot. Then pray that the warden didn't notice that his key ring no longer contained any keys.

But none of our practice had taken into account my sweaty palms, shaking fingers, or gurgling belly, which threatened to derail the whole plot.

"Um, sir?" I said meekly, careful to keep my face concealed beneath my lacy bonnet. "The chef has sent a gift of pecans. He found them at the market and recalled your special fondness for them, sir."

"Eh?" he grunted again, only this time it was a grunt of piqued interest.

The pecans rested at the edge of my tray, ready to fall with the slightest twitch. I stepped up to the warden, took a deep breath, and . . .

The door behind me swung open.

"We got another one, boss!" said the man pushing into the room. I spun around to see who had entered, and as planned, all the nuts went scattering onto the floor. But instead of helping me gather them, the warden rolled his eyes. The soldier who had entered, leading a bound prisoner, stared at me like I was crazy. "Something wrong with that one?"

The warden shrugged. "All these housemaids are missing a screw or two," he said. He kicked at one of the dropped pecans. "Well? Pick them up, girl!"

I set down my tray and chased after the nuts, which had rolled off in all directions. Meanwhile, the warden rose from his seat with a groan, like a man who hadn't stood up in quite some time. He removed the key ring from its hook.

And just like that, my plan was ruined.

I bit back my tears, grateful nobody could see my face—not that they would've noticed anyway. How was I going to rescue Father now? And how would I escape from here myself?

"Another one accused of treason," said the soldier. "Found loads of contraband in his house. Some wacky stretchy stuff . . . Whaddayacallit . . . rubber?" I swallowed the gasp that rose up in my throat. It was Mr. Dudley! From where I was crouched, I could see only his bound hands, gnarled and oil-stained.

"I—I won't do it again," Mr. Dudley pleaded. "I promise, I'll destroy it all. Just don't leave me here!"

"Too late for that," said the soldier.

I rose and came face to face with my friend, now drawn and defeated. My heart ached for him, even as my eyes begged to him not to acknowledge me. He must have understood, because he stared blankly past me. Or perhaps he was too disoriented to recognize me.

"I'll take it from here," grumbled the warden.

"Righto," said the soldier. He turned and pounded on the door for the guard outside to release him.

The warden, still clutching the keys, nudged Mr. Dudley ahead of him toward the cells. When he passed me, he barked, "Hurry up, girl!"

"Yes, sir," I mumbled, hoisting my tray. My only option now was to act the part of a royal servant and deliver steaming bowls of gruel.

The prison cells were cramped and drafty, adorned with

nothing but chamber pots and loose straw for bedding. Most of the men were sprawled on the floor, either asleep or pretending to be, but some of them pounded on the bars and shouted violently. They aimed their anger at the warden and then, in his wake, at me. After all, they regarded me as a lackey of the king. A small gap under the iron bars of each cell gave me just enough room to slide the bowls of mush underneath, which I did from as far away as possible. The ceramic skidded against the stone floor, the gruel spilling out in chunks.

In every cell, I searched for Father, but the men all looked the same—plastered in grime, their hair and beards wild and tangled. Near the end of the row, I paused in front of a man balled up on the floor with his back to me. I squinted hard at him in the dying light. I didn't recognize his clothes or his matted hair, but I knew him by his rounded shoulders and the way they shuddered. I'd seen him in that position before, right after Mother died. He'd been curled up on their bed, sobbing. I felt the same helplessness now that I did back then. I wanted to call out to him, to *reach* out to him, but I couldn't or I'd give myself away. I had to do something better than that.

I had to save him.

I had to come up with another plan.

# KNOTS AND HOW TO USE THEM

I reluctantly left Father and continued down the row, delivering the last bowls of gruel and racking my brain for inspiration. I was still without a plan when I reached the very last cell, where Mr. Dudley sat on the dirt floor, staring at something invisible on an opposite wall. He didn't budge when I slid his food under the bars. He only rubbed his wrists, which were red and raw where he'd been bound by the soldier's clumsily tied rope.

The rope, which the warden had removed from Mr. Dudley's hands and carried with him back to his post at the entryway.

The rope, which gave me an idea.

It dawned on me that I'd been going about this whole thing the wrong way. I was a balloonist, not a thief. I didn't know how to sneak around and steal keys—those were Abi's areas of expertise. But I knew rope. And, more to the point, I knew knots.

The warden was now wide-awake and happily cracking open the pecans with a nutcracker. "Excuse me," I said softly.

He sighed in frustration. "Another spill?"

"No, sir, it's not that. Actually, I just wanted to make a . . . suggestion."

He cupped his ear as if he'd misheard me. "A *what*?"

"A suggestion, sir. About your prisoners."

"Is this a joke?"

"No."

"You're a housemaid, aren't you?"

"Yes, sir."

"I don't take suggestions from housemaids." He squeezed another pecan between the metal arms of the nutcracker until the shell shattered in his fingers.

"But your men are using the wrong knot," I said. "When they tie up the prisoners."

"You insubordinate rat!" he bellowed. He picked up another nut, and without the aid of the nutcracker, crushed it in his fist. "I'm the warden here! Don't tell me how to do my job!"

"Yes, sir," I whispered, my head sinking to my chest. "I'm sorry, sir."

All the air went out of me then, like a deflated balloon. I'd been foolish to think I could pull this off. Just because I'd built a rickety catapult and flown a balloon a few miles (crashing it, no less), I thought I could brazenly break into the royal prison? I was a Goody Gumdrop, not a criminal. I shuffled toward the door.

"But if I *were* interested," said the warden to my retreating back, "which I'm not, of course—what knot would you suggest?"

I turned slowly around. "The pulkker," I said. "The royal guardsmen use a slipwich, which can be easily loosened. I can show you, if you have a spare rope."

"Yes, over there," he said. I retrieved the rope that had bound Mr. Dudley's hands and wound it around an iron bar from the nearest cell, walking the warden through each twist, loop, and fold of the pulkker knot.

"See," I said when I'd finished. "Try and loosen it." He pulled at it, using his considerable weight as leverage, but it didn't budge.

"Not bad," he said. "But I'm pulling on it from the outside. How do I know the prisoner won't be able to loosen it when it's on his wrists?"

"I can show you," I said.

He wrinkled his brow, still reluctant to take advice from someone so far beneath his station. But he finally nodded. He placed his wrists side by side and held them out to me. I couldn't believe what was happening—I blinked a few times to make sure it was real. The warden of the royal prison was actually requesting that I tie him up. He even smiled, pleased as a pig, while I used the rope to bind his hands with a pulkker knot, while the other end was still tied to the bars of a prison cell.

"Well, I'll be!" he said, attempting to extricate himself. "This pulkker knot is really something. I'll talk to my officers about this right away. Now untie me, girl."

"I—I'm sorry," I stammered. Even though he was an awful man who'd imprisoned my father for a meaningless crime, I still felt a twinge of guilt for what I was about to do. I lifted the key ring from its hook.

"What's going on?" he boomed. *"What are you doing?"* As it dawned on him that he'd been duped, his face reddened, and he roared like a caged beast. "I'll find you! When I get free, I'll find you and kill you myself! Or I'll toss you in one of my cells and watch you rot!"

The threats went on and on, but the thundering of my heart drowned out the rest of his rant. I *was* going to pull this off. I was going to rescue Father. And I was going to do it my way.

# BRACING FOR A BANG

"Father?" I gently shook him, but he didn't rouse. "Father, it's me. We have to go. We must hurry." When he finally rolled over, I stifled a gasp. It wasn't his appearance that shocked me, or the smell of him, though both were repellent. It wasn't even that he'd aged fifty years in the last five days. It was the blankness in his eyes and the slackness of his jaw that unnerved me. His chest rose and fell, but that was the only indication of life left in him.

"Prismena?" he uttered through cracked lips. "Is it you?"

"Yes, Father. I've come to take you out of here. It's not safe. We must leave."

"Have I been released?" he asked, rising with a grimace to a sitting position. "Did they catch the smuggler?"

"No, Father. I'll explain everything later, I promise. Just come with me now. Please."

"Prismena." His voice became hard, and his eyes bore into me. There was some mettle in him yet. "I told you not to get involved. Have you done something reckless? Something illegal?"

I lifted the hem of my wide skirt. Where my petticoats should've been, Abi had secured several tightly rolled bundles. A pair of black trousers, patched by the children of Mulberry House.

The purple coat with brass buttons. A pair of black boots in two different sizes. "I don't have time to argue with you. If you stay here, you'll die, for no reason other than your own stubbornness. Put these clothes on. We're leaving."

Father did as I said—not because he believed I was right, but because he didn't have the will to fight me. Luckily, it was now dark outside, because nobody who saw him in daylight would've mistaken him for a soldier. If the stubble and the stench didn't give him away, the frayed, ill-fitting clothes certainly would have.

We crept out of Father's cell into the hallway. The other prisoners were pressed against the bars, taunting the warden. Only Mr. Dudley wasn't participating. I rushed to his cell, where he was hunched over his gruel, oblivious to the chaos around him. "C'mon," I said. "I can get you out of here."

"No, you can't," he said into his bowl. "I'm too old to make a run for it, Prissy. I'll never get past the guards."

"You've got to try," I said. I fumbled through the key ring until I found the one with the skull-shaped head. I removed it and tossed the rest to Mr. Dudley. "Save who you can."

"Prissy!" hissed Father. "What are you doing? These men are criminals!"

"Some of them are merely inventors," I said. "And balloonists!"

I grabbed Father's arm and dragged him to the back of the building. Beyond the last cell, I fell to my knees and felt for the latch on the floor, which was nearly invisible in the dark. When my fingers landed on it, I pulled up, opening a hidden hatch that concealed a steep set of stairs. As Marybeth had promised.

"What is this?" asked Father.

"Just go," I said, practically shoving him through the hatch.

We both stumbled down the steps, and I pulled the door closed behind us, breathing easier as soon as we were out of the main prison and could no longer hear the warden's curses. But we weren't in the clear yet. The exit was at the other end of the cellar. To reach it, we had to traverse a pitch-black underground room—the place where King Michael stored Black Powder.

I took the lead, shuffling slowly along the length of the cellar. A fine powder crunched underfoot, and a peculiar scent filled my nose, like burnt leaves and metal. A few times, my legs collided with one of the waist-high barrels that filled the room. Each time, my heart seized with fear, bracing itself for a bang. It was with great relief that we finally reached the door.

I slid the skull-shaped key into the lock. When the door creaked open, I gulped the fresh air as if I'd been trapped underground for years instead of minutes. I looked back over my shoulder and, in the wash of moonlight, saw that we'd walked through a sea of barrels—dozens and dozens of them—stretching from one end of the wide room to the other. There were also rows of tables in between, littered with tools, scraps of metal, and lengths of rope.

As Marybeth had instructed, I pried the lid off the barrel nearest the door and pressed the key deep inside. When I removed my hand, it was coated in a gritty film of Black Powder. I grabbed a nearby rag to wipe it off, but when I held up the cloth, I realized it wasn't a rag at all. It was a tiny sweater, for a child hardly bigger than Cole. Abi's words rushed back to me: *Kids who don't get claimed by an adult are either sent back over the Wall or taken to the palace to build the king's weapon.* I prayed that someone—the right someone—would find that key.

Father and I emerged from the cellar and found ourselves on a wide green lawn behind the prison. On the other side of the building, shouts—both joyous and angry—indicated that the other prisoners had begun to escape. We could use the commotion to our advantage, but we had to move quickly. We had to make it back to the servants' gate before Quincy went off duty.

"Stop right there!" someone called out to us. A young soldier with a patchy mustache ran over, panting.

"Um . . . we were just . . ." I fumbled for my words. "I was just . . ."

"All guards must report to the main gate!" said the soldier to Father, completely ignoring me. "What are you waiting for?" He dashed away frantically, calling over his shoulder, "There's been a jailbreak!"

Father and I darted from nook to shadowy nook—careful to avoid both soldiers and escapees—until we reached the cart I'd driven into the palace earlier that night, which already felt like a lifetime ago. We climbed in, and I drove to the back gate at a calm trot as though everything were fine. In reality, I thought my heart might burst from beating so hard.

"Who's there?" demanded the guard who approached our cart. He stepped in close, and I tipped my head down to hide my face.

"Marybeth," I said softly.

"I thought that was you!" he replied. I gazed up long enough to see Quincy's friendly smile. I'd never been so happy to see a royal guardsman in my life.

"The chef is sending me on another errand," I said. "To pick up . . . the king's favorite cheese." I suddenly wished I had Abi's knack for lying. And for not dissolving into utter panic at times like these.

"The Gouda?" asked Quincy.

"Yes! The Gouda!" I said, sounding a bit too shocked that my story had worked. Quincy didn't seem to notice. "We have to hurry, before the cheesemonger closes shop for the night."

"Hmm." Quincy frowned. "Nobody's permitted to leave the grounds right now. Some sort of situation at the prison. We're on lockdown."

"Please, can't you make an exception?" I begged. "If I don't get that cheese, the chef will have my hide. I promise we'll be back before anyone knows we're gone."

Quincy lowered his voice. "If it were up to me, I'd allow it, Miss Marybeth. But you know King Michael doesn't make exceptions. Sorry."

"But . . ." I felt tears stinging my eyes. We were so close. We couldn't fail now.

"Have you seen the king when he doesn't get his cheese?" Father's voice rang out like a gong, surprisingly powerful. "If he finds out that you were the one who kept him from his Gouda, well . . . I won't envy you."

I looked at Father in alarm and struck a tear from my eye.

Quincy gulped. "Just to the market and back, right?"

"Yes," said Father.

"All right," whispered Quincy. "Go on. And hurry." He swung the gate open, and we rolled through. As soon as we cleared the threshold of the palace, tears sprang to my eyes again—this time in relief.

But we'd made it only a few feet down the road when something hurtled out of the darkness and onto our path, blocking our way.

"Abi?" I whispered.

"Halt!" shouted a soldier—a real one, as far as I could tell. He was gripping the forearm of a slouching girl, as limp as a bundle of yarn. In fact, he seemed to be the only thing holding her up. I cried out in anguish when I recognized her—curly brown hair, overbite, and clad in just her petticoats.

Marybeth.

# HAUNTING THE HALLS

*Catherine felt like a ghost, haunting the halls of her own palace. Nobody paid her any mind until she stepped beyond the threshold of the East Wing, where she'd be blocked by some dim-witted guard blindly following the king's orders. She thought of her father, who would spin over in his grave if he knew his flesh and blood had been made a prisoner in her family home. She thought of her son, of whom she'd had no news since she'd left him in a balloonist's workshop in the middle of nowhere. She thought of the rebellion, the movement she'd started and had now all but abandoned. What would happen on Savior's Day? What nefarious news was Michael so giddy to announce?*

*Catherine no longer had any influence within the palace, but she still had one thing Michael and his lackeys didn't—an intricate knowledge of the place. As a girl, she'd roamed every inch of it, even those inches that were known only to a few. Like the hidden passage behind the walls that connected the sitting room in the East Wing with the king's private office in the West Wing, designed by one of Catherine's less honorable ancestors.*

*The benefit of being a ghost is that nobody notices when you disappear, as Catherine did one afternoon after her supper plates had been collected. She slipped through the wall into the narrow corridor behind it, thanking her stars that in her solitude she no longer had to wear unruly whalebone cages beneath her skirts. She tiptoed through the dusty, pitch-dark passage until she reached the office. She pressed her ear to the wall and was met with silence. There was a bookshelf on the office side, so she had to throw her entire weight against the wall to make it budge. A clever set of wheels helped things along, but still it groaned and resisted terribly. Had anyone been in the room, she would never have escaped unnoticed. Luckily, it was empty.*

*She rushed to the king's stately oak desk—the same one that had once belonged to her father. She'd often played in this room as a child and had just as often been shooed away, with a gentle pat on the head, by a busy King Reginald. The memory made her heart ache. But this was no time to get sentimental. There was work to be done.*

*She riffled through the king's desk drawers, and it didn't take her long to find what she sought—a marriage certificate formalizing the union of Lord Michael and Princess Catherine. The date stamped on it was the very one on which she had run off to Palma, the day after she married Jaxson. The signature bearing her name wasn't in her handwriting—it wasn't even a particularly good forgery. She now had evidence that Michael had seized the throne unlawfully.*

*She'd expected to find evidence of Michael's betrayal, but something else on that sheet of parchment chilled her blood. The witness to the marriage ceremony was listed as Greta Blake, her lady-in-waiting. If Greta had falsified the marriage certificate so Michael could take the throne, what else had Greta done in his service? Catherine had confessed everything to her loyal servant. She'd even charged Greta with the care of her son. An icy pang of fear struck her directly in the heart.*

*Catherine heard footsteps coming down the hallway, toward the office. She took the certificate and turned to go, but then another document on the desk caught her eye. She scanned the page, her horror growing as she read. She knew Michael had a sinister plan for Savior's Day, but she had no idea just how deadly it would be.*

*She took that document, as well, briefly lamenting the fact that ladies' gowns didn't come with pockets in which to store such things. Then she scrambled back into the space behind the wall and pulled the bookcase into place behind her. And, like a ghost, it was as if she had never been there at all.*

# A BUMP IN THE ROAD

The soldier approached the cart, dragging Marybeth beside him. When he reached it, he dropped the poor maid in a heap at his feet. Then he leaned toward me, his beady eyes glinting in the moonlight. If Marybeth had the likeness of a rabbit, then this man was the human version of a rat. I knew instantly that he was Jensen, the one Marybeth had warned me about. "Excuse me," he said with mock politeness. "It seems Marybeth here has been robbed of her clothes, and she's a bit confused about what happened to them. My questioning seems to have worn her out. I don't suppose you know anything about it?"

I fumbled for a plausible story about the king's cheese, but at the sight of Marybeth, broken and bleeding, all I could do was stare.

"Do you know the penalty for impersonating a member of the king's staff?" he asked.

Again, I merely blinked at him, struck dumb.

"I'll tell you," he said. "It's prison. But breaking out of jail? That's a much more heinous crime. Punishable by death. I don't suppose anyone here has committed such atrocious acts. . . ."

"W-we're just going to the cheesemonger," I finally managed to say.

Jensen laughed, as if our squirming was immensely entertaining. "You may have gotten past Quincy back there, but he's an idiot. Do you think *I'm* an idiot?"

I vigorously shook my head.

"Good. Because I'm not. And when I bring you in, all three of you"—he nudged Marybeth with the toe of his boot, and she groaned—"I'll finally be free of gate duty and can work on cleansing Oren of filth like you."

"Is that all you aspire to?" said a girl emerging from the darkness. "How very boring."

"Abi?" I whispered again, hope swelling in my chest.

"Another accomplice?" said Jensen. "It must be my lucky day. How generous of you to turn yourself in."

"Psh," said Abi. "Don't compare me to these rabble. I've got something to offer you. Something much more valuable than a chance to tackle children for stealing grapes. I can make you richer than your wildest dreams."

Jensen chuckled. "Nice try, urchin. As I've already mentioned, I'm not an idiot."

"Then I guess you're not interested in this." Abi cupped a small object in the palm of her hand. The soft moonlight caught the jewels at just the right angle, making them wink and sparkle.

"Clearly a fake," he said. "Those seem to be in abundance tonight."

"Look closer," said Abi. "It's the queen's monogram. Made especially for her by the royal jeweler. Are you suggesting that the queen wears fake diamonds?"

"Let me see that," Jensen demanded. He took a few fierce strides closer to Abi. The road ahead of us was clear now, but if I took off, I'd be leaving Abi and Marybeth behind. I held the reins still, even as Father moaned softly beside me.

"I don't believe it," breathed Jensen.

Once he'd gotten a good look at the barrette, Abi darted away from him in a quick hop and dangled the jewelry out of reach.

"You stole that, you little thief!" the guard said. "Hand it over."

"As soon as you let these people go," said Abi.

"You think you can make demands of me?" he shouted. He lunged for her, and in one fluid movement, Abi chucked the barrette as far as she could into a clump of bushes. Jensen didn't hesitate to dive in after it, having apparently forgotten his vow to rid Oren of the likes of us. He disappeared in a flurry of leaves.

"Hurry!" said Abi, rushing to Marybeth. The two of us quickly dragged the girl into the cart. Abi sat beside her, stroking her hair, while Marybeth whimpered in pain. Father didn't speak a word as I prodded the horse into a gallop and we left the palace, and the prison, behind us.

Before we reached the main road, I pulled the cart into a clearing. The Royal Guard would soon come looking for us, and we'd be an easy target in a stolen palace cart. We'd have to continue on foot. Abi and I hopped to the ground.

"I'll bring Marybeth to Mulberry House," she said. "They'll take good care of her there."

"Can you do me a favor?" I asked, digging around in my many pockets until I landed on the peach pit. "Can you give this to Cole?"

"Sure thing," said Abi. "Where will you go now?"

"We can camp out at Fletcher's Mill for a few days," I said. "Until Father gets his strength back. After that . . . I'm not sure."

"Do you think he'll help us with *Goldilocks*? Do you think he'll let you fly?"

"I don't know," I said, though I had a sinking suspicion I *did* know. "Once he's had some food and rest, I'll ask him."

"Well, hurry up. Savior's Day is only six days away."

"Believe me, I'm well aware of that. Thanks again for helping me with Father. And for rescuing me. Again."

"Don't mention it," she said.

"That barrette must be worth a fortune. I can't believe you—"

"*Don't* mention it."

"Maybe you're not such a horrid girl after all," I said, grinning.

She rolled her eyes. "Don't get the wrong idea, Prissy. Just because I keep saving you doesn't mean—"

"I know, I know," I said. "We're not friends."

"Exactly," she said. "Now get out of here, Gumdrop."

# THE VERMIN OF SILK VALLEY

The journey to Lollyhill had never been so arduous. Father winced with every step, and when he mustered the energy to speak, he used it to complain about his wayward daughter. "You shouldn't have done it," he said. "Now what will we do? Where will we go? We're fugitives!"

I opened my mouth to tell him everything I'd discovered over the last few days, but the clip-clop of horses' hooves approaching made me clamp my jaw shut. We were alone on a quiet street in Silk Valley in the dead of night. The only other people out at that hour were outlaws and soldiers, and I wasn't eager to encounter either one. I wedged myself under Father's armpit and lugged him into an alley jutting off the street. Two horses thundered by as we slid into the darkness.

As soon as the threat had passed, I let go of Father. He collapsed against the side of a brick building like a sack of potatoes, and I doubled over in exhaustion. Silk Valley was less than halfway to Fletcher's Mill. My wounded arm was throbbing terribly, and Father could scarcely support his own weight. And the Royal Guard was out in full force looking for the escaped prisoners. How could we possibly make it the rest of the way?

Three quick clicks, like pebbles colliding, shattered the stillness of the alley. Someone had struck a piece of flint, and a flame sprang to life. By its orange light, I could make out the form of a man a few feet away from us. We were not alone.

"I see even Silk Valley has its vermin," said the man with a strong Tuleran accent. He raised a flaming strip of charpaper to his pipe, and for an instant it illuminated his face, which was almost entirely nose.

"Jerrick Larue?" I said. We must have ducked behind the dressmaker's shop. I remembered how he'd shooed Abi away from his window, and how he'd sneered at me when I was begging the palace guards for mercy. I didn't expect any sympathy from him. Just the opposite, in fact. "We'll go," I said, tugging Father's sleeve. Father tried to raise himself from the ground, but he faltered and fell.

"Hmph," scoffed the dressmaker. "You'll never make it. The streets are swarming with soldiers. And speak of the devil . . ." The rumble of more hooves sounded in the distance. Mr. Larue puffed his pipe and moved toward the alley's entrance, toward the men searching for us. Without thinking, I grabbed the tail of his coat and tugged him back.

"Please, sir, don't turn us in," I begged. "I promise we'll get out of here as soon as they pass. Please!"

"How dare you!" he howled. "This is the finest wool in all the world, far too good for your grubby hands. Now I will have to incinerate it. Shame on you!" With a huff, he continued toward the street as the soldiers arrived.

"Good evening, sir," shouted one of the men on horseback. Father and I huddled together and barely breathed, trying to blend into the shadows. "We're searching for a band of escaped criminals. Devious ones, dressed as members of the royal staff. Have you seen anything suspicious tonight?"

"Indeed I have," said Mr. Larue. "Foul miscreants right here in Silk Valley! What is the world coming to?"

"I can assure you, sir, we're doing everything we can to remove them from your fine neighborhood. Point us toward them, and we'll make sure they're severely punished."

"Thank you, my good man. I can tell you precisely where they are." Jerrick shot a look in our direction. After all I'd been through, I couldn't believe it would end here, in this alley, because of a snooty dressmaker. I took Father's hand. I could feel his pulse thumping, just like mine. "They took the main road heading west, toward Wilderburg. They're probably as far as Landingham by now."

"Thank you," said the soldier. "Your service to your kingdom will not be forgotten."

"I certainly hope not," said Mr. Larue. As our pursuers dashed off to Landingham, he strolled back to where we crouched behind a trash bin, and offered me his hand.

"B-but . . . ," I stammered.

"Don't make me change my mind," he said. "Let's go."

# THE WARS OF KINGS AND COMMONERS

As soon as the alley was clear of purple-suited soldiers, Jerrick loaded Father and me into his wagon and took us all the way to Lollyhill. The bumps and jolts of our ride were cushioned by Oren's finest fabrics. Jerrick didn't utter a word along the way, just deposited us by the side of the road with a curt nod. He had to stay in character, I supposed. Of all the shocking things I'd learned since my father's arrest, the true allegiance of Jerrick Larue was one of the most astounding.

Father and I entered the mill under cover of night. "I hoped I'd never set foot in this place again," he murmured. As for me, I was visited by fond memories of the night Abi had rescued me from Kluwer House, of listening to the lullaby of the looms with Abi and Cole asleep beside me. I wondered what they were doing now. Had Abi made it to Mulberry House with Marybeth? Was Cole safe and sound, delighted that his peach pit had come back to him?

Father sighed heavily, so I guided him to a soft pile of lamb pelts and set about creating a place for him to sleep. The materials Abi had taken from his workshop were still stashed there. I spread out the balloon tarp once again, to block the damp chill of the ground. Father stopped me. "Is that *Tiger Lily*?"

"Pieces of her," I said. "We borrowed a few things from your shop when we spent the night here."

"You stayed *here* while I was gone?" He gave me a searching look. "Did the Fletchers get you into this mess with the rebellion? I should've known."

"I stayed here after Ms. Stoneman sent me to a children's home, where I was mocked and hit and could've been sold to the Royal Guard. And no, the Fletchers didn't get me into any mess. In fact, Mr. Fletcher saved me and my friends. Believe me, Father, I tried to heed your warnings and stay out of it, but . . . well, I just couldn't."

Father lowered himself, with difficulty, onto the makeshift bed. I rushed over to assist him, but he waved me off. Then, gazing up through the open windows, he said, "A great deal has happened in my absence, daughter. Tell me about it."

So I did. Though both of us longed for sleep, there was too much that had to be said without delay. I told Father more in the wee hours of that night than in all the years since Mother had died—every detail of my adventures with Abi and Cole. He listened without saying a word. He only groaned here and there.

"And when the signal is sent on Savior's Day," I said, nearing the end of my story, "the rebellion will strike at last." A jolt shot through me when I uttered the words. There it was again—something akin to excitement.

"The signal?" grumbled Father. "The rebellion? What utter nonsense! You have no idea what you've gotten yourself into. You're a child playing at being a grown-up. You all are. And I'll have no more of it."

"But, Father—"

"What happens when the signal is sent?"

"The rebellion will strike," I repeated.

"What in blazes does that mean?"

"I—I'm not sure. Not precisely. Halston has it all planned. His men are going to rise up against King Michael in a coordinated attack."

"His *men,*" spat Father derisively. "More like a bunch of disgruntled farmers who don't want to pay their share of taxes!"

"It's not true, Father! Weren't you listening? The queen wasn't really kidnapped—she told me with her own lips! King Michael started a false war in Palma so he could justify the evil things he'd done. And then he lied about all of it. He made Palma look like the enemy so he could defend his deplorable actions. And now . . . now there are orphans living right here in Oren, right under our noses, whose parents were lost because of King Michael. Would you have more Palmerians suffer at the hands of the Royal Guard, on the whims of King Michael? You'd have more children become orphans because of his greed?"

"The business of kings and soldiers is not our business, Prismena!"

"That's precisely how they get away with it," I shouted. I'd never raised my voice to Father before, not once. But I didn't stop, not even when his eyes widened in alarm. "The last signal is a yellow balloon flying high enough for everyone to see. *Goldilocks* will signal the start of the war, and *I* will be flying her. I made a promise."

"No," he said. So simple. So definitive.

"But—"

"No."

"Father, hear me out—"

"I will not participate in an unlawful rebellion against the king, and I will not allow my daughter or my property to participate in one, either. That's final."

"It's not fair!" I gritted my teeth and turned away from him, fuming.

Neither of us said anything for several seconds. The creaking looms filled the silence, but they sounded ominous now—a funeral dirge instead of a lullaby. And then Father spoke.

"Your Mother always said you took after me," he said. His voice was softer now, unsteady. "So precise and obedient. Even when you were a little girl, you colored inside the lines. If you made a mistake, you'd crumple up your paper and start over. But I saw something else in you. I noticed all the ways you were like her. You may have stayed inside the lines, but you were coloring. I never bothered with anything but black and white."

I was still seething, but I turned around to face him. I'd never heard him talk like this before. He'd barely mentioned Mother since she died.

"I sympathize with the orphans and the Palmerians and the queen," he said. "But their cause is not mine. Another man's cause wasn't worth losing your Mother over, and it's not worth losing you."

"But, Father . . ." I walked over to him and knelt down beside him. "You can't put up a wall and expect it to keep you safe forever. That's what I learned while you were away. Even if Mother hadn't come here to nurse Mrs. Fletcher—"

"She didn't," he whispered.

"What?" I said, pulling away from him.

"She didn't come here to nurse Mrs. Fletcher. She came here to help Mrs. Fletcher look for survivors. Some refugees from Palma made it over the Wall in a balloon, but they crashed just east of Fletcher's Mill. The Fletchers asked us to help them dig through the wreckage." Tears welled up in Father's eyes. One tear escaped and swerved down the lines of his face. "I begged her not to go. I told her it was too dangerous, and not our fight, but she refused to listen. She . . . she swallowed so much smoke that night . . . she could hardly breathe. She was laid up here for three days before . . ."

"Wh-what?" I said, my voice barely audible. "She—she didn't die nursing Mrs. Fletcher back to health?" The world went blurry, and I realized I was crying.

"No. Your mother died from the smoke in her lungs."

"A balloon crash," I murmured. "Not far from here."

"Yes."

The pieces clicked into place, like the gears inside one of Mr. Dudley's watches. The last few days hadn't been a random series of events. There *was* something connecting it all.

Mother.

Mother had died in support of the rebellion. She had died helping refugees.

She had died saving Cole.

The realization sucked the breath from my chest. "You lied to me," I said softly.

"I was protecting you," said Father. "That's my job. I couldn't save your mother, but I can save you."

"I don't need protecting," I said, raising my voice again. I stood up. "I don't need saving! I need the truth. That's what Oren needs, too—the truth! I'm joining the rebellion, Father. And I'm flying on Savior's Day!"

"I forbid it!" he said.

I moved toward the door. I didn't blame him for wanting to protect me, but I was Mother's daughter as much as his. And it was her voice in my head telling me I had to go. I only hoped he would forgive me.

# A FACE LIKE SHATTERED GLASS

I walked quickly and anxiously, tiptoeing through grass that was coated with a crunchy layer of frost. I knew every hill of Fletcher's field, but I'd never roamed them in the dead of night before. My dwindling candle cast ominous shadows, and I flinched at the slightest rustle of wind in the leaves.

"Prissy?" someone whispered.

The voice spooked me out of my skin, and I yelped in alarm. The shrouded person hushed me.

I recognized the voice, but only barely. It hadn't called my name in years. I turned and saw Mrs. Fletcher in the shadows, wrapped in a crocheted shawl. She'd grown old. Her face was so full of wrinkles it looked like shattered glass, and her eyes were heavy with a sadness that hadn't been there before.

"I—I was just . . ." I couldn't finish my sentence. I couldn't manage another lie. "I'm leaving."

"I know," she said. "I saw you and your daddy go into the mill. I stayed up to keep watch, in case the Royal Guard showed up. You're doing what you've got to do, and I'm not going to ask for an explanation or try to talk you out of it. But I'm sure as sun-light going to send you off with food in your sack." She dropped a cloth satchel into my hand, still slightly warm. It smelled like fresh bread.

"Thank you," I said.

"I've missed you, Prismena. I know your daddy is still upset about what happened, but you don't have to hold his grudges, you know."

"I know," I said, and flashes of my time with Mrs. Fletcher—drinking chocolate at her kitchen table, digging in her garden—made my heart ache. "I'm sorry."

"Don't be. Just pay me a visit every now and again."

"I will," I said. I turned to go but stopped myself. "Mrs. Fletcher?"

"Yes, dear."

"That night, when the balloon crashed, did you save a child? A baby?"

By the light of my candle, I saw the sadness flare in her eyes. "We sure did. Your mom found him in the wreckage, a tiny wailing thing all covered in soot. She wrapped him up in balloon scraps. She's the one who named him, too. She said he looked like a lump of coal, so that's what we called him. Cole."

I smiled, hoping I'd get the chance to tell him that story. I bet it would make him giggle.

"Your mother . . . well, she got real sick after that. She went quicker than anybody thought she would. I'm sorry you didn't get to say goodbye to her, Prismena. It's always been one of my biggest regrets."

"Did Mother regret it?" I asked. "Saving Cole, I mean. Do you think she'd have done it differently, had she known?"

Mrs. Fletcher sighed. "I can't answer that, Prismena. She never would have chosen to leave you, that I know for sure. But your mother always had to help people who needed it. That instinct was bone-deep in her."

I nodded, tears pooling in my eyes. So often I'd ached to have Mother back, to lie with her in the tall grass again. I would've given anything for more time with her. But having her back would've meant losing Cole. It wasn't fair that such trades had to be made. But sometimes they did. I knew that now.

"What happened to Cole after Mother died?" I asked. "How did he end up in Between?"

"In Between? Oh dear." Mrs. Fletcher clutched her chest. "Cole lived with us for almost a year. We kept him hidden because we didn't know what sort of danger he might be in. But as soon as he got to walking and talking, we realized we were no match for him, being as old as we were. So I called that schoolmistress of yours, Ms. Stoneman. I figured she'd know what to do with an orphan child. I wasn't aware back then of what happens to kids with nobody to speak for them. If I'd known . . ." A sob caught in her chest.

"It's okay," I said. "Cole is going to be all right."

"Is he?" she said, swatting a tear from the corner of her eye. "Thank you for telling me that. It eases my mind a great deal. Now, you'd best get going if you want the night to protect you. The sun will rise in no time. But you come back someday soon. I've got stories about your mama I bet you've never heard. She did much more than save one little boy."

"I will," I said, and took my leave of her.

By the time I got to the workshop, the sun had poked its head up over the horizon, painting the stones golden yellow. I blew out my candle and walked inside. A week ago, entering Father's workshop without permission would've been unthinkable. But the rules had been rewritten since then. Or maybe the rules had stayed the same but I'd finally learned how to break them.

My foot landed on something slippery in the doorway, and I had to steady myself on a workbench to keep from falling. By the light of the rising sun, I could make out what it was that had nearly knocked me down—something slick and bright red. A fragment of *The Flame.*

When I raised my eyes, I didn't recognize the place. The packed-earth floor, normally muddy and dimpled with footprints, was a landscape of color. Every inch of ground was awash in the vibrant hues of our balloons, the fabrics all tangled and twisted together. It would've been stunning if it hadn't been a massacre. Every last balloon had been shredded into confetti, Father's earthbound rainbow obliterated. I picked up a tattered strip of *Goldilocks,* no longer than my arm. She would never fly on Savior's Day. Not to signal the rebellion. And not to save the queen.

# LITTLE ROOM FOR LIGHT

*Catherine spread the paper out on her lap, on top of her embroidery. She studied it once more, trying to make sense of it. It was a diagram of a small object, which consisted of sharp bits of metal and an ample quantity of Black Powder. It was labeled, in Michael's own hand, a "bomb." The diagram also showed a "blast radius" and a "strike zone," terms Catherine didn't understand but that turned her stomach, all the same. This must be what Michael intended to unleash on Savior's Day, and Catherine had no way to pass this information to the rebellion, no way to prepare them for what this simple drawing foretold.*

*Catherine had been confined to her quarters for three days, the monotony broken only by the comings and goings of the servants. Her requests for books and games had been denied—because, her captors said, the king didn't want to tax her overburdened mind. That left her with precious few options to pass the time: gazing out the window, working on her needlepoint, and worrying herself sick about Savior's Day.*

*When the king appeared at her chamber door that day, Catherine quickly concealed the stolen document under her embroidery. Michael's girth flooded the doorway, leaving little room for light to get in around the edges. When he'd been courting her, Michael was considered handsome—slender and strong. But the perks of being king had made him soft and lazy. Without waiting for an invitation, he squeezed into the room.*

*"I see I've lost my privacy as well as my freedom," said Catherine.*

*"I'm the king," he replied. "I can go where I please and take the head of anyone who tries to stop me. Even you."*

*"I'm inclined to let you have it," she said. "I've little need for it anymore."*

*"Don't tempt me."*

*She flicked her eyes up to his reddening face and decided to change the subject. Taunting him wouldn't be worth it. "To what do I owe the pleasure of your company?" she asked.*

*"I'm here to extend an invitation," he said. "There will be a feast tonight with several important guests in attendance, and the queen's absence might cause alarm."*

*"That sounds more like a summons than an invitation," said Catherine. She didn't want to let on that she secretly longed to attend a dinner in the dining room, if only for the sake of leaving her room and having a proper meal. "Might I ask who the honored guests are?"*

*"Winston Vickers and his retinue arrived last night from Tulera," he said. "You know old Winnie, don't you?"*

*"Vaguely," answered Catherine, but hope flickered like a struck match in her heart. Winston Vickers had long been an ally of her family, and, more recently, of the rebellion. During her years in Palma, the silk scarf Winston had given her had been the only fine thing she owned, until she passed it to a visiting balloonist, along with a message. If she could tell Winston what she'd found in Michael's desk, he'd know what to do. He'd send help.*

*"General Sorkin will also be in attendance, along with some of his men."*

*"General Sorkin?" she repeated, again trying to sound neutral. But upon hearing the name of the man who'd murdered Jaxson, a bitter metal taste flooded her mouth. She swallowed it down—a skill she'd perfected by now. "What's he doing here?" Ever since he'd "rescued" the "kidnapped" queen, General Sorkin had been the top military officer in Palma, in charge of all the war efforts there. He ruled over occupied Palma like a king in his own right. He returned to Oren only in rare circumstances.*

*"He's been recalled from his post," said King Michael.*

*"What? For good?"*

*"You've no need to trouble yourself with military matters," the king snapped. "Many things have changed since your impudence got you locked away. In fact, I thought you might be interested in another recent development. The Royal Guard visited the balloonist's workshop in Lollyhill today." He studied her face as he delivered the news. She gave him nothing.*

*"Of what interest are balloons to the queen of Oren?" she said. "It's clear I'm not traveling by air anytime soon."*

*"That's right, my dear. I had all the balloons destroyed. Only royal balloons will grace the skies of Oren from now on."*

*"That's rather extreme, isn't it?"*

*"Not at all. I've received reliable information that the balloonist is in league with the rebels. But hot-air balloons are no match for my men's blades. No balloons of any color but purple will go soaring over Oren, despite what the nursery rhymes say." He bent down over her, his breath smelling of old coffee and sausage. He lowered his voice to a whisper. "My guards are going to find the boy with the crimp in*

*his ear." He pushed back her hair and ran his finger over the dent in her own ear. His touch made her wince. "And when they do, I'm going to kill him."*

*Then he stood, towering over her. "Come to think of it, you're looking rather pale today. I don't think you're well enough to attend a state dinner. I'll give your regards to Winnie. I'll have the maids bring up your food. In fact, Greta has returned to us. I'll have her do it."*

*Catherine knew that each word he uttered was calculated to drive another dagger into her heart, but she wouldn't give him the satisfaction of crumpling in front of him. She waited until he left the room and shut the door. Then she collapsed onto the bed and soaked her fine silk sheets with tears.*

# QUITTING LESSONS

The second floor of Mulberry House was its usual blend of unrestrained voices and joyful mess. But I clomped up the stairs with heavy footsteps and a mood to match. I searched the rooms until I found Abi, admiring herself in front of a chipped mirror, balancing a dainty feathered hat on her head. When she spotted me in the reflection, she spun around, posing with her hands on her hips. "What do you think? I'm putting together my ensemble for Savior's Day."

"Don't bother," I said, letting my knapsack sink to my feet.

"Are you all right?" she asked, leading me to an overturned crate that doubled as a stool. "You look awful. Have you been crying?"

I *had* been crying, and I blinked hard not to start again. "It's over," I whispered.

"What are you talking about?"

"Someone broke into Father's workshop. The balloons are gone. All of them. Destroyed." I picked up the knapsack, tipping it over and shaking out the contents. Frayed pieces of our balloons fluttered to the ground. Abi gasped. "I'm not flying *Goldilocks* on Savior's Day. Nobody is."

"But what about the signal?"

"There won't be any signal, Abi. Don't you get it? There won't be any rescue mission, either."

"But Halston hasn't been able to communicate with the queen in days. He won't be able to warn her. The moment she denounces King Michael on the Wall, she'll be arrested."

"I can't rescue her without a balloon," I said. "There's nothing we can do."

"There has to be another way!" Abi cried, looking around as if the answer were right there in the room. But even the pot couldn't give us a hot-air balloon.

"All of this has been for nothing," I said. "I rescued Father, and now he'll probably never speak to me again. I risked everything for the rebellion, and now we don't have a signal—the one thing Halston said was critical to his plan. Everything was supposed to work together like a machine. But the machine is broken, Abi. The queen is going to sacrifice herself for nothing. What was the point of any of this?"

"We can patch *Goldilocks*."

"No, we can't. Not before Savior's Day."

"But if everyone pitches in, like we did with the catapult—"

"It'll never work."

"There has to be a way."

"There's not," I snapped. "It's over! You have to learn when to quit, Abi."

Her mouth fell open, and for a split second, I thought Abigail Smeade might actually be speechless. But then she set her jaw and said, "I guess I should take a lesson from you, then. Quitting seems to be your specialty."

"I know you think you know everything," I said, standing up and balling my hands into fists, "but you don't know anything about *me*!"

Kids from other rooms had wandered in to see what all the commotion was about. They watched wide-eyed as we faced off, our noses inches apart.

"Of course I know you, Prismena Reece. You're a tourist. You give up the moment things get rough. And you're absolutely right about me—I *don't* know when to quit. Because if I quit, I can't go running back to Daddy. If I quit—if any of these kids do—we'll be arrested or sent over the Wall or worse. Quitting is not an option here. So why don't you slink back to your old life with your stupid balloons and forget all about us, like I knew you would. But just remember this—your mother would never have given up so easily."

Her last words sucked the air from the room. Some kids even gasped and backed silently out the door.

"How dare you," I growled. "Don't mention my mother! You don't know a thing about her!"

"I know more than you do," Abi shot back. "Did you even know she was part of the rebellion? That she delivered supplies to refugees in Between? When I first climbed over the Wall and was living in the woods with nothing but the clothes on my back, your mother and her balloons were the only reason I survived. She fed me more times than I can count."

The blood drained from my head, and all the fight seeped out of my body. I suddenly felt unsteady, like the solid earth beneath me had become wobbly—like I was standing on a rapidly deflating balloon. "Mother was part of the rebellion?" I whispered, mostly to myself. But Abi and the others nodded.

In a way, everything made sense now. This is why kids kept asking me if I was the balloonist's daughter and gawking like I was some kind of celebrity. But in another way, nothing made any sense at all. I'd been told a lie to explain Mother's death, and now, it seemed, what I knew about her life had been a lie, too. Maybe Abi had been right. Maybe I hadn't known my own mother at all.

Suddenly, a vivid memory returned to me: Mother beside my bed, singing. *"Pink to heal you. Red to fight. Green to keep you warm at night. Blue to feed you. White to run. Yellow for the rising sun."* Father stood in the doorway with his arms crossed. Afterward, when they thought I was asleep, they argued, not realizing I could hear them through the wall. "How could you sing that to her?" Father said. "How could you sing that *in our house*?" Mother never sang it to me again.

"The nursery rhyme is a code, isn't it?" I asked.

Abi nodded. "The color of the balloon signals to the kids below what it's carrying. Pink for medicine. Red for weapons. Green for clothes and blankets. Blue for food. White for shoes. Your mother had been smuggling supplies to the Palmerians for years before she died. Then Guernsey took over."

"So all this time, you knew who she was," I said. "And you knew who *I* was."

"Of course I did," said Abi. "It was my idea to recruit you. I figured if your mother was so good, her daughter would be, too. You can imagine my disappointment."

"Abi, I'm sorry. I didn't know—"

"Save it."

"Why didn't you tell me you climbed the Wall, that you're Palmerian?"

"We're not friends, remember? And I don't need your pity." She locked eyes with me. "Stick to what you're good at, Prissy—mending holes in balloons and hiding behind locked doors."

Abi pushed through the crowd of gawking kids and out of the room. The thump of her footsteps echoed down the stairs. The other kids slowly dispersed, but nobody would meet my eye. I stood in the center of the room, alone, not quite sure what to do with myself. Not quite sure of anything anymore. I felt so stupid—so naïve—for having failed to see for so long what was going on all around me.

Suddenly, Cole burst into the room and ran at me like a battering ram, and I was grateful for his childish, oblivious delight. Somehow, he'd missed the entire fight. "Prissy!" he squealed.

"I'm happy to see you, too," I said, halfheartedly tousling his hair.

He spied the balloon scraps littering the floor and grabbed a large swatch of *Goldilocks.* He held it out to me, motioning for me to tie it around his neck. I obliged, fastening it so it trailed down his back like a bright-yellow cape. Then he fluttered around the room with his arms outstretched, as if flying.

As he played, I picked up a square of *The Flame* and studied it. A scrap like this one had swaddled Cole when he was a baby. And provided a bed for us at Fletcher's Mill. And cradled the rebellion's message as it floated into Palma.

Didn't all those scraps, when pieced together, make something whole?

Like all the unseen, unwanted children of Oren coming together to challenge a king.

And just when I'd thought I had nothing left—no balloons, no Father, no Abi—I realized that I was wrong. I had five days left before Savior's Day. I had an idea. I had some fight in me yet.

# A GARMENT WORTHY OF AN UPRISING

The morning sun tinted the streets of Silk Valley a lustrous gold, and the air smelled like spun sugar. Even the birdsong was more joyful than usual. The world seemed suffused with hope for the first time in days, because today was the day I'd put my plan into action. *If* I could enlist the help of two extremely stubborn people who had no reason to trust me. It was a long shot, but at least there was a chance.

When I arrived at the meeting spot, Abi was already there, tapping her foot impatiently. "Well?" she said. "What do you want?" In my message asking her to meet, I'd told her to wear something respectable. She showed up in someone's cast-off formal wear, tugging uncomfortably at the demure high collar. I noticed that she still wore Mother's scarf—clearly an intentional jab at me. Perhaps one I deserved.

"I have a plan," I said, unable to suppress my grin. "And a surprise for you."

"So?"

"Don't you want to know what they are?"

She shrugged.

"I thought of a way to send the signal *and* save the queen. It's unconventional and completely . . . I'll just say it . . . crazy. But it just might work. And I can't do it without you."

"Hmph," she said, rolling her eyes.

"Listen, Abi, you don't have to help me, but hear me out first. If you don't want to be involved once you know the details, you can walk away, okay?"

"Fine," she said, doing her best to look uninterested.

"Good. Follow me."

We walked a short distance before I stopped in front of a storefront with large windows filled with lavish displays—mannequins decked out in dresses as sumptuous and frilly as birthday cakes. As I reached for the doorknob, Abi cried, "Stop!" She shot me a panicked look. "We're going in *there*? Into Jerrick Larue's shop?"

"It's all part of the plan," I said. "Does this mean you'll help?"

Abi gulped. She smoothed the pleats of her stiff dress. "I'm not making any promises," she said. "But I'll come inside."

The bright tinkle of bells announced our entrance into the dressmaker's shop. Jerrick's head rose at the sound, a welcoming smile plastered on his face. But his smile promptly sank when he realized who had walked in.

"You," he said, with an accent more pronounced than usual, expelling the word like a wet cough. "What are *you* doing here?" I hadn't expected him to invite me for tea, but I thought he'd be a bit less disdainful now that I knew his secret.

I glanced over at Abi, whose eyes were darting all over the room, about ready to pop out of her head. Dressmakers' forms draped with fancy frocks were positioned throughout the shop, and expensive fabrics were laid out on every surface.

"W-we want to commission a dress," I said. "And a few . . . accessories."

Jerrick's manicured eyebrows shot up. "You can't be serious."

"I am serious. This dress is for an important client of yours. Your *most* important client."

He guffawed so hard I thought he might actually choke. "And did this client send you?"

"Yes," I lied.

Nobody spoke for several seconds. I held Jerrick's skeptical gaze, even though I longed for the less intimidating view of the carpet. "Fine," he finally said. "Back. Door."

Abi and I returned to the street, then ducked around to the alley where Father and I had huddled in the dark just days earlier. In the daylight, it looked as sparkling clean as every other place in Silk Valley. Even the alleys were pristine here.

Jerrick's head peeked out the back door. He made sure nobody was watching, then he beckoned us into his workroom, which was a cluttered mess of sewing supplies and half-constructed dresses. "Touch nothing," he said, and Abi's outstretched fingers curled back into themselves. "Tell me why you're here." He spoke firmly. Tersely. And without any trace of an accent.

My mouth fell open. "Wh-what happened to your voice?"

"I'm from the Slope, not Tulera," he said. "For some reason, people like buying fine clothes from a man with an accent. It's not fair, but that's life, eh? Now, please, get on with it. I have real clients to attend to."

"We need your help," I said. "Your, um, client wants to put her plan into action on Saturday."

"What makes you think I know what you're talking about?" he asked, staring down at me.

"Because I thought the queen trusted you," I said. "Perhaps I was mistaken."

"Of course she trusts me! I am her dressmaker! I will prepare the perfect ensemble. I've already started making her Savior's Day dress, but I will make a few tweaks for this extra-special occasion. Perhaps epaulets to make her look powerful. Most dressmakers never get the chance to design a garment for an uprising. It will be the highlight of my career."

"Actually, the uprising has hit a little snag. That's why we're here."

"I don't follow," said Jerrick. "What does this have to do with me?"

"We need you to make a few other . . . er, modifications to the queen's dress. And I don't mean epaulets."

"Excuse me?" he said, throwing his shoulders back.

"Here." I handed him a sheet of paper.

"I am not a seamstress," said Jerrick, taking the drawing between two fingers like it might be contagious. "I don't make other people's dresses, and I'm not about to start now for two children. I'm an artiste. That's . . ." His words trailed off as he reviewed my sketch. His eyebrows leaped up the sloped plane of his forehead again, as if ready to launch straight off his face.

"Can you do it?" I asked.

But for once, Jerrick Larue was speechless.

# HAMMER AND FLAME

I jabbed the poker into the furnace and sent a swarm of red-hot cinders skittering in all directions. My hair was tied back, and I'd shed all my clothes except a tissue-thin shift dress. Still, the sweat poured out of me. Father's thick leather gloves came up to my elbows and made me feel ham-fisted as I prodded the fire over and over and over, telling myself each time that it wasn't quite ready. The truth was, *I* wasn't quite ready. Disobeying Father to join the rebellion was one thing. Using his forge and his tools was quite another—a more personal form of betrayal.

Also, I was completely terrified.

I was about to heat a steel rod to the approximate temperature of the sun, then beat it with a five-pound hammer. I'd seen Father do it hundreds of times, but I wasn't convinced I was strong enough—or brave enough—to do it myself. But what choice did I have now? Without the final signal, the machinery of the rebellion would break down, and the cogs in that machine would become twisted bits of rubbish. Only in this case, the cogs were Queen Catherine, Halston, Abi, Gruber, Roz, and the others whose stories I'd heard over the last few days. I had to do my part.

With a deep breath, I picked up a metal rod and plunged one end into the furnace until it was engulfed in flames. When it began to glow bright red, like something otherworldly, I placed it on the cast-iron anvil. I had to move quickly, because the metal became less pliable with each second it cooled in the open air. Bracing myself, I lifted the hammer and let it crash down on the rod with a blast of sparks and a piercing clang that reverberated up my arm. And the metal gave way. It bent too much, crimping at a ninety-degree angle instead of forming a gentle curve, but it bent. *I* bent it. It was a start, at least.

"I don't think I'll ever get used to Prismena Reece swinging a giant hammer," said Abi, watching from a safe distance. She was stringing thread through a glinting needle.

"I'm not sure I will, either," I said, shouting over the roar of the furnace. "This is going to take some practice." I held up the mangled metal. It was only one-quarter of one steel hoop, a tiny fraction of what I needed to make before Savior's Day.

I plunged the metal into a bucket of cool water, and it released a hiss of steam. Then, as I'd seen Father do so many times, I used my glove to wipe the sweat from my brow.

"I'm impressed, Gumdrop."

"Thanks," I said, dropping onto a bench beside her. Abi was hunched over a strip of lace, practicing a stitch Jerrick had taught her. After an effusive show of protest, he'd finally agreed to help us, and now he and Abi were working together on the queen's dress.

"Some girl at Kluwer House said I could never be a Vine

with these arms," I said. "I wish she could see me now." I flexed, showing off a meager muscle.

"Hmph, try climbing a hundred-foot wall," mumbled Abi. "Then we can talk."

"What was it like to climb the Wall?" I asked.

"I told you, Prissy, we're not here to exchange our life stories. We're not—"

"Don't say it, Abi!"

"Friends! I don't *have* friends."

"I hate to break it to you," I said, "but you do now. You might as well get used to it."

Abi groaned and leaned more intently over her work.

"I'm here, Abi. I'm not going anywhere."

"That's what they all say," she said without looking up. "Before they leave. Or die."

I placed my hand over the lace, which nearly got me skewered by Abi's needle. She huffed at me. "I can't promise I won't die," I said. "But I'm really in this fight."

She snatched the fabric out from under my hand. "Can you scoot down the bench, Prissy? You smell like a farmhand."

I sighed and stood, returning to the furnace to select another strip of metal. Steel, I'd discovered, was far easier to ply than stubborn Abigail Smeade.

Then I heard her voice behind me. "There's a tree at the east end of the Wall. On the Palma side."

I paused where I stood.

"If you climb to its tallest branch and stretch as far as you can, you can just reach the top of the Wall. But it's a thin little branch—more of a twig, really—so you have to be light as a feather to make the climb. And nimble as a monkey, too. That's why most of the Vines are children."

"It must be terrifying," I said.

"It's not so bad if you don't look down. Especially if you've got someone down there, urging you on. It's better not to see what you're leaving behind."

"Did you have someone down there?"

"My mama," said Abi. "She was so sick by then she could barely hold herself upright. She knew she wouldn't be around much longer, and it was her last wish to send me over the Wall. So we trekked through the woods. I had to support her the whole way. We camped there, and I trained for days and days, sometimes falling so hard I thought I'd broken my skull. By the time I was ready, Mama was even more wasted away than when we'd started, brittle as a bunch of matchsticks. At the last minute, I refused to go. I stamped my feet and pitched a fit. Mama didn't raise her voice or anything—she couldn't. She just said, 'Please.' So up I went. And I didn't look down, not once. I would've lost my will."

"I'm so sorry, Abi." I pretended not to notice the tear that fell onto the delicate lace in her hands.

"I kept my eyes up," she said. "And the next day, a hot-air balloon came floating by. A green one. Something fell over the side, and I dove into a bush to hide. But what came fluttering down was a dress made of lovely blue linen."

"Mother," I whispered.

"Yes. Those balloons became the only bright spot in our lives, no matter what they brought. They meant someone was out there. Someone cared. The funny thing is, we all wished to see the yellow balloon more than any other, even though it wouldn't be bringing us food or clothes. Knowing the rebellion had begun is what we hoped for the most."

"And now you'll know," I said. "Everyone will."

I drove another metal rod into the belly of the furnace. With fire in my eyes, I watched it turn from solid steel into something I could bend.

# TOMORROW ANYTHING CAN HAPPEN

As the day of rebellion neared, my life flipped utterly upside down. At the hour when respectable Orenites were blowing out their candles, I was just getting started. I'd creep to the workshop and light the furnace, twisting molten metal until the sun came up—and, thankfully, getting better at it as the nights wore on. In the morning, I'd hitch a ride on a milk wagon back into town, tired, sweaty, and soot-covered, and drop like a stone onto the floor of Mulberry House.

With what little energy I had left after my trips to the forge, I worked alongside the other children—measuring, cutting, sewing, and fastening. If we wanted to be ready by Savior's Day, we needed every pair of hands we could get. If anyone was caught sitting idle, Roz would give them a needle, some thread, and a stern look, until every kid was busy toiling.

As we worked, the kids of Mulberry House taught me Palmerian rhymes I'd never heard before, and I sang them the traditional Lollyhill work songs Mother used to sing. They also passed the time trying to predict what we were making with all that metal and fabric, but Abi and I refused to give them any hints—not that we knew all the details of the rebellion's elaborate plan. We simply told them it was for Halston and Wren, and that was enough to convince them to help, even as they complained of numb and calloused fingers.

Abi buzzed around like a honey-drunk bee in those days, smiling for no reason and twirling her frilly skirts more than usual. She'd been spending more and more time at the dress-maker's shop, helping Jerrick with his part of the plan and using my scraps of rubber to create skirts with stretchy waistbands, which even impressed the old snoot himself. She started most of her sentences with "Jerrick says . . ." and wrinkled her nose when she saw the state of my clothes—littered with holes from the forge. "Just because the world thinks we're gutterpups," she said, "doesn't mean we have to dress like it." It's a wonder she didn't adopt a fake Tuleran accent and start smoking a pipe.

Neither of us dwelled on the things we'd recently learned about each other—that my mother was a rebel, that Abi was a Palmerian refugee—because there were far more pressing mat-ters to occupy us. We kept our eyes fixed on Savior's Day, and at last, its eve arrived. By then, most of the pieces were in place, but there was still one last thing to do. So Abi and I snuck to Jerrick's shop in the middle of the night, both of us drop-dead exhausted. We stood side by side, propped against each other, while Jerrick dragged a dressmaker's form into the center of his workroom with its back to us.

"Ta-da!" he said, spinning it around in his typical dramatic manner. Bleary-eyed and awestruck, we gaped at the queen's dress. Together, Abi and Jerrick had designed a glorious gown with layers of bustled yellow silk trimmed in lace and a dainty waist that billowed into a wide skirt that would sway like a bell when the queen walked in it.

"I can't believe it." Abi beamed. "My first real dress!"

"It's gorgeous," I breathed.

"Wait," said Jerrick. He crouched beside the headless form, fiddling with the final bits of ribbon and lace. "It's the details that separate a lady from a queen. Every last stitch must be perfect." He flounced the skirt once more and stepped back to examine it. "It's fabulous," he concluded. "Now I, for one, am ready to call it a night and catch up on my beauty sleep. If I'd known saving the kingdom would result in such ghastly undereye circles, I would've declined."

But Abi and I had revived at the sight of the dress. Abi whooped and twirled around the shop, her gossamer skirt floating around her. Then I joined in, round and round. When I was in motion, even my brown burlap sack somehow looked ethereal. Jerrick leaned back against his workbench, watching our celebration with an amused grin.

We'd done it. We'd actually done it. Our plan could still go wrong in a million different ways, ending in disaster for the rebellion, for the queen, and for all of us. But at least we were still in the fight. Laughter spilled from my throat, and tears leaked from the corners of my eyes. I lost my bearings, growing dizzy and light-headed. I felt like I could spin forever.

But I couldn't, of course.

I abruptly stopped when someone pounded on the back door, the one leading to the pristine alley. My bubbled-up dress floated back down to earth and settled against my legs. A booming voice rang out: "Royal Guard! Open up!"

The three of us flashed one another panicked looks. Our laughter had given us away, and it was too late to pretend nobody was there. Jerrick creaked the door open, and a soldier marched inside with brisk and confident steps. He ignored us at first, pacing the length of the room as though merely browsing, picking up this and that, muttering to himself. Abi and I stood with our heads down and our hands behind our backs, like scolded schoolchildren. But Jerrick slipped right into character, accent and all.

"Hello, sir, how can I help you this evening? Perhaps a splash of wine has left you in need of a cravat? One never knows when the need for a fine frock will arise."

"I'm not here for clothes," said the man. "I heard voices in your shop and found it rather odd, given the late hour. I thought I'd come check things out. An abnormality of this kind usually means laws are being broken. And I see I was correct in that assessment."

"I can assure you, sir, no laws are being broken here. I am merely working on a gown for Queen Catherine with my young assistants here."

"Oh, really?" said the man. He stepped closer to us. The floral scent of his laundry soap mingled with the stale beer on his breath. I held my nose. "Where do you live?" he asked Abi.

"Sir . . . ," began Jerrick.

"Silence!" he barked. "Let them answer."

"In the Slope," said Abi.

"With your parents?"

"Yes, sir."

"And you?"

"In Lollyhill," I said. "With my father."

"You're a long way from home."

"Yes, sir."

With an inscrutable "hmph," he kept pacing. If he intended to make us squirm, it was working. Finally, he spun on the heel of his polished boot to face Jerrick. "I know what's going on here," he said. "Don't think for a moment that you've got me fooled."

"Sir, I—I . . ." Jerrick fumbled for words, uncharacteristically stumped.

The soldier's stone face hovered just inches from Jerrick's reddening, sweaty one, and I held my breath. Then the soldier laughed. Oddly enough, a grinning soldier can be far scarier than an angry one. None of us knew how to react.

"Believe me," said the soldier, "I know what it's like to try to make a coin in this kingdom. Not so easy, even for a fancy shop owner. And the urchins from the children's home come so cheap. What are you paying them with? Plums?" He chuckled again and clapped Jerrick on the shoulder in a gesture of solidarity.

Jerrick, now in on the joke, responded in kind. "You get it, then! I give them a bag full of candies, and they work all night. How can I resist? Besides, look at their tiny fingers. They can make the most delicate stitches."

The soldier nodded. "I sympathize completely, my good man. But that doesn't change the fact that such practices are against the law. I'd be derelict in my duties if I didn't report this to my superiors. You understand?"

"But sir . . . can't you overlook this one minor infraction?"

"I'd like to, but King Michael feels quite strongly about such things. He's made it a priority to keep unwanted elements out of Oren." He gave Abi and me a cutting glance. "I'm afraid my hands are tied."

"You strike me as a reasonable man," crooned Jerrick. "There must be something we can do. Some arrangement we can make."

"But Mr. Jerrick, I'm afraid I can't be swayed by plums and candies, like a child."

"I'm sure I can offer something more to your liking," said Jerrick. "Are you a married man?"

"Of course. An upstanding family man."

"How would your lovely wife enjoy a dress as fine as this, made of the rarest, most expensive silks?" Jerrick motioned to the queen's ball gown.

The soldier stroked his chin. "I think she might. But then, I fear my daughter would be jealous, and that would make things very unpleasant for me."

"In that case, you'll need a matching pair!" said Jerrick. "Bring your girls in next week for a fitting. They'll feel like royalty the moment they step through that door, I assure you."

"That is too kind of you, Mr. Jerrick. Oh my, look at the hour! My shift is coming to an end. I'm afraid I won't have time to file any reports tonight. Just make sure this doesn't happen again, eh?"

"Of course not," said Jerrick, ushering the soldier out of the room. With a few more hearty claps on the back and a solid handshake, the man left the building.

When the clomp of his boots had faded, Abi collapsed onto a stool. Jerrick rubbed his tired eyes and moaned. Nobody spun or whooped.

Abi and I crept back to Mulberry House under cover of night.

My nerves were still tingling from our narrow escape, and my body hummed with excitement over the monumental thing we'd done, and were about to do. On the other hand, I was overcome by the need for sleep. I longed for my cramped patch of floor, to close my eyes at last.

But when I arrived home—to Mulberry House, that is—the children were wide-awake, dancing in the halls, gorging on sweets, and dressing up in the finest clothes the pot had to offer. Tomorrow was Savior's Day! Tomorrow was rebellion! Tomorrow anything could happen!

Sleep didn't stand a chance in the face of all that.

# A HEAP OF COLORFUL RUBBISH

Jerrick clambered over the cobblestones with a ball gown shoved into the belly of a wheelbarrow. Normally, the queen would send a lavish carriage for the dressmaker and his creation—as Jerrick had taken great pleasure in informing us—and he'd conduct a final fitting at the palace, in the queen's chamber. This time, however, he'd received a different set of instructions. Apparently, the king had forbidden all vehicles in and out of the palace grounds, after a recent incident at the prison.

Abi and I spied from across the street as Jerrick struggled with the wheelbarrow, cursing when its wheels got caught in the grooves of the road, then cursing harder when it burst free and crashed into him, knocking him over like a bowling pin. When he stood back up, a dark splotch of dirt coated the rear of his tweed trousers. Jerrick made matters worse by spinning in the center of the road to assess the damage, like a dog chasing on its own tail. The soldiers posted at the palace gate nudged one another and pointed. Even Abi and I had to muffle our giggles. Jerrick's face turned a deep radish red, but he valiantly stiffened his lip and wheeled our dress toward the guards, in spite of their heckles.

"Well, well, well," said the first soldier, burly and mustached. "If it isn't Mr. Fancy Pants."

"His pants don't look so fancy now, do they?" laughed the other, scrawny and hairless. "Where's your carriage, Mr. Jerk?"

"It's *Jerrick,*" said Jerrick, dropping the handles of the wheelbarrow, throwing his shoulders back, and jutting his chin outward. "It seems the royal carriage is indisposed. But carriage or not, the queen needs her ball gown with all due haste for today's festivities. Now, if you'll please step aside, gentlemen."

"Are you pulling my leg?" asked the burly one, peering down at the bright bundle of material. "She's gonna *wear* that?"

"I can assure you, this is the latest fashion," spat Jerrick. "My designs are not meant to be piled up in wheelbarrows, like manure."

"I'll never understand women," said the scrawny one, shaking his head at the colorful heap.

"I think they'll manage without your understanding," said Jerrick, grasping the handles again. "Now, if you please . . ."

"I'll bring it to her," said the burly one, placing his bulk in Jerrick's path.

"Her Majesty insists that I deliver her dresses personally," said Jerrick.

"It's not up to her," snapped the guard. "Nobody's permitted to see the queen. King's orders."

"Whyever not? I'm always permitted to see the queen."

"We dunno," said the scrawny one. "Marital spat, I guess."

"Shut up!" the burly guard growled at his companion.

"That's just what I heard," said the scrawny one with a shrug.

"We don't need to hear what you heard!" roared the burly one. "Now let's inspect the goods." He elbowed Jerrick aside and reached into the wheelbarrow.

"I wouldn't do that if I were you," warned Jerrick.

"Why, whatcha got in here? A bayonet?" The guards shook with laughter.

"You'll see," said Jerrick.

The burly one lifted an edge of lace with pinched fingers.

"Big mistake," said Jerrick.

The guard lifted the lace higher, until it was at eye level. "Whaddaya suppose this is?" he asked, squinting at the tucked fabric and billows of silk. Then his eyes widened as it dawned on him. He dropped the garment as if it were, in fact, the sharp edge of a bayonet.

"The queen's pantaloons," said Jerrick. "How do you think King Michael would feel about you pawing through the queen's undergarments?"

The scrawny one doubled over with laughter.

"Take this to the queen!" the burly one barked to his companion. "And don't touch it!"

I beamed. Putting the pantaloons on top of the pile had been my idea. Jerrick looked back at me and winked.

"I guess our work here is done," said Abi, as we watched our dress rumble through the palace gates, on its way to the queen.

"What are you going to do now?" I asked.

"All the shops in Silk Valley will be unattended while everyone heads to the celebration," she said with a mischievous grin. "I'm gonna check for unlocked doors."

"You're impossible."

"Thanks."

"Once again, that's not a compliment."

"Says you. What are you going to do before the festivities?"

"I have to go back to Lollyhill." I sighed. "I have something to take care of."

"Oh," said Abi with a sympathetic smile. "Good luck."

"Thanks. Good luck with those unlocked doors."

"Speaking of stolen property," said Abi, "it's about time I gave you this." She began to unwind the scarf from around her head.

"Actually, will you hold on to it a little longer?" I said. "I can't go shoving it back into an oak tree at this point. Besides, it looks good on you."

"Yeah, I think so, too," said Abi, retying it in her hair. "See you at Savior's . . . I mean, Traitor's Gate?"

"Yeah, but how will I find you?" I asked. "The place will be packed."

"Don't worry, Gumdrop," she said, skipping off. "*I'll* find *you.*"

# WHO CARES ABOUT A FROCK?

*The scrawny man who entered Catherine's chamber wouldn't make eye contact. As queen, she was used to people avoiding her gaze, but his face was a shade of red normally reserved for tomatoes at the peak of a Palmerian summer.*

*"I've got your dress 'ere, Your Majesty. And your . . . um . . ." Without completing his sentence, he rolled a wheelbarrow into the room. The kind used by gardeners. Not, to Catherine's knowledge, by dressmakers.*

*"Are you sure that's it?" she asked.*

*"I—uh . . . well, no . . . I didn't . . . I wouldn't dream of . . . I'm told it's a dress."*

*"All right, then. Leave it over there." She waved toward the wardrobe. Try as she might, she couldn't bring herself to care in the least about a frock. She could step onto the Wall in her pantaloons, for all she cared.*

*The royal presentation would take place on top of Savior's Gate, one hundred feet up, where Michael would parade her in front of his adoring fans. On the Oren side of the Wall, people would cheer for the ruler who had brought them prosperity and security by defeating the brutal Palmerians. On the Palma side of the Wall, the echoes of that celebration would only serve to taunt those who had been robbed and starved and left for dead by that same ruler.*

*And then there was the matter of General Sorkin's sudden return. Over the last few days, Catherine had spied his men from her window—scores of them traipsing the palace grounds. It seemed there wasn't an Orenite soldier left in Palma, which didn't bode well for the rebellion. Halston's ragtag forces were already outmatched by the Royal Army. With additional soldiers back from Palma, they wouldn't stand a chance, especially since they no longer had a signal to trigger Halston's attack. On top of all that, it seemed Michael had a deadly new weapon at his disposal. In other words, their plans for the rebellion were unraveling, and their chances of success had gone from small to nonexistent.*

*So what did it matter what she was wearing?*

*A rap at the door startled her out of her thoughts.*

*"Breakfast, Your Majesty," Greta announced, entering without waiting for an invitation. The china, embossed in gold with Catherine's family seal, rattled on the tray. Catherine was almost impressed by her former maid. The nerve it must take to commit the ultimate betrayal and then arrive with tea and biscuits. But Greta did exactly that without batting a pale-blond eyelash.*

*"Go away," said Catherine.*

*"Yes, ma'am. Would you like me to dress you for the ceremony?"*

*"I'd sooner jam hot coals into my eye sockets."*

*"Very good, ma'am. And will you be wanting supper when you return from the festivities?"*

*"I don't intend to return," said Catherine.*

*"As you wish, ma'am," said Greta, unfazed. Catherine briefly glanced up and noticed Greta had acquired a new brooch, heavy*

*with jewels, pinned conspicuously to the collar of her uniform. A gift from the king, no doubt.*

*The maid's footsteps receded down the hall, and Catherine rose and stretched like a cat. She had grown so used to lying around and doing nothing that her body ached with the movement.*

*She glanced into the wheelbarrow. Her "dress" was a wrinkled crumple of color. It wasn't lovingly laid out for her, as Jerrick would normally do. And that wasn't the only unusual thing about it. Catherine thrust her hands into the wheelbarrow and felt something buried in the fabric, something unexpected. Jerrick hadn't just delivered a dress, the clever old cad. He'd delivered something far more exciting.*

*It even had a helpful pair of pockets.*

# GHOSTS IN THE MILL

The ghosts in the mill were working furiously when I poked my head inside on the blustery morning of Savior's Day. "Father?" I whispered, my voice echoing through the empty room. "Father?"

I took a few cautious steps inside. When there was no sign of him, the possibilities sprang vividly before my eyes. Maybe the Royal Guard had searched the mill and found him, weak and crippled by obedience, refusing to hide. Maybe they'd dragged him back to prison. Or maybe he'd had a row with the Fletchers. Maybe he'd stormed off, seething with disappointment in me. Maybe I'd never see him again.

But then, out of the shadows, he materialized, quiet and somber and barely more than a shadow himself. Another ghost.

"Father," I said. "Are you well?" His face was pale and drawn, but some of the flesh had returned to his bones. His hair and beard had been washed and trimmed. The Fletchers were taking care of him.

Father wouldn't answer or look at me. He sat down heavily on a bale of hay and twisted a piece of it around his finger.

"It's Savior's Day," I said, stepping closer to him. He smelled like soap, a far cry from his scent the last time I'd seen him. "We're making our first strike against the king."

"We?" muttered Father.

"Don't worry, I'm not involved in the fighting. I've been helping in the most unexpected way. I—I was hoping you'd come with me today, so I can show you what I've done. I made something special, something you'd be proud of. Will you come?"

"I can't, Prismena. I'm a fugitive, remember?"

"You can wear a cloak. I'm sure Mr. Fletcher has something—"

"No," he said. The word hung in the air between us, like the clouds of smoke our breath made in the frigid building.

"I'm sorry," I said. "I know I've hurt you and disobeyed you. I know I'm not the person you thought I was. But I hope you can find it in your heart to love the person I am now."

His shoulders slumped further, and he focused on the brittle piece of hay in his hands.

"I think Mother would have wanted me to do this," I said.

"Just go," he said.

I moved toward the door, toward the fierce winds that blew outside, with an icy ache in my heart.

"Prissy . . . wait," he said softly, his voice hitching on my name. I turned. "I don't want you to do this, and I won't pretend otherwise." He sucked in a deep breath. "But I've never doubted that you *could* do it. Not for a second."

My throat constricted, and my chest welled up with all the emotions that had lodged there over the last few days. I wanted to run over to Father, to bury my face in his shirt and stay there. To let the rebellion happen without me.

But then the door to the mill swung open, and a little girl—disheveled and breathless—appeared on the other side.

"Roz?" I said. "What are you doing here?"

"Halston told me to fetch you. The Royal Guard found us, Prissy. There was a raid on Mulberry House."

"What?" I gasped. "Is everyone all right?"

"No. They attacked at first light. Everyone was runnin' and shoutin'. Some kids sent for Halston, and he held the soldiers off." Her voice shook. She looked so young, all of her brash confidence gone. "By the end of it, lots of kids were hurt."

"What about Cole?"

"Nobody can find him. The rest of us took shelter at the Dead Man's Trough. I'm to bring you there."

I glanced back at Father.

He shook his head.

I didn't know what else to say to him.

I ran.

I didn't ask Roz where she got the wagon that whisked us through the streets of Oren. With everyone gathered in the South for Savior's Day, the heart of the kingdom was deserted. We stopped in Market Square, several blocks away from the pub, and made sure we weren't followed before we barreled down the alley beside the Dead Man's Trough. The scarred alley-keeper grunted at me but let us pass.

We burst into Halston's office, and the bitter scent of blood flooded my nostrils and turned my stomach. Kids, all of them banged-up, bruised, and bleeding, packed the room, slumped against the walls. They were moaning and whimpering; some of them were crying. In the center of it all, Gruber moved with the same agility he'd shown in the kitchen, only this time his instruments were bloody rags and bandages. "Keep the pressure on," he called over his shoulder, "and wrap it up tight."

Marybeth was standing over the rickety table, speaking to someone splayed out there. Her face was splotchy and red. "You can't fight in this condition," she was saying.

"You're right," croaked the boy on the table. "The fight will go on without me."

"Halston?" I whispered. I hadn't recognized him until he spoke. His tan skin was drained of color, his dimpled cheeks slack.

"But, Hal, we can't do this without you," Marybeth went on.

"Of course you can," he said. "This was never about *me.* It was always about the cause. Now, tell me, did you make the final delivery?"

"Yes," said Marybeth, sniffling. "I handed it off last night."

"Good, then we move ahead as planned. This is what we've been working for. What you risked your life for. Don't let it go to waste. Make sure they finish the job."

Marybeth nodded, tears glistening in her eyes.

"Is Prismena here?" he asked, lifting his head with difficulty.

"I am," I said, stepping toward him. Up close, I saw that his face was twisted in pain, his hair matted with blood and dirt. Gruber approached him from the other side and pressed down on the dressing wrapped around his abdomen. A bright-red splotch was quickly blooming through it.

"Halston, you're hurt," I breathed, growing light-headed at the sight of him. "You need to rest."

"Ah, this is nothing," he said. He tried to smile, but the effort made him grimace instead. "Is the signal ready to go?"

I nodded.

"Good," he said. "It has to fly today. This whole operation depends upon it. King Michael is plotting something, so we must be ready. Everything must go according to plan." He paused to catch his breath. "Where's your partner in crime?"

"Abi went to Silk Valley," I said. "To . . . steal things."

Halston attempted a chuckle. "That's Abi for you. I need you to give her a message for me, all right? Tell her she was always my best soldier. I know she thinks I underestimated her, but she's wrong. She was the only one I trusted with Cole."

"You can tell her yourself," I said. "When all this is over."

"I know, but . . . just in case. Promise?"

I nodded again. I wasn't sure I was capable of speech.

"And one more thing. I need you to . . ." He clenched his teeth in anguish as Gruber pressed down harder on his wound. When the pain subsided, he continued. "I need you to find Cole and keep him safe. He trusts you."

"Of course," I said, biting my lip to keep from crying.

"This is no time for tears," said Halston. "I'm going to be fine. I've got the best medical team in Oren." He gave Gruber a wink and let his head sink back against the table. His eyelids dipped low, almost closing. "Prismena, do you remember the day we met?"

"Y-yes, Hal." Now I knew he was delirious. We'd met only days earlier, in that very room.

"Not last week," he said, reading my thoughts. He focused on the ceiling, as if watching an entirely different scene unfold there. A better one, I hoped. "It was over three years ago. You came to the market with your mother. She came to my stall."

The memory came flooding back. Mother buying apples from a boy with deep dimples. *That's* where I recognized him from.

"You were looking at the watchmaker's trinkets," Halston said, "so you didn't notice when your mother handed me something. She gave me a peach pit, in the shape of a bird. She met my brother on one of her trips to Palma. She told me he was alive. And somehow married to the queen! Expecting a baby."

So that's how the peach pit got from our mantel to Cole's pocket. It was a message, passed by a balloonist from one brother to another.

"Your mother gave my brother back to me," he said softly, through dry lips, "even though I never saw him again. She told me he was happy. Then I knew his choice had been worth it. I knew . . ." His voice was a mere wisp now. I had to lean close to his mouth to hear the words. Gruber stood on Halston's other side, still holding the rags in place, with tears shining in his eyes. "I had a nephew. I had . . . something . . . to fight for."

He opened his mouth to say something else, but I shook my head. He was too weak.

"You did the same for me," I said. "You gave my mother back to me. I didn't really know her until you and Abi found me. Thank you."

The merest hint of a smile passed over his lips before he closed his eyes.

"Go on, now," said Gruber, wiping away a tear. "Go find the prince."

# SAVIOR'S DAY

From the richest noblemen to the humblest tradesmen, everyone in Oren turned up for the Savior's Day celebration. Savior's Gate was strung with banners, and the broad cobblestone square in front of it was packed with people. Vendors were lined up around the perimeter, peddling cotton candy, sugared nuts, and giant turkey legs. Musicians, magicians, sword swallowers, and jesters roamed the street, entertaining people for spare change.

How was I possibly going to find one little boy in the middle of all that?

I worked my way methodically through the crowd, keeping my eyes at three-year-old level. I spotted every manner of toddler—chubby-cheeked and gaunt, doted on by parents and bounding along alone, gorging on candy and picking pockets—but none of them was Cole. I scanned the people gaping at the fire-breather and those waiting in line to be lifted by the strongman. I scrutinized the faces mesmerized by the mind reader. Still no Cole. Several kids from Mulberry House greeted me with knowing winks, but none of them had seen Cole. Nobody had.

"Prissy?" someone cried out to me. I turned and saw Guernsey, our clumsy pilot and secret rebel, weaving toward me. Before I could respond, he wrapped me in a hug. I'd been wrong about Guernsey—his sloppy flying had actually been a series of detours taken for the cause—but I didn't have time to make amends now. I had to find Cole. "Thank you," he said as I squirmed out of his grasp.

"Thank *me*? For what?"

"For saving me." He looked like he wanted to hug me again, but he restrained himself. I'd almost forgotten that Guernsey had been arrested for treason, like Father. He must've been one of the dirt-covered men in the prison that day, but I hadn't recognized him.

"You're welcome," I said.

"I've got something for you." He removed a string from around his neck, with a shiny, skull-shaped key dangling from it. "The kids in the prison cellar got out. All of them. Because of you." He placed the key around my neck, and I clasped the cool metal in my hand.

Then, over Guernsey's shoulder, a tent caught my eye. In it, a troupe of actors was performing a pantomime, reenacting King Michael's most famous feat: charging into Palma and rescuing the queen. Rescuing Queen Mama.

With a hasty apology, I pushed past Guernsey and made my way to the makeshift stage. A gentleman with three days' worth of facial hair was impersonating the queen, in a shimmering gown and a sparkly crown, cooing about the bravery of King Michael. Cole didn't seem fazed by this hairy imitation of his mother. He stood front and center with an amused grin, clapping his pudgy hands. I relaxed at the sight of him there, happy and safe. I started toward him.

"We meet again," said a gravelly voice behind me. I recognized it instantly, and a shiver skittered up my spine. I turned around and came face to face with the soldier who'd discovered us in the dress shop the night before, the one who'd blackmailed Jerrick. "I was hoping I'd run into you again," he said.

"Why?" I asked. My eyes darted back to Cole, still smiling at the novelties all around him. I was determined not to lose sight of him.

"My superior officers were impressed when I led them to Mrs. Mulberry's School of Music," the soldier said. "But I never would've found it without you and your little friend. I owe you my thanks."

"Wh-what?" I stammered. "I don't understand."

"Sure you do," he said, a wicked smirk spreading over his face.

And then, suddenly, I did understand. And it gutted me.

He'd followed us home the night before. That's why he let us go so easily—not to secure a pair of dresses, but so he could find out where we lived. We'd led him straight to Mulberry House. To Halston. I started to tremble.

"I see you get it now," he said. "Lucky for you, you have one more opportunity to do your civic duty. I'm looking for a little boy. A relation of the queen apparently, with a crimp in his ear just like hers. The king is offering a hefty reward for whoever finds him. And since I'm on a winning streak . . ."

My heart seized up. "I don't know any little boys," I said. But my traitorous eyes sought out Cole again, instinctively.

"Is that so?" whispered the guard. He cast his eyes in the same direction as mine, fixing them on Cole. "What about that one?"

"That little urchin? I don't know him."

"I can always tell when people are lying," said the soldier. "It's an important skill in my line of work." His hand landed heavily on my shoulder, holding me in place. "Now, if I rush for the boy, I'll scare him off. He'll disappear into the crowd faster than I can blink. I need you to call him over here. Do that, and I'll let you go. Then you can crawl back into the gutter you crawled out of. I only want the boy."

He squeezed my shoulder, and his fingertips dug into my skin. I couldn't move.

"It's you or the boy," he whispered. "It's up to you."

I heard Father's voice in my head telling me this wasn't my fight. I heard Mother's voice, too, urging me to save Cole just like she had. I saw a little boy who'd come to trust me, alone in a vast crowd. I felt the hot breath of the soldier on my neck. And I spotted something shimmering out of the corner of my eye.

"A-all right," I said. "I'll call him over." I took a deep breath and cried out to Cole. At the sound of my voice, he looked around and spotted me. His face lit up.

The soldier smiled, too.

Cole weaved around people's legs to get to me.

The soldier released me and reached out toward the boy.

Then the crowd surged forward and issued a rousing cheer. There was movement up on the Wall. It had begun.

# THE KING'S ANNOUNCEMENT

*After what felt like an endless climb, Catherine emerged on top of the Wall. The view from that height humbled her. Above her stretched an endless sky. Below, a sea of people—a moving, breathing mass of indistinguishable specks. She thought about Cole among that throng, one of the tiny blobs of color looking up at her tiny blob of color. It made her happy to think of him down there. And sad, too.*

*She glanced over her shoulder at the Palma side. Nothing stirred in the woods, but she knew they were there. Waiting for the signal. The king roughly grabbed her arm and turned her attention back to Oren. As custom dictates, she stood behind him in the procession. She was followed by General Sorkin, whom she'd not had the strength to look in the eye. He probably took great joy in having broken her, but today that would come to an end—one way or another.*

*She walked against a punishing, howling wind that she feared might pick her up and carry her off. It stung her face, but Michael didn't seem the least bit ruffled. He smiled a big openmouthed smile and swept his arm in a wide arc over his head, waving to the whole kingdom at once. He basked in the roar of the crowd below, as if it were producing a heat that warmed him.*

*Nobody paid any attention when Catherine dropped her gray wool cloak and revealed the dress beneath. The hoop of the skirt extended several feet in either direction, which made walking—and climbing steps—difficult. The bell shape made it look buoyant, but to the wearer, it was heavy and clunky. To make matters worse, it had a cape hanging off the shoulders, an extra stretch of fabric that was prone to being stepped on by the black boots of soldiers. It's true what they say about the price of beauty. Jerrick had produced a stunning but rather annoying dress.*

*Once they took their places, the ceremony began. A line of men in purple uniforms marched onto the Wall's ledge in perfect formation. In unison, they lifted shiny gold trumpets to their lips and blared a bold and patriotic song. The crowd cheered. People danced in the streets, kicking up their heels and whisking loved ones into their arms. The kingdom rejoiced, but the festive mood unsettled Queen Catherine. The brash notes of the trumpets sounded to her ears like a wailing alarm, like a warning.*

*When the musicians had finished, another group filed in to replace them. These men held similar metal tubes, but instead of music, they propelled small glimmering objects into the sky. The onlookers fell silent and craned their necks back to see what was drifting toward them. Based on the hollers of appreciation below, Catherine guessed that it was candy. It takes so little to bribe a kingdom. Michael returned to the edge of the Wall to lap up the cheers of his subjects. Catherine had to restrain herself from breaking ranks and shoving him, letting him fall right into the arms of his adoring fans.*

*Finally, the moment people had been waiting for arrived. The king stepped up to the platform. "Citizens of Oren," he said. "Please join me in celebrating this most joyous of all days! Not only is this the anniversary of the day I laid the final stone on the Wall and brought security to our kingdom, it is also the day I bring you peace. Today, I am thrilled to announce that the war with Palma is officially over!"*

# A DARK SHADOW IS CAST

Everyone stared with rapt attention at the royal family above us. They danced when the trumpeters played; they cheered when sweets came falling from the sky. Then they roared when King Michael addressed them directly. But all I could focus on was Cole, rushing right into the arms of a soldier.

"Prissy!" squealed Cole, a trusting smile on his grubby face.

The soldier stepped in front of me to intercept the boy. But just as his hands were closing in on Cole, the man suddenly lost his balance. He toppled over, face-first, like a felled tree. People in the crowd leaped back so he wouldn't collide with their legs. He squirmed on the cobblestones like a caught fish, much to the amusement of onlookers. His ankles had been bound together with something shimmery and colorful—a familiar silk scarf.

"I guess my babysitting duties aren't done after all," smirked Abi, crouching near the soldier's feet. "What would you do without me, Prismena?"

"Do you really want me to answer that?" I said, pulling her up by the forearm. She paused to adjust her Savior's Day outfit—three tulle skirts in red, blue, and yellow (the colors of the Oren flag). I rolled my eyes. "Let's get out of here before he recovers."

"But the scarf—"

"Leave it," I said. "That thing has gotten me into enough trouble already." We grabbed Cole and ducked into the crowd, letting its current carry us away from the angry soldier. Hopefully, his fancy new scarf would be a distracting consolation prize.

"Wait," said Abi, pausing. "Listen."

"I am thrilled to announce that the war with Palma is officially over!" said King Michael, his voice spilling over the crowd.

"Did you hear that?" I gasped. "The war is over! Do you know what that means, Abi? We don't need a rebellion now! We don't need a signal!"

"No," said Abi, her face darkening. "Just the opposite. Good news from King Michael is never good news. It always means he has worse things in store."

As she said it, the people around us began to titter and nudge one another, pointing to something behind us. We turned as a gigantic wooden structure on wheels slowly moved into the center of the square, parting the crowd. It was being pushed by what looked like an entire battalion of soldiers, flanking either side of it. Its wheels groaned under the tremendous weight of a platform. Ropes attached to each of the platform's four corners restrained a massive balloon, fully inflated, in dark royal purple. It was the largest hot-air balloon I'd ever seen. And it cast its dark shadow over all of us.

# A WEAPON TO END THE WAR

*Catherine had to give Michael credit—wheeling a hot-air balloon into the middle of the crowd was a shrewd move. Balloons were lovely and bright. Nobody ever associated them with war. As the people marveled at the royal vessel in their presence, Catherine's stomach sank. The rebellion needed the people's support in order to succeed. But the people loved a good show.*

*"Citizens of Oren," the king continued, "what you see before you is more than just a hot-air balloon. What you see before you is a symbol of freedom! This balloon is going to end the war!"*

*Confused murmurs drifted up from below.*

*"I know you're wondering how that can be possible. You may have heard rumors of a powerful substance developed by the Palmerians, known as Black Powder. I regret to inform you that those rumors are true. The Palmerians have used Black Powder to build a weapon with the capability to destroy entire cities—even strong enough to blast through the Wall."*

*His words roused terrified screams and angry shouts from the crowd.*

*"But you needn't fear! We are going to beat the Palmerians at their own game. I have developed a weapon of my own—an un-*

*rivaled weapon called a bomb that will drop Black Powder directly on enemy sites. And this balloon is going to deliver it! It will teach them that Oren is not to be trifled with! We will win the war once and for all!"*

*Riotous applause erupted. Michael stepped to the edge of the Wall, where his subjects' exuberant gratitude rose up to meet him.*

*And now his schemes made sense. He didn't recall the soldiers from Palma so they could fight the rebellion. He did it to spare them, to clear them out of Palma before he destroyed it. Catherine had to stop him. It was her turn. She walked to the ledge with shaky steps.*

*"People of Oren," she said. Her voice wafted through the air, but nobody cheered for her. She closed her eyes and sucked in a breath. She was supposed to recite a list of clichés about loyalty and bravery and the king's surpassing brilliance. But this was her chance—her only chance—to tell Oren the truth. Would they think her mad, even if she spoke honestly at last? Would they listen, or shout her down? Would she have enough time to convince them before the Royal Guard ran for her?*

*She could stick to the script, or she could start a rebellion.*

*She cleared her throat. She opened her mouth to speak.*

# A DUET WITH THE QUEEN

"He's going to drop weapons from the sky!" said Abi, her face ashen. "He's going to destroy what's left of Palma, and they won't even see it coming! They won't be able to stop it!"

"But *we* can stop it," I said. "This isn't over yet."

"We've got to send the signal," said Abi, reaching for the satchel slung over her shoulder. "Now!"

"Not yet," I said, stopping her hand. "It starts with *her*."

We both looked up at the Wren, standing on the Wall in the yellow dress we'd made. I was too nervous to delight in the fact that the queen of Oren was decked out in our creation. I was too nervous to do much of anything but clutch Cole and stare up at her.

And then the queen's voice, crisp and loud, rang out over the crowd.

*"King Michael is a traitor!"*

---

*The soldiers on the Wall didn't react at first. Some of them weren't listening, expecting the usual platitudes. Others were confused, wondering if this was all part of the show. But Catherine knew their inaction wouldn't last long.*

*She spoke quickly, the words gushing from her mouth like blood from a wound: "King Michael is not the savior of Oren! For years, he has told you nothing but lies. Starting with this." She slid her hand into her pocket and produced the marriage certificate. "With this paper, Michael claimed the throne, but it is a forgery! We were never legally wed. The throne of Oren belongs to me alone. And he lied about my kidnapping. I was never a prisoner in Palma—I was happy there, with a husband and a son—yes, the rightful heir to the throne! It was Michael who waged war on the innocent people of Palma, not the other way around. The Palmerians have no weapon. He's using your own fear to manipulate you!*

*"Most of you think me mad, but I can assure you that I have all my wits about me, and I can prove the truth of my claims!" She waved the false marriage certificate over her head. "Do not let him fly that balloon! Do not let him destroy an innocent kingdom full of innocent people because of a lie! Do not let him put blood on your hands!"*

---

She did it. The queen spoke the truth, and everyone was momentarily stunned by it. It was as if she'd frozen time at that instant. People stopped talking. Children stopped fussing. Vendors stopped hawking their goods. Even the royal guardsmen sprinkled throughout the crowd—hunting for the boy with the crimped ear—turned their attention to the drama unfolding onstage.

For a few seconds anyway.

Once the shock and confusion passed, everyone started talking at once. People checked with their neighbors to make sure they'd heard correctly. The royal guardsmen remembered who they worked for and started pushing through the crowd, more intent than ever on finding the lost boy, whose value had suddenly become clear.

One soldier in particular chucked people out of his way to clear a path to Abi, Cole, and me, twisting Mother's silk scarf in his clenched fists. "Did you think you could stop me?" he growled. "Did you really think a bunch of kids could outmatch me?" He grabbed Abi and me by our wrists and, in one quick jerk, pried us away from the cowering Cole. He tossed us aside like banana peels and yanked Cole up by the hair. The little boy bawled and fought, but he couldn't break away.

"No," I cried, beating at the man's chest with my fists. "No, no, no, no." The word bubbled up and out of me, over and over, the only word that I could manage. *No, no, no, no, no.*

---

*By the time the last words had escaped Catherine's lips, the king's men were upon her. "Get her!" cried Michael, his face a mask of sputtering rage. The two nearest soldiers unsheathed their swords and crept toward her slowly, as one would approach an escaped animal that might get spooked. Catherine moved away from them, closer to the ledge of the Wall.*

*"Stop right there!" demanded one of them.*

*"You've got nowhere to run," said another.*

*He was right. The heel of her left shoe inched dangerously near the edge.*

*"Come with us, Your Majesty," said the first soldier, extending his hand. His tone was softer now, as if he were speaking to a child.*

*Catherine knew they wanted to arrest her, not send her toppling off the Wall. How would it look for the king if his guards drove the queen to her death in front of the entire kingdom on Savior's Day?*

*"You'll be fine," the soldier said. "You won't be in any trouble."*

*That was a lie, of course. Catherine knew Michael well enough to know precisely what sort of trouble she'd be in.*

*Her left foot slipped. For a split second, it flailed out into the open air before she pulled it back onto the solid stone and steadied herself. In that instant, her stomach dropped with the sickening sensation of falling. The crowd below her gasped and then went quiet—eerily quiet—as if they were all holding their breath at once.*

*The soldiers came closer.*

*Catherine reached into her pockets with both hands. All she had to do was . . .*

*"Don't move!" yelled the officer.*

*His voice startled her. Her left foot slipped away from the Wall again, but this time she didn't catch herself. This time, she fell.*

*In that moment of free fall, Catherine's world spun out of control. Up and down, ground and sky, friend and foe—it all collided. All those little specks below violently whirling. The wind tore her hair loose and whipped it into a wild froth. She heard panicked screams from below and above—from everywhere. In her pockets, she felt the cold, comforting touch of metal against her palms. She held it tight. And then her plummet was met with a sudden jolt that rattled her bones.*

---

I screamed, just like everyone else. It wasn't supposed to happen like this. She wasn't supposed to be a bright-yellow streak in the sky, dropping like a rock. I was supposed to save her. I squeezed my eyes shut.

"What's that?" cried someone in the crowd.

Someone else gasped—but not in fear. In awe.

I cracked my eyes open and saw a flash of silver.

And another.

Two spindly metal arms sprang from the waist of the queen's dress—the retractable rods I'd hidden in the lining. They were attached to the billowy cape, which stretched over her head, trapping the air. The queen was suddenly suspended, as though someone had caught her by the scruff of the neck.

The dress's fabric was balloon-grade, made of *Goldilocks* herself. It could withstand the high winds and speeds of a fall without tearing. And the cage underneath—the ladder of steel hoops that kept the garment's shape—wasn't the traditional whalebone. It was made of steel, forged during my late nights in the workshop. It was solid, ready for flight.

The queen was a bright-yellow bubble drifting to earth, the signal the rebellion had been waiting for.

Along with all of Oren, I gazed up at her in wonder. She'd been falling, and now she was flying.

But it was far from over. The queen's descent was only the first part of the plan.

"Now," I cried.

---

*When Catherine next opened her eyes, she was floating in midair. The crowd beneath her was near enough that she could make out their faces. Their fear had turned to awe. Most of them were cheering or smiling, reactions the Mad Queen wasn't accustomed to. A few purple coats weaved through the crowd, trying to pinpoint where she'd land. Their faces wore hard scowls. But they were outnumbered.*

*Her high-heeled shoes slid off her feet and cartwheeled to the ground. People clambered after them as though they were jewel-encrusted. The wind that had buffeted her was gentle now, cradling her on her way to the ground. She wouldn't have minded staying there, suspended between the rage above and the chaos below. For she knew this wasn't the end of their fight. It was just the beginning.*

*A single voice in the crowd shouted, "Now!"*

---

"Hey, mister!" said Abi, tugging at the soldier's arm. He still held Cole with the other.

"Go away!" he barked, swatting at her like she was a mosquito. But he must have noticed the object in her hands, which looked like a bright-yellow ball the size of a cantaloupe, because he turned back with a furrowed brow. "What is that?"

"Watch," she said. She flung the thing into the air, but it didn't come back down as it should have. It kept floating, higher and higher.

"What on earth . . . ?" said the soldier, his eyes tracing the path of the steadily rising yellow object.

"Yellow for the rising sun," said Abi. "It has begun."

*"What?"* he roared. He didn't know what any of it meant, but he was smart enough to realize it meant *something.*

In fact, the thing gaining height in the sky was one of the lanterns we'd built over the last few days, the ones that had made us cross-eyed and turned our fingers into pincushions. As it rose, the soldier hesitated, looking from Cole to Abi to the lantern. Finally, reluctantly, he shoved Cole to the ground, placing a boot firmly on the boy's chest to keep him in place. Then he removed his sword from its sheath and began to swing at the lantern with its blade.

He couldn't dislodge it from the sky. That little yellow beacon rose well above the crowd, where it joined the others. Hundreds of them. A whole skyful.

At my command, children had emerged from under the bleachers, from darkened alleyways, from every shadowy hiding place. They had streamed out into the light, growing bolder as their number increased. And their small, dirty hands launched the yellow lanterns, flooding the sky and dyeing it *Goldilocks* yellow. Soon the lanterns would top the Wall. Soon the signal to start the rebellion would be visible for miles. A rising sun to usher in a brand new day. A rising son to reclaim the throne from the usurper. A signal that was just like them—fragile and formidable all at once.

With a roar, the soldier holding Cole started leaping for the lanterns and swatting them out of the air with his bare hands. He knocked a few of them down, sending the limp packets and their expired candles to the ground. But they were quickly replaced by new ones. And while he was doing this, Cole rolled out from under the big black boot. He rushed to Abi and me, and we ran, all the while clinging fiercely together, like three broken pieces of something finally made whole.

---

*As if this moment could get any more surreal, Catherine sank into a sea of tiny balloons that matched her dress. She gently kicked them as she descended, and they bobbed out of her way, floating past her on their way up to the clouds.*

*The wind pushed her toward a copse of pine trees, and the reaching treetops scratched at the soles of her bare feet. She jerked the metal bars of her contraption to steer away from them, but the branches tore at her dress and their prickly needles held her in place. People scampered into the trees to untangle her and lower her to the ground.*

*She was disheveled, her dress tattered. She hadn't made the graceful entrance she would've preferred, but nobody seemed to mind. The people swallowed her up and shielded her from the Royal Guard, using their own bodies to protect her. Then they began a chant she'd never heard before, but one she quite liked the sound of: "Long live the queen!"*

---

The first time I'd seen Queen Catherine part a crowd, she'd been impeccably dressed, surrounded by soldiers, and tossing disdainful glares at her subjects. This time, her escorts were farmers, tailors, and produce sellers. Hands reached out to her, and she clasped all that she could. She smiled, though her chest still heaved for breath. Her hair was wild and windswept, her dress shredded, her cheeks flush with adrenaline. She'd never looked more beautiful.

I lifted Cole onto my shoulders, his legs dangling around my neck. "Mama!" he cried. Abi and I joined in, screaming and jumping up and down. Our cries blended into the general mayhem of the crowd, as people released their voices into the sky. Whether they believed the queen's words or not, they'd just seen her jump off the Wall and survive. That alone deserved a celebration.

Queen Catherine spotted us, and recognition lit her face. The beginnings of tears clung to her lashes and made her eyes glisten. With the aid of the crowd, she glided toward us. She reached out to her son. Cole held up his chubby arms.

But before the queen could get to him, the first explosion rang out, like the crack of a giant whip. Like hot oil popping on a skillet, only ten times louder. The stones beneath our feet rattled. The sky bloomed with bright tendrils of fire and clouds of smoke. Terrified screams replaced the whoops of joy, and we all cowered where we stood. All around us, the world burst into pieces.

# THE BATTLE BEGINS

Cole and I huddled together, our arms wrapped around each other's necks and our eyes shut tight. For seconds that felt like years, the rumbling continued. But so, too, did our heartbeats and our ragged breathing. We were still alive somehow. When I cracked open my eyelids, I saw Abi and the queen standing upright, without a trace of fear. The violent pops continued, one after another, and a familiar, pungent smell wafted on the air.

"Black Powder," I gasped. "Is it King Michael's weapon?"

"No," cried Abi. "It's the rebellion!"

*"What?"* I shouted, wondering if I'd misheard because of the ringing in my ears. "The rebellion unleashed Black Powder? On its own kingdom?"

"Sort of," she said, grabbing my arm. "I'll show you." She led Cole and me to the edge of the crowd, to the very tree that had recently caught the queen in its branches. She climbed it with the agility of a squirrel, and Cole followed, just as nimbly. I brought up the rear, more accustomed to climbing ropes than trees.

The air was thick with smoke, casting a haze over everything. When Abi pointed into the distance, to the east of Savior's Gate, I could make out only indistinct shapes and movement. Then another boom rang out, and a flash of orange light illuminated the scene. An explosion at the base of the Wall sent heavy stones blasting into the air. People nearby dove away like scattering bugs as rocks and debris came raining down.

My mouth fell open. "Are they . . . ?"

"Yep," said Abi, grinning down at me from her perch. "They're tearing down the Wall."

"Celebrate Savior's Day with a *bang,*" I whispered.

"This is what we signaled," said Abi. "The rebellion planted explosives at intervals along the Wall. Halston planned to set them off simultaneously, to bring down huge sections at once, before King Michael could react."

"Incredible," I breathed, squinting through the billows of smoke at the spectacle of the once-impenetrable Wall being reduced to rubble. "But how did the rebellion get Black Powder?"

"Marybeth and the kids who worked in the prison cellar have been pocketing the stuff for months, taking handfuls at a time and passing it to the rebels through the palace gate."

I clasped the skull-shaped key around my neck. "A bunch of children did *that,*" I gasped.

"And it's not over yet," said Abi. "Look."

The thunderous booms of Black Powder had been replaced by a softer thudding, like a drumbeat growing steadily louder. A hearty chorus of huzzahs rose from the other side of the Wall. Then I saw them—scraggly, scrawny figures marching over the wreckage. They had to scramble on their hands and knees over certain sections of the unsteady rocks, but they kept coming. "The Palmerian army!"

"They're here," said Abi. "We did it!"

Before long, they were stomping right past our tree. They wore military jackets of faded blue, with an emblem of a rising sun—the symbol of Palma—sewn onto the sleeves. Their weapons were dented, rusting, or missing entirely. They paused to bow to Queen Catherine as they marched toward the center of the square. All the while, they whooped and smiled—not at all how I'd envisioned an advancing army. But then again, so many things had turned out differently than I'd imagined.

The people of Oren who'd gathered for Savior's Day were struck dumb by the rapidly shifting course of events. They stepped aside to let the Palmerian army pass. Some of them even joined the march, so moved by the queen's words that they were prepared to take up arms against King Michael. The army eventually converged with Halston's rebel forces, wielding pitchforks and machetes. Together, they were still a shabby bunch, and only a fraction of the size of the sophisticated Oren army.

Above it all, on one of the sections of the Wall still standing, the king stepped forward to speak to the crowd, his voice shaking with rage. "What you've seen here today is *treason*!" he cried. "The Mad Queen and anyone who fights alongside her will be executed for their crimes—that I can assure you!"

His threats didn't deter the rebel forces. They reached the Orenite soldiers amassed in the middle of the square, and for a moment, everything remained still. Then the smiles of the Palmerians dropped. And the fighting began.

"We have to get out of here!" I cried. "We have to get *Cole* out of here!"

"Are you thinking what I'm thinking?" asked Abi, cutting her eyes to the giant purple balloon in the center of everything, bucking against its ropes like an untamed horse.

I craned my neck all the way back, taking in the spectacular machine. It was almost twice as big as any of Father's balloons, its landscape of rope and knots more complicated than anything I'd ever seen—let alone anything I'd ever flown.

"Abi, that thing is massive. And incredibly complicated. And . . . and . . ."

The skirmishes beneath us intensified. The clang of colliding swords rang in my ears.

"And . . . ?" cried Abi.

"And . . ." I trembled with fear and doubt. I'd be crazy to climb down from this tree and wade into the middle of a war, with the future king of Oren in tow, only to attempt an impossible flight. I'd probably get us all killed anyway.

On the other hand, I'd promised the queen a ride.

"I'm going to fly us out of here," I said.

Abi's face split into a big, toothy smile.

# YOU'VE GOT THIS, GUMDROP

I scampered down the tree and scooped Cole up in my arms. I carried him through the tumult, shielding his eyes so he wouldn't see the things I myself was trying not to see, like men wounded and wailing and gasping for breath. I didn't want him to see his mother, either—a shivering mound of bright yellow, cowering as swords clashed all around her.

"We have to rescue the queen," I called to Abi.

"Uh . . . no we don't," said Abi, her jaw falling open. We watched the queen rise, wielding someone's mislaid sword. She hadn't been cowering at all—she'd been retrieving a weapon. She lifted it over her head and immediately stopped an Orenite blade on course for her neck.

"Whoa," Abi and I gasped at the same time.

We jumped up and down, waving our arms to catch her eye as she held off her attackers with a series of impressive parries and ripostes, showing off the skills of someone who'd learned the fine art of fencing in a royal court. When she spotted us, she smiled. We gestured for her to follow us to the royal balloon. She nodded and began to lunge in that direction. Meanwhile, Cole, Abi, and

I crouched and crept through the fray, sidestepping falling men and flashing steel.

*We just have to make it to the balloon,* I told myself. Reaching it wouldn't necessarily solve our problems, but at least hot-air balloons made sense. Even giant complicated ones had a logic I could figure out. Unlike rebellion and war and . . . pretty much everything else I'd been involved with lately.

At last, we got to the platform and climbed onto it. Oren's soldiers had left the balloon unguarded, so it stood empty and waiting, its fire crackling above. When the queen joined us, Cole ran to her while Abi and I dashed for the tethers. We'd have to climb them—about eight feet of taut rope—to get on board. But before we got started, the queen turned around and looked out at the brutal scene around us. The color drained from her face.

"C'mon," said Abi, tugging her arm. "We have to go!"

"It's him," said the queen, transfixed by something in the distance. "General Sorkin. He's coming."

A man with a chest full of medals was moving toward us at a steady clip, weaving through the battlefield as if he were tramping through a field of flowers. He kept his eyes on the queen, a sinister smirk on his lips.

While Abi urged the queen to hurry, I grabbed one of the tethers and pulled myself up, hand over hand. Eventually I reached the basket and hoisted myself over the side. I tumbled like a bowling ball into a mound of round metal objects, each the size of a grapefruit with a long white fuse poking out of it. They were so heavy they didn't budge when I barreled into them, and I instantly knew what they were. Weapons full of Black Powder. Unassuming hunks of metal powerful enough to flatten a city. Bombs. I held my breath and scampered away from them.

I stood and peered over the edge of the basket. The others were climbing up the tethers behind me, with Cole clinging to his mother's back. General Sorkin was still cutting through the crowd, but he was quickly nearing the platform. When a member of the Palmerian army stepped into his path, the general unsheathed his sword and felled the man in a single stroke. I screamed but bit back my rising nausea. I had to keep it together long enough to get us out of there.

Abi had almost made it to the basket, but the queen was inching slowly up the rope, weighed down by a squirming three-year-old. And General Sorkin was only steps away. If he reached her dangling feet before she made it into the basket, he'd pull her down by the ankles. And Cole along with her.

"I've got this," said Abi, letting go of the rope and dropping back onto the platform.

"Abi, no!" I yelled. I wanted to warn her about what I'd witnessed—that General Sorkin wouldn't hesitate to strike her down—but she'd never hear me over the din of battle. All I could do was watch as she picked up a discarded sword, raised it over her head, and brought it down hard on the rope the queen was climbing.

The queen and Cole shrieked as the severed rope whipped through the air, but they didn't lose their grips. The loose corner of the vessel rose, tossing me to the other side of the basket. I barely had time to recover before Abi moved to the next corner of the platform, slashing its rope. Again, Cole, the queen, and I scrambled to hang on.

By the time Abi reached the last rope, General Sorkin was within a few strides of her. She raised the sword and held it there long enough to flash him her signature grin. "Too slow," she said, bringing the blade down with all her might. The rope sprang free, and Abi caught it in midair, wrapping her lanky body around it.

Now that the balloon was untethered, it started to rise quickly. I tamped the fire to slow our ascent, but still we gained speed. And the higher we went, the more violently the ropes swung in the wind, dashing the others around like clappers on a ringing bell.

When the queen's hands finally reached the ledge, I hauled her and Cole into the basket. But no sooner had they got their bearings than we were all drawn back to the ledge by a shriek from Abi loud enough to pierce the whoosh of the wind and the blazing fire. General Sorkin had caught the bottom of her rope. And he was almost at her heels.

"You can't win!" he called up to the queen as he advanced with ease. "I'll catch you, and I'll see you all punished. But first, I'll toss this brat to the ground like a rag doll." His threat sent chills through me, because I had no doubt he'd carry it out without flinching. Abi was an excellent climber—she'd even made it over the Wall—but he was quickly gaining on her.

And then, in what seemed like no time at all, he reached her. His hand clamped down on her ankle, and she cried out. I searched for something to throw at him, but I couldn't risk hitting Abi by accident. But there had to be something I could do. I looked up.

Abi kicked, trying to dislodge the general from her ankle,

but he held fast. With his other hand, he reached up and seized her calf, his fingers digging into her flesh.

I stared at the dangling ropes. I selected what I hoped was the right one. I curled my fingers around the coarse weave.

"Abi!" I called down to her. "Wardrobe change!"

She looked up at me and smiled her crooked smile.

General Sorkin grabbed a handful of Abi's red skirt. At the same instant, I held my breath and yanked down on the rope. The balloon pitched in Abi's direction, and she swung her legs free. The rubber waistband of her skirt slid off her narrow hips, helped by the weight of the startled general. He lost his grip and went flailing from the tether, still clutching a handful of red tulle as he fell.

Abi joined us in the basket moments later, panting and shaken. "I knew those extra skirts would come in handy," she said. I rushed over and hugged her. She didn't object.

"Are you ready to fly us out of here?" the queen asked me.

I nodded numbly.

"You've got this, Gumdrop," said Abi, nudging me with her elbow. "Just try not to crash this time."

"No pressure," I mumbled, stepping over a pile of deadly explosives.

The royal balloon had a completely different mechanism from our Dudley Valves, but I managed to keep us steady and on course for Lollyhill. I gave the others one order—keep the bombs away from the fire—then dashed around the basket, tightening knots, adjusting valves, and figuring out how it all worked. When we reached the height of the Wall, I paused and let the vessel float for a moment. King Michael was still standing there, on top of Savior's Gate, all alone. Even from that distance, I could feel the fury coming off him like heat. In both directions, his wall had been decimated. It looked like the giant from my bedtime story had come to life and taken huge steps all along its length.

Below us, the fighting continued unchecked, the melee overtaking the square.

To the north, Oren looked the same as always. But I felt like I was seeing it for the first time: the broad green fields of the perimeter, the gilded wink of the palace, the stalls of Market Square, the vibrant crush of the Slope. From that height, the kingdom was a collage of shapes and colors, like a child's drawing. The world became so much simpler, it seemed, when we left it behind. But eventually we had to come back down.

I soon got the hang of the ropes and pulleys in the royal balloon, even tucking away a few ideas for our own fleet—if Father and I ever had one again. I guided the balloon into the clouds, where it felt like we'd plunged into one of Mr. Fletcher's lamb pelts. But when I reached out to touch them, my fingers closed on empty air. I'd gone well above the legal limits set by the Ministry of Balloons, but none of that mattered now. The old rules had been chucked overboard like dead weight.

When our balloon reemerged above the clouds, we could see far beyond Oren. Abi's hand suddenly landed on mine, and she leaned against me for balance. I wondered if it was the altitude affecting her, until she pointed and said, "There!"

To the south, Palma was a flat patch of land, appearing and disappearing below the drifting wisps of cloud. The ocean was just a shimmering line against the sky, but it winked at us, proving it was still there.

"Thank you," Abi whispered, with tears on the ledges of her eyelids. Then she squeezed my hand so tight I wondered if she'd leave a mark—purple and blue and blossoming.

# GOODNESS, MULTIPLIED

Abi and I sat on the front porch of my house, with our legs dangling over the side. We were devouring a hunk of Mrs. Fletcher's corn bread, letting the crumbs sprinkle into our laps. We'd recently finished our shifts in the workshop, repairing the Aerial Fleet—an important-sounding name for our hot-air balloons. I'd been stationed at the furnace, forging metal for new baskets, while Abi had been mending the damaged envelopes. Popping the last bite of corn bread into her mouth, Abi held her hands in front of her, stretching her fingers wide and showing off a landscape of pinpricks and bruises. "Ballooning isn't glamorous work, is it?"

"Tell me about it," I said, examining my own collection of scrapes and burns. "But if I recall correctly, dressmaking wasn't much better."

"That's true," she said. "But I love it. Something about it is just . . ."

"Right?"

"Yeah."

"I know the feeling."

The workshop and adjacent fields bustled with activity as

volunteers prepared for the upcoming flights. Soon, rebuilt balloons would carry blankets to the weary rebels at Savior's Gate, deliver Black Powder to troops in the capital of Palma, and drop dolls and toy cars to the orphans still in Between.

Children traipsed from our house to the workshop with muffins and pots of coffee, supplying fuel to the hungry workers. A group of men congregated by the workshop door, laughing and watching the smoke of their breath curl into the cold air, until a gangly man with a crooked nose emerged to shoo them inside with a string of indecipherable curses.

"Did you tell him your idea?" I asked Abi.

"Lord, no," she said. "Jerrick isn't ready for ladies' breeches. Not yet."

The front door creaked open behind us, followed by Father's heavy tread on the porch. He cradled a mug of coffee. Deep circles permanently ringed his eyes now, yet somehow, he seemed renewed. He never told me exactly what had changed his mind about the rebellion or why he'd offered to help. I liked to think it was the day he looked up at the sky and saw it teeming with yellow balloons—that it reminded him of Mother and her big buoyant spirit. Of how every act of goodness she'd committed had rippled and multiplied in ways we'd never fully know. But he never said that outright. He was still a man of few words.

"Break time is over," he boomed. "Let's go."

"But we have ten more minutes," I said.

"Up!"

With a groan, Abi and I rose and followed Father into the fields. When we turned the corner, I found myself bathed in a deep-red shadow, while Abi was tinted apple green.

*"Halston!"* I said, grinning up at the colorful patchwork balloon strung up on the masts. Father had allowed Abi and me to name the first mended vessel of the Aerial Fleet, the one made up of scraps from all the others. I could think of no more fitting tribute to the fallen rebel than that balloon, awaiting its orders.

"Notice anything different about him?" asked Father, with an uncharacteristic grin.

I studied the towering balloon for a few seconds before I saw it, protruding from the back side of the basket—a lightweight propeller. "Really?" I gasped. "Does it work?"

"There's only one way to find out," he said. His crew was busy stoking the fire in the brazier. The envelope had already begun to inflate. "How'd you girls like to take the first ride?"

Abi broke into a sprint. She careened headfirst into the basket, startling the crew and sending sparks flying.

"I guess that's a yes," chuckled Father.

"I think you're right," I said. "Are you sure about this?"

"No," he said. "But I don't imagine that would stop you." He winked and nudged me ahead. I ran after Abi and climbed into the basket beside her. One of the crew presented me with a rope, which I tied to the metal frame using a pulkker knot. I made sure it was good and tight before nodding to Father to release the tethers.

The balloon lurched, then steadied itself.

My heart did the same.

And then we rose.

# ACKNOWLEDGMENTS

Writing is a solitary activity, but publishing a book requires the hard work and dedication of many. My heartfelt thanks go out to everyone who helped make this book a reality:

To my agent, Erzsi Dek, for plucking this story out of the slush pile and believing in it from the very beginning.

To my editor, Wendy Loggia, for bringing her incredible vision to this book, for taking immense care with my words, and for helping me transform this story into something better than I ever imagined it could be.

To everyone at Random House who contributed to making this book: Elizabeth Johnson, Colleen Fellingham, Tamar Schwartz, Alison Romig, and Beverly Horowitz.

To illustrator Emma Cormarie and designer Carol Ly for bringing Prissy, Abi, and Oren so stunningly to life.

To my incomparable critique partners—Amy Board, Maria Linn, Cheryl Caldwell, DK Brantley, Gail Schmidt, and Kristy Hinson—for sharing their time and talents and making this writing journey a less lonely one. To my parents, for a lifetime of encouragement and letting me spend the better part of childhood with my nose in a book. To my little brother, for being my first creative collaborator. I'm convinced that's where it all began.

To Edmund, for reading the lousy first drafts, buying me Goldilocks-yellow roses, and giving me the time, space, and support I needed to pursue this dream.

And, last but never least, to Harper, for reminding me why I do this in the first place.

# ABOUT THE AUTHOR

When she's not writing for kids, CHRISTYNE MORRELL is busy raising one. She is a corporate attorney and in her spare time enjoys reading, baking, and watching *House Hunters* marathons. She lives with her family in Decatur, Georgia. *Kingdom of Secrets* is her debut novel.

christynewrites.com